I0825784

Invasive Species

By

Steven Streeter

www.DarkInkBooks.com

ISBN: 978-1-943201-62-4

Library of Congress Control Number: 2021941930

Cover by Alicia C. Mattern

www.AMInkPublishing.com

This book is dedicated to the welcoming people of the Yorke Peninsula.

And to David & Larissa.

Chapter 1

We bonded properly over a haircut.

Just writing that makes it seem so juvenile, not the sort of thing thirty-something-year-olds would do. But that's the way it happened. Going back long before then, Anthea had been in the year above me at school, and when she repeated the final year, we found ourselves in a few classes together. We were friendly enough to say, "Hello," and have a chat at times when we bumped into one another in the street or at the shops, but that was the limit of our relationship for the next twelve years.

Twelve years later was when I was her daughter Emma's teacher during the year Anthea and Leroy divorced. I became a surrogate counsellor to Emma and even listened to Anthea a few times, but that did change things between us afterwards. We still greeted one another, but it was not the same. There was a better connection than we'd had since we'd known each other. She even came in to talk to me a few times after school; I had the feeling her friends didn't really understand what she was going through, and she needed a non-judgemental sounding board. We actually became friends. Still, even that didn't seem to matter. It wasn't like we hung out in the same circles or anything.

And then, a couple of years later, came the fundraiser. It was for a few of the local sporting clubs in the town she lived in and I taught in, a Friday night all-ages event with the theme of "the 80s." The teachers were sort of expected to go, support the local community, that sort of thing, but if ever there was a theme that I could get into, it was the 1980s. I was born in 1985, and my parents always thought I'd been exposed to too much of their music and likes because it was all I listened to or got into until well into high school. I went all out. I went to my parents' house the weekend before – they'd moved to Adelaide by this time – and hunted through their wardrobes until I had the look of Duckie – the character played by Jon Cryer in the John Hughes classic *Pretty In Pink* – down pat, from the hat to the perfectly rolled sleeves and the sunglasses, the works.

I arrived with a few of my fellow teachers, all of whom had made a token effort to look the part, and we walked into the school's hall where the event was being held, doing a bit from the group dance from *Footloose*, with me taking on the Kevin Bacon lead role. We received a round of applause and a lot of laughter as we mingled.

The place was already packed. The kids had obviously taken the dress-up aspect seriously and it looked like the old Blue Light Discoes my parents had attended in their youth, judging by the photos I've seen. Amongst the adults there was a lot of denim, a lot of Day-Glo and way too many men mimicking the looks of Crockett and Tubbs. The music was a steady stream of 1980s pop and rock numbers, with enough of them being yelled by everyone in attendance to give it the feel of something really joyous.

It must have been an hour into the evening and I was talking with a couple I knew, having just danced with the mother of one of my current students to the Communards' cover of 'Don't Leave Me This Way'. I was having way too much fun, and I knew that the few members of my current batch of eight-year-olds who were in attendance would not let me forget it in class on Monday.

That was when I saw Emma. Her long hair was up in a side ponytail and she was dressed in something that would not have been out of place in Kylie Minogue's 'Locomotion' video. "Hey, kiddo, how's it going?" I asked her as she waltzed past.

She looked at me and smiled. "Good, Mr Kincaid," she said. "You look like something out of one of mum's movies."

I grinned at her, then looked around. "Speaking of which, where is your mum? I thought she was one of the ones running this show."

Emma's face fell. "She's out the back getting the food ready," she muttered, then beckoned me to come closer. I bent down. "I think she's upset," she whispered.

"Why?" The question came automatically.

She shrugged. "Some of the other ladies laughed at her haircut." She looked at me seriously. "You wouldn't do that, would you?"

I shrugged. "Probably not," I replied.

Emma nodded as sagely as a ten-year-old could, looking at me strangely. "No, you're one of the good ones," she said before flouncing off to join a group of similarly dressed girls. I watched her go and then looked around. On a whim, I decided to see just how upset Anthea really was.

'Out the back' was a room with a small kitchen area and a larger empty space that made the hall more attractive for community hirers, reached by a corridor that went past the toilets. The end was blocked off by plastic cones festooned with signs saying '*Authorized persons only*' printed off on what looked like one of the school's cheap student printers. I ignored it and went directly to the door of the so-called Community Room.

I opened it and half-poked my head in. "Everyone decent?" I called.

"Who's there?" a voice responded. I stepped all the way in. "Oh, Mr Kincaid. It's you."

"Come on, it's Brayden," I replied, closing the door behind me. I turned and that was when I saw her. For as long as I'd known her properly – since the end of high school – she'd worn her hair the same: a bob cut that touched her shoulders, sometimes longer, and a fringe that often hung in her eyes. But this haircut was very different, a lot shorter than I'd seen on her before. I must have been looking at her strangely because her face scowled.

"You going to make fun of me as well?" she demanded, touching her head as though it was a scar.

"You look just like Lucinda Dickey in *Breakin'*," I said.

Her eyes widened and her mouth fell open. Then suspicion clouded her visage. "Did Emma tell you that?"

"She just told me you were upset because people made fun of your haircut, but… wow." I reached a hand across and pushed a short piece behind her ear without thinking, then quickly withdrew. "Sorry," I muttered.

"You know the film?" she asked as if I hadn't done anything.

"Of course." I smiled and saw the first glimmer of a smile touch her lips as well.

She now took me in and the smile became an actual grin. "Duckie, right?" she asked.

"Not one of the people out there got it." I shook my head. "But I wasn't game to go the whole hog like you." I rubbed my face and the beard I'd worn since my second year of university.

"Yeah." The grin faded and she touched her head again.

"What's wrong?"

She shrugged, shook her head and turned away. "It's the whole… Look, I'm sorry. You're here to have fun and I've got some stuff to do here so…"

"Tell me." I sat on a chair and kept eye contact with her.

"Well, it's not just the hair," she said. "I mean, them laughing at me made me feel like crap because it wasn't done in fun, they were poking fun. But I could deal with that. No, it's…" She stopped and turned away, paused, then walked to the kitchen area. I followed her, but kept my distance.

"Go on," I said. "You know I'll listen."

She seemed to consider this as she continued to spread party pies and sausage rolls over a series of trays, then she muttered, "Yeah, and you already know some of the shit." She stopped doing what she was doing, leant on the counter in front of her and bowed her head. "Leroy's getting remarried," she said. "I can handle that," she went on quickly. "At least, I think I can. But he's moving interstate and he's getting a lawyer so he can fight for fifty-fifty custody. Now I have to get a lawyer as well, and Emma's ten so the court might decide she needs a children's rights advocate because Leroy and I are arguing so much, and… Oh, shit, Bray, he's screwing me over! He didn't want anything to do with her for the first year after the divorce and now he wants to share custody? And with a new wife, won't a judge see that as a better family relationship? What if I lose her, Bray? I couldn't handle that. I can't lose my little girl. I can't!" And the tears started, pouring down her flushed cheeks, but the expression on her face was one of pure anger.

I stepped across, turned her around and wrapped my arms around her and stroked the back of her short hair – everything I believed I should not have done. But she leant into me without really a hesitation and I let her cry against my vest. Then, quite suddenly, she stepped back and wiped her eyes. "Sorry," she muttered.

I shrugged. "No need to be," I said. "But if you need someone to talk to, I'm a friendly ear."

A smile slowly appeared, touching her eyes as well as her mouth. "Just like Duckie in *Pretty In Pink*," she said. "You know, I always thought he should have ended up with Andie."

"I don't know, that friend thing is probably a lot more permanent," I replied with a shrug, then straightened up my clothes.

She suddenly stopped me and held the lapels of my jacket. "May I admire you?" she asked.

"If you wish," I replied instantly, finishing the movie quote.

Her laugh was filled with relief. "You actually do know the film," she said.

"And you actually do look like Lucinda Dickey," I replied.

"Not quite," she said and slowly slid the dress she was wearing down, revealing a leotard with sash around the waist. "Now?

"Now," I agreed and we both started laughing. The music we could hear coming from the main hall changed to 'Wake Me Up Before You Go-Go' by Wham! Without thinking I started to do the moves from the video clip. Anthea was beside me quickly, and we did the whole thing, singing along, then broke up into gales of laughter as it ended.

"I haven't done that in too long," she panted.

"Same here." I smiled and shook my head as I collapsed onto a chair.

"Ooh, I like this one as well," she suddenly said. I strained and made out the gentle strains of Tiffany singing 'Could've Been' in that sweet little way of hers. "Come on." She reached her hands out to me.

"What?" I asked stupidly.

"Come on," she repeated and took my hands, dragging me to her. She rested her head against my chest and I placed my hands on her shoulders and we swayed back and forth on the spot, in the manner of teenagers everywhere since pop music had become a thing. She knew all the words and sang along; all I could do was hold her and go along with the flow.

Halfway into the song, the sound of the default Samsung ringtone erupted and she let go of me and went to a handbag on the counter where she fumbled inside until she pulled out her phone. She looked at the screen, then tapped it and pressed it against her ear. "Yeah, Donna, what's up?" I watched on in curiosity. "I told you I wasn't available tonight." She rolled her eyes and started to pace. "Why can't Keith go?" She stopped. "He's what?" Her demeanour became sterner. "If he's drunk again, so help me, he's gone." She listened again and this time she shook her head. "Okay, text me the address. I'll be there as soon as I can." A briefer pause. "It's not your fault, but Keith is a dead man. Thanks, Donna." And with that she disconnected the call.

"Problem?" I asked.

"Call-out, property up the highway at Wills Creek. The guy who's supposed to be covering tonight went off on another call two hours ago and he isn't back yet." She was not happy.

"At night?" I asked. Anthea ran a snake catching service under the auspices of National Parks and Wildlife; although she was not the only one on the Yorke Peninsula, I had the feeling she had a very good reputation. In addition, she'd told me once during our chats that she milked venomous ones to help create anti-venom. Not a job I thought I could do.

"It's in a house." She shoved the phone in her bag

and grabbed her dress. "Shit," she suddenly groaned.

"What?"

"I got a lift down with Liz Carmody, the woman in charge of the netball. Now I'll have to drag her out of there, get someone else to take this over, tell Emma we've got to go, find a babysitter, and then..." Frustration was coming to the fore; after what she'd told me already tonight, this did not look good.

"Get yourself ready," I said. "I'll drive you back home. You see if one of Emma's friends can take her to their home if you're not back before this ends, and I'll go get someone to take over in here."

"Bray, I can't let you..." she started.

"You're not letting me," I interrupted. "I'm doing it to help a friend who's going through too much shit at the moment to let something else get on top of her."

"Are you sure?" she tried. "I mean, it won't take much for me to organize everything."

"I know, but I am offering." She stared at me, then nodded slowly.

"Thanks, Bray."

"Well, I can't let my dance partner down, can I?" I smiled. She actually giggled. I indicated her clothing. "This is a really volcanic ensemble you're wearing, it's really marvellous," I finished, throwing another quote from *Pretty In Pink* at her. When I left, she was trying desperately not to laugh too loudly.

We bonded properly over a haircut. And a love of the decade we had both been born in.

Chapter 2

I lived in the small town of Port Clinton, the first town you come across on the eastern coast of the Yorke Peninsula when you come from Adelaide, capital of South Australia. Seven kilometers down the coast was Price. Running south from Price was the Wills Creek Conservation Park, and at the southern end of that was the town of Wills Creek, consisting of a tiny church building that was now a junk shop, four dozen houses at most, a caravan park we all knew as 'the campsite', and an empty building that had been a general store until only a few months before all of this. Keep going south you eventually reach Tiddy Widdy Beach, then Ardrossan, twenty-five kilometers south from my place via the Yorke Highway, which was where the school was and where Anthea lived. Writing it like that, it seems that the place is crowded, but the drive is filled with huge gaps of nothing except farmland punctuated by lines of trees and some hunks of native vegetation. Only two hours away from Adelaide, the state's capital, and you might as well be in another world.

By the time the two of us organized everything – getting someone to do the food ended up being the hardest bit – it was twenty minutes later and I took straight to her house, a little way out of town, on the opposite side of the highway. The snakes were the reason she lived out here; you didn't have a bunch of live snakes in the city limits, even if it was a place with less than fifteen hundred residents and the animals were secured. I waited in the car while she went inside, emerging only moments later with jeans and a polo shirt emblazoned with the company name – AB's Serpent Service – under an open jacket. She waved at me and climbed into her four-wheel drive. I started to reverse, but over the sound of my Ford's engine I heard her car not even turn over. Again and again she tried, but she got no response. I returned and climbed out. "Problem?" I asked.

She looked at me and I saw in the car headlights the moisture glistening on her cheeks, but that defiant anger on her face. "Won't start," she snapped. "Now I've got to wait for the RAA, and…"

"Grab what you need, throw it in the boot, I'll take you," I said.

"Bray, you've already done more than enough," she said, and I could sense a distinct reluctance in her tone.

"So what's a little more? Look, I'm not catching the stupid thing, I'm just transport," I countered.

She glared at me and her shoulders actually slumped so noticeably it looked like she was going to face the principal or something. "Thanks again," she muttered.

"Let's do this," I said and opened the boot, then helped her cart a lot more stuff than I would have thought necessary from her vehicle to mine.

The conversation of the drive from the school to her place faded on this second leg of the journey. She looked angry and I didn't want to press my luck with anything else. After a few minutes of silence, I opened the console between us, pulled out a CD and put it into the car's stereo. I wasn't sure what one I'd grabbed, but the first track told me it was Dire Straits' *Brothers In Arms* album. Without thinking, I started to sing along, the lyrics of 'So Far Away' coming to my mind as readily as my own telephone number or address.

But when the song ended, she stopped it. "Sorry," I said. "Not a fan of Dire Straits?"

"Why are you doing this?" she asked.

"What? Helping you?"

"Yes, helping me. Why?" There was still a hint of anger there and probably also suspicion.

"Dunno. Emma said you were upset, and after what happened with Leroy way back when, and you telling me about what you were going through, I guess I feel protective." Honesty has always been my policy; it helps when you're teaching inquisitive children.

"Yeah, I suppose I've told you a lot of stuff over the past two years, haven't I?" She gazed out of her side window. Then: "I thought you were after something back then, when Leroy left me. But you didn't try anything. Can I ask why?"

I snorted. "I was doing it to help, not for anything else," I said. "When you stopped coming to chat, I thought you were getting over it, so I let it be. And when you started again, I was still in that frame of mind. I wanted to help, I really wasn't doing it for anything else." I smiled. "Besides, even if I did, I was seeing someone. I couldn't go behind someone's back, even to flirt."

She looked at me square on. "You know, I almost believe you," she said. I shrugged, but didn't respond. She kept on looking at me for a few more moments, and I felt like there was more she wanted to say. But, instead, she simply shook her head and opened the centre console. "Sorry, but I'm not in the mood for Dire Straits tonight," she said, then pulled out another CD. "This, however…" She replaced it and soon we were singing along to the *Footloose* soundtrack as if it was something we did together all the time.

We turned the music down only when we entered Wills Creek. "We want Creek Road," she said, looking around. "Know where that is?"

"Yep." It was the road that ran along the coast, at the top of a series of cliffs that lead down to a rocky beach. It was the oldest part of the town and the houses all looked it.

Upkeep was not high on the agenda of the predominantly older population who lived there.

I turned and slowed right down so we could make out the house numbers. "We need number fifteen, but it's marked with the name 'Here Yam'," she said, dropping her voice as if we were in a library.

It didn't take long to find it in the light from the late evening sun. We climbed out of the car to be greeted by a woman with dishevelled grey hair and wearing a dressing gown. She looked us up and down. "Who are you supposed to be?" she demanded. She did not look impressed at all.

"We were at a function," Anthea replied tersely. "If you want, we can go straight back there." She held the old woman's gaze and that plus her tone of voice saw the poor woman crumble straight away.

"It's in the living room," she whimpered, opening the door. "Straight down and on your right." It was obvious she was going to make no attempt to enter with us. Yes, us. I simply followed Anthea like a serving boy.

The light was on and that meant the errant reptile was easy to spot, coiled up beneath a rocking chair covered in blankets that created a sort of a cave. "Christ," I whispered, "that's a big one."

"It is," Anthea agreed, her voice sounding distant, her eyes not once leaving the snake.

"What sort is it?" I asked, just happy to have the sound of a voice.

"I don't know." She said those words slowly, and that worried me. "Okay, I need you to go and get the pole with the wire hook on the end. There's a few bits of extension pole, add three to it."

"Three, right," I repeated.

"And the blue bag on the pole, and the largest plastic

box," she added. I started to leave, slowly and quietly, then she went on, "And three of the orange straps. You'll see them."

"Right." And I was out of there. She was so calm, cool and collected while I felt my heart going at a million miles an hour and a very real sense of panic threatening to overwhelm me completely. Despite that, and maybe it was also because of macho bullshit, I was quickly back with everything she'd asked for.

"Thanks," she said, holding a hand out, still not shifting her gaze. "Give me the hook and have the bag ready and the box open." I passed her the hook, glad she could not see me shaking, and watched in wonder. She reached in and managed to get hold of the tail of the reptile. It opened its mouth and hissed angrily. She stepped back and I followed suit. But what she was doing was dragging it out. It was probably close to two meters long and appeared to be black in color and its head did not look like any snake I'd seen before, but I had to admit my experience with snakes was limited to the odd sighting in the bush and David Attenborough wildlife specials, and what I saw in that room was only in passing, really. She was working so quickly. It hissed and tried to strike at Anthea, but she held it at arm's length and kept moving so that it could get no sighting on her, I guess. "Bag," she said. I handed her the pole. She tilted it so that it fell open and, with a flick of her wrist, she had the animal's head inside. She quickly dropped the rest of the snake in after it and withdrew the hook, then spun the top closed. "Box." I slid it across and she dropped the bag inside, then detached the pole. "Lid." I placed the lid over the bag and looked at her. She nodded at me. The bag inside was moving and thrashing about. "Bad mood," she grumbled, and then grabbed one of the orange straps. She carefully lifted one side of the box; the creature in the bag reacted violently but she took her time sliding it underneath, then securing it. The next two went on a little faster.

And just like that she'd caught a snake. She lifted the box with ease and I followed behind again, carrying the hook and bag's handle. "All done," she said to the woman as she walked past. I felt my stomach knot up as the box was deposited into the boot of the car, but I said nothing. It was well-secured and my biggest worry was not it getting out, it was just having it so close to me while I was driving. I placed the tools beside the box, still moving a little, although not as much as it had been when we were in the house, and then closed the boot.

Anthea nodded at me and went to the woman. I stayed where I was and saw some agitation cross the woman's face, and then a sudden burst of fear. She looked across at me, then sighed and the two of them entered the house.

I felt very uncomfortable and made my way back to the front of the vehicle and sat on the bonnet, trying to be as casual as I was definitely not feeling. I could not shake the unease at having a snake in my car. It was some time before Anthea reappeared. "Ready to go?" she asked.

"Sure," I shrugged and within moments we were away. I left the music to her, but, to my surprise, she turned the volume down and stared out of the window, an expression of concentration on her face. I decide that discretion was the better part of valor and left her to her own thoughts.

We were maybe halfway back to her place when she turned to look at me. "Did you notice anything odd about that snake?" she asked.

"Sorry," I replied, "my knowledge of snakes comes from TV and the projects my students do."

She managed a slight grin. "At least you're not

bullshitting me about what you know." She fell silent again, then asked, "Okay, as someone who's seen snakes on TV, did you notice anything at all?"

I shrugged. "When I first saw it I thought its head looked wrong," I offered.

"Yeah," she muttered, "me too."

"What sort is it?" I tried.

She shook her head. "Don't know, and that's not a good thing."

"Why?"

"Well, it's big, so the chances of it being a new, never before seen species are pretty much zero. That leaves, to my mind, one thing – an invasive species. You heard of the Burmese python problem in Florida?" I shook my head. "Well, people were getting these pythons as pets, but when they got too big, they were let go. Now they are overrunning the everglades. They even eat alligators. That's all we need here – a species like that."

"Great," I muttered.

She reached across and touched my leg. "Thank you for helping out tonight. And for not freaking out."

"Close call," I replied. She glanced at me, then smiled. "Seriously, having that thing in my car… not anything I'd choose. But I will do this for my dance partner."

"Your…" She shook her head and upped the volume, enabling us to sing along together until we pulled into the driveway of her place.

Chapter 3

Saturday morning and I was up early. Every day of the week except Sunday (and that was not hard and fast) I went to the only gym in Ardrossan – a "24/7" gym, so I had an access tag – before, on weekdays, going to work, where I'd shower and dress properly. Saved me a bit on my water bills and it kept me in shape. I saw what my father had become and I was not going to put myself through that. But on this day, I arrived at the gym a good hour later than normal, after the activities of the previous night. Following our adventures in snake-catching, I'd managed to get back to the fundraiser, even though Anthea stayed home to look at her new acquisition, and I gave Emma a ride back there at the end of the night. Had to carry her inside; it was a late night for her. I managed to get out of staying for a cup of coffee, but still got home late, and hence my later than usual arrival.

I was in the middle of a set of squats when my phone sounded out. I cursed and managed to get the bar into its hooks and ran to my bag. The name that came up on my screen was a simple 'AB', and I rammed it against my ear. "Yeah?" I barked. Someone on my contact list, but not anyone I called too often.

"Is that Brayden Kincaid?" came a hesitant female voice.

"Yeah." Now I was the one who was unsure.

"I didn't get you up, did I?" the woman asked.

"No."

"Look, I… hang on, sorry. This is Anthea, Anthea Bowman."

"Oh, Anthea, okay." I relaxed instantly.

"Yeah, okay. Look, I know this is an imposition, but how soon can you get to Ardrossan?"

"I'm here," I said. "I'm at the gym."

"Oh, thank God," she breathed. "Look, I left some stuff in the back of your car last night. Is it okay if you come by and drop them off on your way home?"

"Not a problem," I said. "But on one condition."

"Oh?" Immediate suspicion.

"The coffee's got to be hot."

Her laugh was light, a giggle like I'd heard the night before in the kitchen at the hall. "And if you're a good boy, I'll even get the chocolate out."

"Well, I'd better start being good," She laughed again. "How soon you want me there?" I asked.

"Finish what you're doing and come on by."

"Okay. See you soon."

"Yep. And thanks, Bray." She hung up and I shook my head. Last night had been quite a night for everyone.

So it was, that about twenty minutes later, sweating like a pig, I pulled up in front of Anthea's place. It looked much bigger in the daylight, with a windowless extension attached to one side of the house that had just appeared as a black shape the previous night. She came out to greet me, trailed by Emma who looked like she had just woken up. "Thank you," she breathed in relief as she came to the back of my car. She turned to Emma. "Grandma will be here soon. You need to get ready."

"But I want to say hello to Mr Kincaid," she whined.

I squatted down. "Hello," I said and smiled. "Now you better do what your mum says."

"Okay," she sighed and trudged back inside.

"You working today?" I asked as I helped her lug the plastic containers we hadn't used and some of the extra pole extensions to the back of her car.

"I hope not," she grumbled. "No, I want to look at that snake we caught and I need to do it without worrying about what she's doing alone in the house." She shook her head, then dropped her voice. "This one's got me beat. I can't find it anywhere on the databases from around the world. I've sent photos to the herpetologists I know and haven't heard anything back yet. It's a weird one."

"Now, I believe you promised me a coffee," I said, trying to drag her away from a discussion on snakes and catching them.

She looked at me and the smile slowly broke across her face. "I did, didn't I? Come on, then." And she led me inside.

The house was incredibly neat and tidy. The walls were bare apart from a few photographs of Emma at various ages and Anthea's university graduation picture. Not even a painting or poster print anywhere. I sat at the kitchen bench on a stool while she put the kettle on. Emma emerged a few moments later dressed in the standard clothing of a child in the middle of a cold autumn – nothing too trendy, just comfort and warmth. She had a backpack on her shoulder and looked a little down. "All ready?" Anthea asked.

"Yep."

"Got the iPad's charger this time?"

"Yep."

"What's wrong, Em?" Anthea hugged her from behind and the youngster fell into her embrace straight away.

"I want to stay with you." It sounded to me like she was putting on an exaggerated emotion to get some sort of response, but I said nothing; none of my business.

"I know, and I hope we can spend tomorrow together." Anthea made no promises, which I thought was a good move. And she had clearly seen this form of pouting before.

"Okay." She trudged into the living room and switched on the television, settling down to watch the music video programme *Rage* on Channel 2.

I watched her go and shook my head. "What?" Anthea asked.

"Just wondering what it'd be like to have one of my own," I said.

"Oh." That seemed to make her a little uncomfortable. She poured the drinks. "Milk? Sugar?"

"No milk, two sugars, thanks."

"No problem." She added a lot of milk to her own and two sugars as well. "I think you'd be a good dad," she said finally as she placed the mug in front of me.

"Thanks, but that would require there being more than one of me," I laughed.

"I thought you were seeing Lynda, the one who works behind the bar?" She sounded like she was just being conversational, and that honesty thing kicked in again.

"We broke up last Christmas," I replied with a deliberate casual tone, then sipped the cup. "She decided that one guy was not enough for her. I didn't make her choose between us, I just got out of there." Short, sharp and shiny. The fact I saw her nearly every time I went into the hotel for a drink, and saw him too often there as well was not anything I needed to tell her. She had her life weighing on her; I was not going to add mine to that.

"You were together for a while," Anthea pressed. "I mean, you were together when you were Emma's teacher."

"Five years. We'd been making plans to stay together, but with the way she was, I couldn't commit." The words came out, even though a huge part of me didn't want to even think about reliving it. "The last year, maybe the last eight months, we were together were tough, but then, quite out of the blue, she seemed…" I stopped. "She was happier. And that was because she found someone not me."

"Probably for the best," Anthea stated coldly. "You know what they say – once a cheater, always a cheater."

I knew from our conversations of the past two years that that had come from bitter experience; Leroy had finally gone off with the third woman he had cheated on Anthea with. At least, that she knew about. I felt uncomfortable going back there for her sake, and continuing to remind myself about Lynda yet again, and so instead I asked, "Can I see the snake?"

She looked at me curiously, and again I had the feeling she wanted to say something else, but didn't. "When Em's gone, sure," she smiled. "How were things when you got back to the fundraiser?"

"Not as much fun without my dancing partner," I replied and winked at her. She giggled, which made Emma turn around to look at her as though that was a sound she didn't hear very often.

"Yoo-hoo, anyone home?" called a voice from the front end of the house, startling both of us.

"Gran'ma!" Emma cried despite her earlier misgivings and ran to the front door, disappearing from view.

Now, I knew Anthea's mother. When I had started work at the local school – the same school I'd gone to myself – she was one of the senior Student Services Officers, and she was assigned to my class in that first year. We got along fine, and so when she saw me, she simply said, "Good morning. And how are you, Brayden?"

"Good, Mrs Bowman. You?"

"Semi-retirement sucks," she said, then dropped me

a wink. She walked up to Anthea – I saw then they were actually the same height – and gave her a quick hug. She pulled back and looked at her critically. "Don't like the haircut," she said. Then, before Anthea could reply, she went on, "What's the work today?"

Anthea's tone was clipped. "Bray and I caught a snake last night and it's a new species. I need to see what it is, then hopefully my car'll be back on the road so I can get back to Wills Creek and see if there is a nest or if it's a one-off."

"Hmm." She cast me a glance. "And what are your plans for the day?"

"Got to make sure my lesson plans for the week are all up to scratch, Mrs Bowman," I replied with false cheer.

"Hmm. Okay." Her attention returned to Anthea. "Give me a call when you want the cherub back," she said. "But not till after three. We're going to head to Kadina."

"Shopping?" Emma asked excitedly.

"Maybe," smiled the older lady. "See you, dear."

"Bye, mum." No hug this time, still a note of stress in her voice.

"Goodbye, Brayden."

"See you, Mrs Bowman," I said as she disappeared. I saw Anthea's whole body tense up until she heard the front door close. "You okay?" I asked.

She shook her head. "She does my head in," was the quiet response. She ran her hand over her head. "And the first thing she says? She doesn't like this. I can't win."

I didn't know what to say, so I took a big mouthful of the coffee. Anthea came around and sat on a stool beside me. The silence we sat in was uncomfortable and growing worse with each passing second. I finally reached across and brushed my hand over her hair. "I don't care what anyone else says, I like it," I said, then added in my best Jon Cryer voice,

"May I admire you again today?"

The hint of a smile touched her lips. "Thank you, Bray."

I shrugged and let my hand return to my coffee mug. She looked at me for a few moments longer, then returned her gaze to her own drink. "You don't deserve all this shit," I said. "You're now a single mum, running a successful business, and dealing with external crap. If people want to pick on you because of a haircut, then they have the issue, not you."

She looked at me out of the corners of her eyes before shaking her head. "No wonder you're Emma's favorite teacher," she said.

That was something I hadn't been ready for, but before I could say anything, that same Samsung ringtone from the previous night sounded out, and the phone on the bench moved a little as it vibrated. She looked at the screen, tapped it, and then held it at her ear. "What's up, Donna?" She sounded defeated already. Her expression changed to one of confusion as this Donna person spoke for a reasonable amount of time. "Can you get him on the phone?" Anthea asked. Then: "Have you called the police or the hospitals?" She closed her eyes and ran her hand over her face. "Nothing?" She looked at me but I couldn't get what she was trying to say. "Text me the address." Pause. "Yeah, thanks, Donna. I'll call you if we find anything." Pause again. "Yeah, I know. Thanks again." She disconnected the call and looked at me and now I did recognize it – that was a hopeful expression.

"What?" I asked.

"They came and took my car away this morning to be repaired," she said, "so can I ask you a huge favor?"

"Where we going?" I asked.

"Look, I can call my mum, get her to take me, but if there's a snake problem… Look, Keith, the guy who works for me, hasn't called in from his job last night. He hasn't come here to drop off whatever he found, Donna at National Parks hasn't heard from him, and we're a bit worried. I need to get out to where he was going and see if he actually turned up."

"Lesson plans can wait," I said. "I'll take you."

"No, really, you don't have to." But her eyes were almost begging me. Almost. Maybe it was more a sense of hope; I think she just wanted a friendly face with her, especially if it turned out her employee wasn't doing his job. Just something else to add to the crap she was going through, I supposed.

"I don't have to, but I want to," I said, then finished the coffee. "But you'll owe me another one of these," I said, holding up my empty mug.

"God, you're cheap," she said with mock seriousness. She couldn't maintain the façade and giggles soon burst through. "Okay. I'll go change and then we can get going. Okay?"

"You're the boss," I grinned.

She laughed again, and then, quite suddenly reached across and kissed my cheek. Just a peck, but it caught me by surprise. "Back in a sec," she said as she went, then she turned and said, "Thank you, Bray. I mean it."

"No problems," I returned. She stayed there for a few seconds longer, and then she was gone. I didn't think anything of it. She was a friend in need, and this snake stuff – frightening though it was – was fascinating. And, honestly, I wasn't really thinking about me.

Chapter 4

Keith had been working for Anthea for about six months, part-time and on-call, mainly to give her a break, especially with her being a single parent. She'd had a few problems with him occasionally drinking when he was supposed to be working, but he was a very good snake wrangler, having learnt his trade in Queensland where getting two meter brown snakes – some of the most poisonous in the country – was apparently not uncommon. Unfortunately, this was not the first time he had really messed up. Anthea didn't give me any details, but I had the impression if he had done the wrong thing this time, that would be it and she would have to look for another employee.

She was angry and conversation was minimal, the music at a low volume. She gave directions coming from her phone, going towards a farmstead on the western side of the Yorke Highway, taking a road opposite the town of Price and then spending a good fifteen minutes traversing several dirt roads; she said very little else.

I pulled to a halt at the end of the driveway. We could see the house on top of a low rise, looking very still. "Drive up," Anthea said. "Donna told me she hadn't managed to get hold of them this morning, so there might not even be anyone here."

I didn't say anything but just did as I was told. The track was in a better state of upkeep than most of the roads we had just driven over, so the approach was easy. And yet I found myself going slowly, while a quick glance at Anthea told me she was not in a real hurry either. There was just something that could be felt in the air. A relatively new Toyota four-wheel drive was parked in front of the place, but the driveway continued around to the rear. I followed it all the way.

"Stop," Anthea said, but she sounded distant again, like she had in that house in Wills Creek. I did as she said. Ahead of us were three vehicles – a battered Toyota Landcruiser attached to a large trailer, a tractor and, behind this last, a Subaru all-wheel drive that looked like it had seen far better days. "That's Keith's car, the Suby," she muttered.

"So, he stayed here the night," I suggested.

"Then why hasn't he answered his phone? Why hasn't Mr Haviland answered his phone? No, something's not right here." She opened the car door.

"Shouldn't we call the police or something?" I asked.

"Or something," she replied, heading towards his car. I swore under my breath and simply followed her. She looked around the car. It was unlocked and a few plastic boxes and lengths of pole extension sat in the back seat, along with an empty bottle of Scotch, a lot of soft drink and energy drink cans and the sort of brown paper bags most bakeries seemed to use, all screwed up and just dropped in the passenger side footwell. I gazed up at Anthea and saw that she had pulled her phone out. She tapped at the screen a couple of times, and then held it to her ear.

From the house came the sound of some repetitive tune. She lowered the phone, looked at me with concern on her face, and then, without saying a word, started toward the rear screen door. I caught up to her as she opened it. The ringing of the phone stopped and she held her own phone to her ear. She scowled and shoved it into her pocket. "Ready?" she whispered.

"Sure," I replied, wondering how I'd explain to the principal what I was doing trespassing in the house of someone I didn't know if we were caught here.

The door opened onto the kitchen-cum-dining room. It was untidy, dishes sitting in cold water in the sink, a few flies buzzing around. "Keith?" Anthea called suddenly, making me jump. "You in here?"

The only response was the sound of the flies and, somewhere outside, a cow lowing across a field. Anthea looked back at me and I saw very real worry on her face. She waited for me to reach her. "What's up?" I asked.

"Can't you smell it?" she returned, her voice so quiet even in these surrounds that it was no more than a whisper on the wind.

I inhaled deeply and gagged a little. I knew that odor – that was rotten meat. "What is it?" I asked stupidly.

She shook her head and led the way through the dining area to a sliding door at the far end of the room. She seemed to steel herself, and then slid it across. The noise seemed ridiculously loud.

"Oh, fuck," she whispered.

I couldn't say anything.

She leant back against me and my hand automatically rested on her stomach, but neither of us could take our eyes from that room. There were two people inside, one at the far end, resting against a second sliding door that was still closed, the other, wearing a similar polo shirt to the one Anthea had on, was in the centre of the floor, lying face down.

That second looked fine from where we were, apart from a puddle of something black and viscous around the head. But our attention was attracted to the other person. He looked to be in his late middle age, with close-cropped grey hair and carrying a little too much weight. But it was what we could see of his right leg that drew our attention. The pants he was wearing had been torn open, revealing the lower limb… or what was left of it. The bone was clearly visible, with a few strings of sinew and muscle attached here and there, all the muscle and skin that lined the edge of this wound that we could see was stained black, and the whole thing was in a puddle of that same dark liquid that was under the head of the other.

Anthea finally moved away from me and stepped into the room, looking all about. She reached into her back pocket and pulled out a pair of disposable rubber gloves which she slid on with practised ease, then squatted beside the other body.

Slowly, carefully, she placed her hands on the shoulder and hip and flipped him over. "Oh, for fuck's sake," she groaned, stumbling backwards until she ran into my legs. I reached down and helped her up, then turned my head and stumbled away, through the house until I was leaning against my car.

"You okay?" I heard behind me. I opened my mouth to answer but what came out was a stream of liquid vomit. It tasted foul, but I could live with having thrown up. I did not think I could live well with what I had just seen.

The whole left side of the face of that man was gone, the dirty skull showing through blackened body tissue, one eyeball glaring out of a pool of thick black ooze, the other gone, the visible teeth forming a half-grin…

I threw up again and this time felt two hands on my shoulders. I caught my breath as well as I could and wiped my sleeve over my mouth. "Sorry," I muttered.

"For what?" she replied, her eyes .wide but staring right at me.

I wanted to say something pithy and cool, but was afraid if I tried I'd just throw up yet again, so I shook my head and offered her a pathetic smile.

"Yeah, I know," she muttered. I wiped a tear from

her eye and she stepped back, then sighed and came in closer. She wrapped her arms around my chest and I let her stay there. I slowly moved my hands to hold her as well, and she almost collapsed against me. Finally, she moved away and I let go straight away. She'd been crying a little. "Guess I should call the police," she muttered.

I nodded and tried to smile again, but this time I failed. She touched my arm before moving away. It sounded like a standard phone call to the authorities, with her giving the address and the fact we discovered two bodies. Then she said, "The deceased are Mr Ian Haviland, owner of the property, and Keith Phillips of Maitland. Both are showing signs of advanced necrosis, and may have been dead for some time." I just stared at her. She looked at me curiously as the person on the other end was talking, then continued, "No sign of probable cause. Sorry. We have left the area and will stay here until you arrive." She mouthed the word, "What?" at me and I shook my head. "Okay, thank you," she finished and disconnected. Now she voiced it, "What?"

"You are so calm," I said. "There's two… I mean, there's… One of them… Shit, I don't know how…" I dropped my eyes. "Sorry," I muttered.

"Look, it's part of the job, I guess," she said and came back to me. "But I'm glad I'm not here alone." She hugged me briefly. "Thank you." Her eyes searched mine for something I could not understand.

"So, what do you think happened?" I asked.

"No idea," she muttered. "I haven't seen anything like that before."

"But you knew what it was. Necrosis, you said."

"Yeah, I know," she muttered. I didn't know what else to say, and she was clearly waiting for something that didn't come, and the awkward silence was only broken by her saying, "You'd better move your car so the ambulances and police can get in."

"Right." She stayed where she was and watched as I reversed, and the guided my car a little way down the drive. I noticed she'd come around to the front of the building, watching me, maybe making sure I didn't leave her there, and then, quite suddenly, she turned, looking at the front window which, I would have guessed was the window that looked into the room that held the two bodies. But her interest was not what was inside the room, but something at the base of it.

"What's up?" I asked as I neared her.

"Stay there," she hissed, holding a hand up, then took a hesitant step forward. She squatted and used a stick to prod at something. Her face took on an expression of concentration and she did something odd with the stick, then reached forward and grabbed something. As she stood I saw that she had a snake by the tail. "It's okay," she called out gently.

"Think I'll stay here," I returned.

"It's dead," she said as though she was trying not to be as condescending as she felt.

"Sure?"

"Oh, yeah. This can't be any deader," she said and there was something about her tone of voice that broke through my fear and encouraged me to approach her. I was quite near before I saw why she was sure it was dead – the thing had no head.

"Wow. What killed it?" I asked, daring to look at it a little closer.

"Well, it's a brown, and the only thing that really attacks them and gets away with it is eagles and hawks, the bigger raptors. But they wouldn't bite the head off and leave the body." She shook her head. "This is getting really weird."

But I was a little distracted by what I was seeing. The headless end of the body looked odd. I moved even closer. "What's up?" she asked.

"Have you looked at this?" I asked.

"At what?" She placed it carefully on the ground, pulled her gloves out of her back pocket and, without putting them on, used them to poke at the ragged end. "That looks like the two" – she swallowed – "two guys in there. Definite signs of necrosis, rotting even along the scales." She stood up and stared down at it. "I don't get it," she muttered, then shifted her gaze to me.

"Don't look at me," I said. "This is the closest I've been to snake, dead or alive."

"It's not the snake," she stated, and I could sense that tension rising again.

"Okay, is this, this necrosis common?" I asked.

"Not at all."

"Then finding a snake with similar sort of things wrong with it as the two people in there would seem to indicate they're related."

"That's what I'm thinking," she murmured. "But it doesn't tell me how."

"Shouldn't we leave this for the police?" I offered.

She sighed and shrugged. "Yeah, I suppose you're right." She shook her head. "But Keith…" She glanced at the window, then turned away quickly. "I wonder if this was what he came out to get, or if it was something else. But what could have done that? And his face…" Her eyes met mine again and I could see she was fighting to stop from crying. "Shit, Bray, this is bad. This is really bad. What could have done that? And Keith… Stupid, drunk, friendly…" The tears started again and I went into protective mode, taking her by the shoulders and guiding her away and back to where I parked the car. She sat herself on the bonnet and wiped her face staring at the ground in front of her feet. I sat beside her and she slid so that her shoulder was touching mine. "He pissed me off, but he was a nice guy and now he's gone. Gone. Just like that…" Her voice drifted off; she looked to me like she was in shock. I risked putting my arm around her shoulders. She took that as an invitation and fell against me, nestling her head in the crook of my neck. I felt I should say something, but was not sure what, so I shut up.

Turned out, that was a good choice. She stayed where she was until we saw the clouds of dust indicating approaching vehicles. "Thank you," she said.

"For what?" I laughed.

She looked at me curiously, then smiled. "For… just, thank you," she finished, and then made her way to meet the authorities.

Chapter 5

The police asked a lot of questions and went through things three or four times with Anthea. Me, they asked me once what I was doing, I told them I'd driven Anthea there and was helping her out for the day, but they really didn't want to know the rest. I was not worth their time and effort, it seemed, and so I sat in the car and watched, being forbidden to even speak to Anthea for the duration. An ambulance showed up and disappeared around the back, but didn't reappear. I was under the impression that only a doctor could say if someone was definitely dead, so maybe that was what they were waiting for, but what did I know?

I was relaxing, eyes closed, some *I ♥ Radio* classic rock station playing through the car's stereo via my phone when a hand on my shoulder gently disturbed me. I opened my eyes and saw Anthea looking at me with an expression of defeat on her face. "Sorry for keeping you," she said, "but they want me to hang around until the forensics guys get here from Adelaide. They're on their way, so it shouldn't be long, but I don't know how long they'll keep me here."

I looked at the clock on the dashboard; it was almost half past ten, so we'd been here for close to two hours. "That's cool," I said.

"No, it's not. I've called mum and she'll keep Em until after dinner. When I told her what had happened she…" She shook her head. I didn't press it. "Anyway, she's fine looking after her. I rang the garage and told them I wasn't sure when I'd be in to get the car, because they close at one. Well, they said they were going to call me a little later on because, at the moment, they don't think they can get the parts they need.

They were going to wait until they were sure…" She stopped herself again. She was clearly frustrated; much like the previous evening, today was not turning out to be a good one. "Look, I'm sorry," she went on suddenly. "I'll get one of the local police to give me a lift back to Ardrossan. Thanks for everything this morning. I don't want to keep you…"

"I'm staying," I interrupted.

"Bray, you really don't have to." She looked like my staying was going to make her feel uncomfortable, but I didn't feel right just abandoning her, as I saw it.

"Don't have to, I want to," I said and smiled at her, then reached across and took her by the hand. "You're going through absolute hell out here and I can't leave you to it."

She squeezed my fingers, then let go, dropping my hand. "Why are you doing this?" I was sure I could hear suspicion was in her voice.

"Because you need it," I said simply.

"Do you do this for all the parents of your former students?"

"Only the ones who dance with me." A flicker of a smile touched her mouth, but I got the very definite feeling a joke was not going to be good enough. "I like to think I would help anyone going through a hard time."

Her expression became a little more deflated, then she forced a smile onto her visage. "One of the good ones," she sighed. "Well, I suppose I should go back and wait for…"

I stepped out of the car and offered her the driver's seat. "Relax. I'll let you know when the next car gets here," I told her.

"Bray…"

I almost pushed her towards the empty seat until she relented and slid in, letting Lynyrd Skynyrd wash over her. I looked at her and received a grateful smile in return. I watched her until she relaxed enough to close her eyes, then went for a brief walk.

Okay, look, I did think she was attractive, and I did like Lucinda Dickey and the 80s, but that was not what I was thinking about. Physically, I preferred girls with longer hair and a different body shape in my dating life, and there was always that strange thing about being too friendly with parents of students, especially in a smaller community, that could have been sitting there. But no, I was thinking about helping someone I had known for a long time, and who I had been able to be there for when she needed me.

And helping Anthea made me not think about me. Focus on somebody else. Perfect avoidance technique. Okay, Lynda and I had split five, maybe six months before and I saw her nearly every time I went into the hotel. I had a job where I saw other people's children and I went home to an empty house. I worked, went to the gym, watched too much TV, read not enough, and went for walks when the feeling struck me. This whole thing with Anthea felt like a nice diversion from a mundane life.

I stood at the fence and gazed across at farming country that had not seen enough rain in too many years, at native trees that stood defiantly in the midst of an agrarian setting, as if daring anyone to mess with them, at fields that would now most likely not even be harvested when the time came and suddenly I felt I was the only person in the world, on the edge of a scene of post-apocalyptic calamity.

It freaked me out for reasons I can't really explain and I turned to hurry back to the car.

That was when I saw it. A snake, staring directly at me. Its head looked a little too large for its body, covered in ridges, and with an almost square snout, like a snub-nosed crocodile. It was black or dark in color, except for its yellow eyes which regarded me coldly. It opened its mouth a little and hissed, but it was a lot more guttural than any snake I'd heard before. It seemed to be watching me closely, and then it slowly started across the dirt path. Its body was thick and I could not see where the tail ended. Its tongue flickered in an out, the forked ending staying there for a moment longer than it should have. And then it reared up and opened its mouth wide.

The top fangs were like sabre teeth, sliding out of grooved pockets in the lower jaw, and a single drop of purple glistened on the end of one, catching the morning sun like dew on a flower. It was now halfway across the driveway, and its head, lifted like that was about the level of my knees. This was huge. I took a very slow pace backwards, my heart beating in my chest telling me I should run, but everything I'd been told during a lifetime living in rural areas telling me to be slow and careful.

The head darted forward, the movement quick. I jumped back and tripped over my own feet before crashing heavily and painfully to the ground. There was no way it was going to reach me, and yet I'd reacted on instinct. The yellow eyes narrowed and the tongue licked at the air again.

Its progress was even slower. It moved in a wide arc around me, but its eyes remained on me the whole way. It was watching me and stalking me, keeping out of the reach of my arms, but it was clearly not afraid. It stopped when its head was in line with my stomach. Its gaze held mine.

Slowly, it lifted itself up, higher and higher, so that its head was over my waist, as if examining me.

It opened its jaws wide again, those fangs sliding out of their grooves like daggers from sheaths.

It leant back a little and I swear it cast me a glance. It was as though this damned reptile was enjoying this!

And then its head snapped around and it dropped to the ground and slithered back the way it had come with an unusually rapid velocity. I had been so terrified I hadn't even noticed the vehicles – two cars and a van – coming up the drive. They rumbled past while I was still on my back, the driver of the van looking at me curiously, and then they went around to the back of the house where a police officer was directing them. I climbed to my feet and just ran until I was back at the car, my eyes remaining on the place in the grass where I'd last seen that serpent.

I didn't realize Anthea was beside me until she touched my arm. I jumped and cried out, and then simply stared at her before almost collapsing, needing to use the side of the car to hold me up. "What's wrong?" she asked urgently.

"Miss Bowman?" The police officer who had been guiding the new traffic was approaching and I shook my head.

"Later," I murmured. She looked at me with genuine concern. "Go. They need you," I urged and shooed her. She touched my arm again, and then turned to face the officer.

"Yes?" she asked.

"Have you got a few minutes? I think once you've seen these guys you can probably go." The guy was young and so I found myself wondering how many dead bodies he'd seen before these two. And if he had seen any, I wonder what state they had been in, especially compared to the rotting corpses in that building...

She looked at me once again and I nodded. She sighed and muttered, "Sure. Let's get this over with." She followed the uniformed guy to the house, but she cast me one last glance before she rounded the corner.

As soon as she was gone, I spun my head and surveyed the paddock in front of me. I guessed at one point in its life it had been a front lawn, but now it was overgrown with brown grass a foot or more in height, with a series of dead shrubs pock-marking it like ancient warts. I took in every square meter of it, but nothing stood out.

Of course it didn't; what was I expecting – to be able to see a snake hiding out there? But I was sure I could feel its cold gaze watching my every move, as if angry it had let me get away…

It had been going to attack me! Snakes did not attack unprovoked – that was simply something you learnt. They attacked things small enough to eat or because they were themselves afraid and did it in self-defense. Keep away from them and they'll keep away from you. But this one made a point of going for me. Was it going to try and eat me? Was that even possible? The merest thought sent shudders running through me and I once again had to keep myself upright by leaning on the car.

But I did not let my gaze drift. Every movement out there, everything that even seemed like it could have been out of place, made my head whip around like a crazy person. I was so close to just getting in the car and driving off, but sanity somehow prevailed and so I merely continued my futile sentinel duties.

A crow, large and black flew out of one of the bushes and I gasped as I jumped back, watching it soar into the sky. "What's got into you?" laughed a voice behind me.

I turned and had to control myself from just grabbing Anthea and hugging her tight. "All done?" I asked, my voice sounding pathetic even to me.

"Yeah, I can go." She looked behind her and grunted. "If they need anything else, they'll be in touch. But, yeah, we can go."

"Cool." I went around and opened the passenger door for her then almost sprinted to the driver's side. Before she could say anything, I was gone, driving too fast until we reached the edge of the property where a police car was parked, the lights on the roof flashing. I came to a halt and wound the window down. I noticed a dirty motorbike parked by the rear of the vehicle, a man dressed in jeans and riding leathers leaning against it, his helmet under his arm.

"Slow down," the cop said with a grunt, then asked, "How are things going up there?"

"Slowly," Anthea said, leaning across me. "But it's… it's nasty."

"Yeah, glad I'm down here," he replied, and he clearly meant it. The other man came across, but the officer turned on him. "No questions," he growled. The man shook his head and returned to the bike. "How much longer do you think it'll be?" the cop asked.

"Forensics only just got there, so probably a little while," Anthea said.

"Great." He stepped back and then glared at me. "And slow down," he repeated before stepping back.

I didn't do anything except turn to head back towards Ardrossan. We drove on in silence for two songs before Anthea turned the stereo off. "Okay, I'll bite – what's up your ass?" she growled.

"Huh? What?" I responded stupidly.

"You've been acting weirdly since the forensics van got there. What's wrong?" Her anger was real, and directed at me.

I sort of guessed what she wanted was a shoulder to lean on now that we were gone, and all I was offering was sullenness. "It…" I stopped myself. She didn't need my shit right now. "It's nothing," I mumbled.

"Nothing. Right." And she stared out of her window at the passing scenery until that Samsung dial tone rang out of her pocket. She took the phone out and, without even looking at me, said, "Hi, mum, what's up?" Her voice was weary. "Yeah, after dinner, you said…" Her brow creased. "Angela's kids as well? Mum, are you sure?" Her eyes closed slowly and she bowed her head. "Yeah, it's been a pretty crappy day," she muttered, casting me a sideways glance. "Thanks, but I think spending some time with Emma will…" She rubbed her other hand over her face. "You already promised her, right. Well… yeah. Okay, I guess. What time tomorrow?" The hand stayed over her eyes. "When will that be?" Her head leant backwards. "Fine. See you then." And she disconnected the call even though I was sure I could hear Mrs Bowman still talking on the other end of the line.

"Problem?" I asked.

"Emma's staying at mum's tonight with Angela's two kids," she replied automatically. I knew Angela – Anthea's older sister. "Then they're going to watch the eldest play netball tomorrow." She shook her head. "I don't want to spend…" She shut up and looked at me. "Look, just take me home, and then you can go on your way and do your lesson plans or whatever and I'll try and work."

"Are you going to be okay?" I asked.

She just looked at me. I could see not only anger there but also hurt. "I'll be fine," she eventually stated.

"No you won't," I sighed. "It's been a shitty day, so why don't…"

"Bray, I…" She shook her head and went back to looking out the window.

This was not good and I felt I was at least in part to blame. "It was a snake," I said. "Black, long. I mean, really fucking long. It stretched across the driveway and I still couldn't see its tail. And it had these long fangs and there was purple and the head was like…was like… was like someone had squashed a croc's face to half the length. And its eyes were yellow. And it was stalking me. Snakes don't do that! They don't fucking stalk people! Then it must've felt the cars coming because it went back into the grass…" I let my voice trail off. I'd just meant to tell her I'd seen a snake, but the rest came pouring out. There I was, trying not to dump on her, but I had.

Silence greeted my statement, and she continued to stare out the window. "Are you sure?" she asked after a while, and there was a hint of accusation in her voice.

"Why the hell would I make that up?" I replied, a little too loudly.

She now looked at me. "Take me home," she said.

"Yeah," I sighed. "Okay. Not a problem…"

"I have to show you something." There was something about the look in her eyes that told me I had better do what she was saying.

"Okay," I agreed, "but one condition."

"What's that?" Suspicion again.

"Afterwards, you let me take you out for lunch."

There was a hesitation before she answered, "Deal," she finally said and I had the distinct impression she felt like she'd just made a deal with the Devil. I had no idea what was going on here, but I decided to go with the flow. What was there to lose?

Chapter 6

She led me past the living room down a small corridor to a plain, brown door that was not only dead-bolted but also had a keypad lock on it. "Pretty elaborate security," I noted.

"Needed it to get permission to have this set up here," she replied, then looked at me. "Do you mind?" she said. "The only people who have the code are me and K…" Her composure almost faltered. "Just me." Her voice was subdued.

I didn't press it and turned my head. Four monotone beeps sounded and then I heard a key in the lock. I turned slowly. "All done?" I asked.

She opened the door. "My lab," she said with little enthusiasm. "What Emma calls 'the snake room.'"

I'm not sure what I was expecting, but it wasn't this. I guessed from the way we had come I was in the windowless attachment to the house, with light coming in through two skylights and fluorescent tubes recessed into the roof, and that gave me more than enough light to see by. And what I saw was a nightmare for ophidiophobes everywhere. One entire wall was lined with what looked like plastic lockers, each with a glass or perspex window, revealing that most of them held a snake or two. On the wall opposite the entrance was another door, and a glass cages set onto metal shelving, these looking from this distance like they were holding lizards in basic terrarium settings. The final wall was dominated by a long bench with two computers and a set of test tubes, a pair of microscopes, a whole lot of stuff I hadn't seen since doing general science in my teaching degree, and some things I don't think I'd seen before. The end of it closest to the entrance had been cut away to fit in an enormous refrigerator that hummed noisily to itself. "Come on in," she said, and led me to the bench.

I stood there like a student watching a teacher demonstration as she lifted a dark plastic box resting near on one the computers. Beneath was a container made of a double layer of glass, inside of which was a coiled snake, resting on top of what looked like an old towel. It was very dark in color and almost looked like it was dead. "This is the one we caught last night," she explained. "I ended up having to sedate it before I could do measurements." She took a piece of paper she had tucked beneath its corner. "Length – one point eight one meters; weight – twenty-two point four kilograms; maximum girth – two sixty-two millimeters." She shook her head and gazed at me. "Means nothing to you, right?"

I shrugged and shook my head. "Sorry," I muttered.

"Length is standard, but for that length, it weighs a deal more than usual and that girth is way beyond norms for the length. I've sent photos and the data to the Adelaide University, but I don't expect to get a response until Monday. I also sent some off to a person I met online from England who seems pretty knowledgeable. No idea when or if I'll hear from her." While she spoke I bent in closer and looked at the reptile.

"Why bring me in here to tell me this?" I asked.

She hesitated and then tapped the glass.

The movement inside the glass case was quick and made me stumble back a few paces. The head seemed to appear out of nowhere, striking at the glass hard enough to make the whole thing appear to actually move a fraction. The yellow eyes stared at the finger for a few moments and then the head retracted slowly back into the coiled body. "Fuck…" I hissed.

"Was that the sort you saw out at the farm?" she asked, her voice clinical.

I nodded. That strange crocodilian head was unmistakable. "But it was at least four meters long," I muttered, "and there was more of a bulge at the end of the neck." I looked around. "Got a pen and paper?"

She passed me what I wanted from a drawer and I drew the way the creature appeared. But as I sketched – badly, admittedly – I realized what I was drawing. "It looks like a legless lizard or crocodile," I mumbled.

"And you say what you saw was around twice the length of this one?" She was not mocking me, but was actually interested.

"Yeah…" Realization struck me. "So, what are you saying – that this is a baby?" I asked.

"Well, a juvenile. Judging by what you saw, yes, I think so." I looked at her and I'm not sure what expression I had on my face, but she managed a smile. "Bray, it's just a snake."

"Is it?" I sounded as scared as I felt, just being that close to it.

"Of course."

"A nasty one," I returned. I gazed back at the glass container, appearing exactly as it had when we had first entered. "Have you seen its fangs? Is there purple on them as well?" I asked, feeling like a child even as the words came out.

She shook her head. "I didn't want to go near the mouth until I knew what it was," she replied. "Safety."

"Okay, fair enough." I risked moving closer to the container again. The head moved and the eyes regarded me. I had a flashback to the farm and shuddered. "It does not look like a snake," I whispered.

"I agree," Anthea responded quietly. "If the

university can't tell me what it is, I'll send them a blood sample and maybe they can do a DNA analysis. But at the moment…" She looked at me, but I was still focused on the reptile. "Earth to Brayden; come in, Brayden."

I shook my head and tore my gaze away from the animal. "Sorry," I murmured.

She looked at me closely and yet I found my eyes drifting once more to those yellow eyes, still watching me intensely. "Come on, let's get out of here." Her voice came through my fog of thought and then I felt myself being almost dragged away. We left the room and she locked the door behind her before she stared at me, drawing in so close that her face filled my vision. "Brayden?" Her voice was very mum-like and I forced myself to focus on her.

"Sorry," I repeated and shook my head, trying to clear my mind. "Sorry," escaped me for a third time. "That snake out at the farm… Shit, Anthea, it was… And seeing that one in there…" A shiver ran through me like an earthquake and I fell back against the wall. She took me by the forearm and took me to the kitchen. "Wow. Here I am freaking out over a snake, and you're the one who's been through all the crap this morning."

"How much did you exaggerate what happened?" she asked.

I considered her question, then shook my head. "I don't think I did," I finally mumbled. "It stalked me, and then it seemed to wait before striking, and then the cars came and it disappeared." Another tremor ran through me and I snorted a laugh at myself, then shook my head. "Here I am acting like a frightened schoolboy and you're the one…"

She placed a glass of water in front of me. "Yeah, it's been a day, hasn't it?" she murmured, but her eyes weren't looking at anything in particular.

"What's wrong?" I asked.

She shook her head. "Doesn't matter," she said. "Job stuff."

"Try me."

Her gaze did not leave mine for a few moments before her body slumped down where she stood, her eyes dropping to the water in front of her. "Bray, what am I going to do without Keith? I struggled before I hired him and now… what am I going to do?" She looked at me again. "And this snake thing's got me worried. I mean, really worried. This is not an Australian species, so we've got an invasive, and it's one I haven't been able to find in any database from around the world. And if this one here's a juvenile, and you've seen a four meter one, that could mean trouble. I'm not sure what I can do." I saw her mouth start to form into a thin line, the eyes moistening, but she was fighting to make sure none of her emotions came out. "And now I'm on my own, and I have to try not to think about what did that to Keith and… to Keith… Keith… Shit, Bray!" She couldn't do it any longer and the first tears trickled down her cheeks. I went around and wrapped my arms around her. She stiffened at first under my touch, but relaxed into my embrace as the crying hit her in earnest. "His face… His face…" was what she kept on saying, over and over and that image came to me as well, striking me like a slap.

My own tears dripped onto the top of her head. I didn't know the guy and yet what I'd seen…

I stepped back from her and she looked up at me as I wiped my own face. She smiled and removed a tear from the tip of my nose as I ran a thumb underneath her eyes. "What a pair we are, huh?' she laughed.

"Yeah." I wiped my face once again. "And I reckon I promised you lunch."

"You did," she responded and looked at the clock on the microwave oven. It was not quite midday, still early, but I reckon she just wanted out of this house, to go somewhere where she could ignore the memories. "Let me get dressed in something not work-related."

"Take your time," I smiled and watched her go to the other end of the house. I wandered around the kitchen and saw a few of Emma's school drawings on the refrigerator. She was quite a good artist for a youngster. They were all of animals, but the two snakes she had drawn – both in just lead pencil – were very impressive. I took one off and looked at it more closely.

"That's your fault, you know." I looked up and smiled. Anthea had changed into denim jeans and a shirt tied across her stomach over a 'Choose Life' t-shirt. "You like?" She spun around slowly, arms out.

"I feel so wrong decade," I laughed, then held the picture up. "She's good."

"You told your class that whatever they liked to do they should do it the best they can. She took that to heart. She spends hours drawing pictures."

"Sorry," I said as I placed the image back under the magnets.

"Don't be. At least you gave some advice that was decent." She came across and hooked her arm through mine. "Are you ready to go?"

"My lady," I laughed, and bowed a little, and then let her guide me to my car. She was smiling, and it appeared to me to be genuine. There was still a hint of redness about her eyes from her tears, and her cheeks had a slightly flushed look about them, but she seemed like everything was over and done with. I only hoped I looked the same.

It had not been a good morning.

Chapter 7

I drove past the front of Ardrossan Hotel Motel and parked a little way up the road.

I knew that red Toyota Prado with the Port Power stickers all over the back window that was parked at the corner. Anthea started to climb out of the car, but stopped when she realized I wasn't moving. "What's up?" she asked.

"Let's go up the road to the café instead," I suggested.

She shrugged. "I think we could both use a beer," she replied. "Why?"

I sighed. "Ross is in there. I'm guessing that means Lynda's in there with him or working. I don't know if I can face the two of them together."

"And Ross would be the new guy, right?" she asked. I shrugged, then nodded slowly. "Look, we've had a shitty enough morning. Don't let them get to you." She waited for me to get out of the car and lock it before she grabbed my arm and guided me towards the pub.

I let her take me down the road and up to the front doors. As I pushed them open, she grabbed my hand and kept hold as we made our way in and found an empty table. A few glances were cast in our direction and I saw people bowing their heads to whisper. She let me sit down, then, with a cheeky grin on her face, said, "I'll get us something to drink."

I smiled at her and she made her way to the bar. People were still trying not to look at us too blatantly, and it actually made me smile as I thought about it. I noticed that Lynda served Anthea and that Ross, sitting at the far end of the bar, kept his head down low. With her one simple action, Anthea had changed everything, and her grin when she came back to the table was close to being a laugh. "Well done," I whispered.

"Lynda didn't say anything," she replied and lifted her glass. I did likewise and we tapped them together. "Want to order now or have a drink first?"

"Drink first," I said with a nod. Then I closed my eyes and shook my head. "I'm going to face some questions at school on Monday."

"Ooh, what will you answer?" she said, leaning across the table a little.

Her face was close to mine. "None of their business," I said.

She suddenly lunged and kissed the tip of my nose. "Well, that should get them talking even more," she giggled as she sat back and downed half the beer. I laughed and shook my head. We didn't talk, we just sat there, drinking, and yet it wasn't awkward. Being here, together, the only people who could understand what was going on with each other, it was just that that made us comfortable here.

I finished my beer and held my glass up. "Ready for another?" I asked.

"Let's grab some food first," she suggested.

"Sure. I'll go get…" The ringtone from her phone sounded and she pulled it out of her jeans pocket. She glanced at the screen, and then looked at me apologetically. I sat down again and watched her.

"What's up, Donna?" she asked. As soon as she said that name, I knew we weren't going to be getting anything to eat soon. Anthea rolled her eyes a little, then suddenly she was sitting up. "Really? But we took…" She looked at me and I saw concern on her face. "No, I'll get there as soon as possible." Hope now crossed her visage. "No, I won't be alone," she stated, staring directly at me. I nodded my agreement. "Tell her we'll be there A.S.A.P. Yeah, no, no problems. Thanks, Donna." She tapped the screen and looked at me.

"We've got work to do, huh?" I sighed.

"Sorry," she muttered. "Look, raincheck on lunch?"

"Of course." I stood and offered her my hand. She took it. "So, where we off to?"

"Back to Wills Creek," she replied. "Same house as last night."

"Everything the same as last night?" I asked, unable to hide my nerves.

She grimaced and shrugged. "No idea." She reached across and took both my hands. "I understand if you don't want to come. I'll get the police to get me out there, and I won't be alone…"

Now it was my turn to reach across and kiss the tip of her nose. "Let's get moving," I said. "We need to get back to your place and pack the car."

"Thank you, Bray," she whispered, and made a point of taking my hand as we walked out.

But on the outside drinking and smoking area we were stopped by a man holding a motorcycle helmet. "Ms Bowman, of AB's Serpent Service?" he asked, smiling slightly.

"I'm busy," she said. "Call our number and I'll get to you when I can…"

He gazed down at our entwined hands. "Yes, I can see you are busy," he stated. She let go of me straight away. "No, I just need to ask you some questions."

"You don't look like a cop," I stated.

His eyes met mine and I held his gaze with ease. "No, my name is Adam Lynch. I'm a…" He hesitated, then continued a little reluctantly, "…a freelance reporter. I saw you at the Haviland property. I just want to know what's going on…"

"You'll need to talk to the police," Anthea responded.

"Come on," he smiled. "This could be great publicity for your business. What's going on up at the Haviland house?"

"We have no idea," I stated. "We were called in to get rid of a brown snake, that's all."

Anthea reached across and took my hand again, squeezing it. "And that's too much information," she added. "Now, we have to go. We've got work to do."

"Come on, you don't expect me to believe…" he started, but I stepped forward, shouldering him out of the way as I went. "Hey! That's assault!" he called.

Anthea looked over her shoulder, "And I'm sure the police would love to know what questions you were asking," she called.

By the time we reached my car, he was out of our sight. I unlocked it and we climbed in. "Sorry, but I had to say something," I said as I started the engine.

"No, that was cool," she nodded. "Something believable without giving anything away. Not that I was told to not say anything."

"Me neither, but I don't want to answer questions about… yeah, about what we saw."

"Yeah." She fell silent. I reached across and squeezed her thigh; she offered me a wan smile but didn't say anything, and remained silent until we were pulling up in front of her place. I started to load the same things into the boot we had taken the previous night while she went inside to put on her work top. I had most of it done when she emerged, carrying what looked like a toolbox with a stylized green snake picture beneath a red circle with a line through it marked on all sides and the lid. "Nice job," she said, looking over everything I'd done. She added a few extra bits and pieces, then placed this odd box on the back seat. I didn't bother to ask; if I needed to know, I was sure she'd tell me.

She found a CD to play as we drove on – *One Hit Wonders of the 80s* – and she sang along to the first track, then turned the volume down. "Bray, what's going on here?" she asked.

"Going on where?" My ignorance was not put on.

"Between us. You and me."

I stopped my mouth saying the first thing that came to mind, and let myself think things over. "I think that, somehow, in less than a day, I've found a good friend," was what I eventually came up with.

"A friend," she repeated.

"A good friend. One I hope I'll see more of now." I don't know why, but I felt like I was not giving her the answer she wanted.

"Okay. Cool." She reached across as if to turn the volume up, then suddenly leant into me and kissed me on the cheek. Before I could say anything, she turned up the volume very high and was belting along with Limahl. I didn't join in; I was missing something that I knew I should have seen. She didn't turn the volume down again until I had taken the road that led toward Wills Creek.

"We're going back to Mrs Robertson's place," she explained, "but it's different this time. She told Donna that she killed a snake this morning with a gun of some sort, but she was sure she heard another one. We're going to do a check of the place. I shouldn't ask you to do this – you're not qualified or trained or anything like that – but I feel like I'm caught in a bind."

"How so?"

"I should be waiting for someone to come from wherever I could get them, but I feel like I need to do this now." She was serious and I slowed the car.

"Why now?" I tried.

She shook her head. "I don't really know. Call it a gut feeling. There's a whole lot of little pieces and I think I'm putting them together, and I don't want to risk waiting until maybe as long as tomorrow." She shook her head again. "I'm missing something, but I don't even know why I should be seeing something. There's something going on here that does not make any sense. I can't even tell you what I think it is, but, yeah, I don't know. What do you think?"

I was stunned into confusion by the question. I wanted to ask a question of my own, maybe what she meant, that sort of thing, but that was not what she needed. I finally said, very slowly and carefully, "If there is a feral snake out here, and it's breeding, then you need to get on top of it. If this woman has got two more of them in her place after having one, she might even be near a nest, and that could be bad for her. I mean, are these things poisonous?"

Anthea chewed the inside of her cheek. "I didn't test for that." She looked down at her hands in her lap. "This is going to sound stupid, but I didn't want to touch the head, even when it was knocked out. I should have milked it, but…" She shook her head and then looked out the window at the passing farmland. "I'm not supposed to be afraid, but this snake freaks me out. Yes, it's the head. And the eyes. They watch. Snakes don't have good eyesight; this one, I'm sure, can see as well as us."

"Yeah," I muttered, the memory of the way the snake that morning had been looking at me springing to mind unbidden and unwanted.

She seemed to ponder everything, then nodded, more to herself than me, and reached across and touched my arm. "Thank you, Bray." She smiled. "Yeah, good friend. That's cool." There was something in her tone of voice that sounded odd, but I forced myself to concentrate on negotiating the road.

We pulled up in front of the house in short order and left the car at the same time. The house was silent and the woman did not come out to greet us this time. I looked at Anthea. Her face was a mask of concentration. She opened that strange box she had placed on the back seat of the car and went to work. Only moments later she was wearing elbow-length gloves, but not just any gloves. They looked like they would not be out of place in a Medieval combat situation. I looked closer and whistled. "What the hell are those things?" I whispered.

"Gloves," she replied simply, then actually smiled. "Three layers. Leather, woven Kevlar and two perpendicular layers of steel mesh on top. Cut and puncture resistant. An adult croc might be able to get through them, but no snake can." She punched one hand into the other. "Uncomfortable, but possibly necessary here. So, if you could bring the hook and bag?"

"Of course." I grabbed what I needed and stayed behind her. She looked like she was going into battle, and, further, that she had done this before and knew what she was doing.

And so, with her protected and me feeling like I'd rather be anywhere else, we approached the front door of a house that we had visited less than twenty hours before, unsure of what we were going to find, but both of us sure it was not going to be pleasant.

Chapter 8

The front door was unlocked. "Mrs Robertson?" Anthea called as she opened it, her voice firm and emotionless. The only response was the sound of a breeze disturbing a distant wind chime. She pushed it open a little further, revealing the short corridor that led directly into the living room, where we had found the snake the previous evening. "Mrs Robertson?" she tried again. Still nothing. She turned to look at me. "Please stay behind me," she whispered. I nodded. I had no plans to do anything else.

The sun coming in through a side window cast the room in a yellow light, the old style tube television set attached to a set-top box in the corner to our left showing some programme I didn't recognize, but with the sound muted. And in front of it, the remains of a snake. It was in two pieces, that crocodilian head with its open eyes staring at nothing some distance away from its lower body, a charred hole in the carpet between the two sections, blood and pieces of black spread across everything, leading back beneath the set. Good shot, and it had made quite the mess.

If Anthea noticed it, she didn't let it distract her like it had me. Instead she took another hesitant pace further forward. "Mrs Robertson? This is Anthea Bowman, the snake catcher. Are you here?" she called.

There was no response, nothing at all. She squatted down and took a flashlight out of her pocket I hadn't seen her put in there. She shone it underneath all the furniture. "Nothing else in here unless it's found a drawer or something," she whispered. "But that means it should be safe enough for us to keep on going."

I nodded, despite every fibre of my being screaming at me to get the hell out of there.

To our right was the door to a bedroom, wide open. Anthea shone the torch in, but it seemed to be empty of both human and reptile occupants. The next door was closed. Anthea pressed her ear against it, then shook her head. We went through a door at the far end of the living room where we entered a corridor. Off to the same side as the bedrooms was the bathroom, while the hallway opened up to a small dining room at the end of which was a doorless opening through which we could see the refrigerator, and so guessed it was the kitchen. Again, she used the light to look first in the bathroom, then under everything in the dining room. I took the opportunity to glance into the back yard. It was an overgrown mess of weeds and bushes, rusted orange objects half-covered by the vegetation, trees half-dead in the middle of it all. The perfect home for snakes, I decided. "Mrs Robertson?" she called yet again, but this time there was a shakiness to her voice that made me feel even more uneasy than I already did.

She stayed where she was, her back to me, but I could see her body tighten. Then she exhaled slowly, a long deep breath and she strode to the kitchen. As instructed, I remained behind her until she cried out, "Fucking hell!"

I was next to her in an instant, and it took a lot of willpower not to run out of that house right there and then. The woman I had seen the previous night, who had argued about money with Anthea, was on the floor in the corner of the kitchen. Next to her a hole had been blasted in the kitchen cupboard by the shotgun we could see on the linoleum beside her legs. From one side of the hole was a length of black snake, the other half was on top of her fingers. It had wrapped itself around her hand, but was now dead. I guessed it had bled out from the gaping wound that had cut it in two.

But what I struggled to draw my eyes away from was Mrs Robertson's arm. That same necrosis we had seen earlier in the day was there, but so much worse. Her entire forearm was a mere bone covered in shreds of black flesh, the palm of the hand the same, only the fingertips showing full form, though their color was also dark. I swallowed hard and bumped into the wall; I had not even realized I had been moving backwards. Anthea turned and looked at me and I saw my own horror reflected back at me. "Go," she grunted from between clenched teeth.

"Yeah," I think I replied but I couldn't move. What I was seeing could not be happening.

"Bray," Anthea growled.

"Look at her arm," I whispered, my voice cracking. She turned with reluctance. Her pace backwards told me that I was not seeing things. Along the inside of her upper arm a black line was creeping up, along the vein or artery. Slowly, like a living creature, it made its way towards her armpit until it stopped just short, tapering out like a pen that's run out of ink. The skin above this line bubbled, each pop leaving a black dot that joined with one another. These dots opened, growing larger, leaving holes in the skin, until there was another line of rotted meat that was opening even while we continued to watch.

Then, from out of the end of the arm, above the bone, a large drop of dark liquid, thick like molasses, fell to the floor out of our line of sight, landing with an audible and sickening splat. "Fu-u-uck," I groaned and turned my head.

"Bray, we need to get the police here, right now," Anthea said in my ear and pushed me out of the kitchen. I wandered as if in a dream, but could not help but gaze in the direction of the other dead serpent. A shudder ran through me and I hurried outside, not stopping until I was leaning against the car, catching my breath and trying not to throw up. Anthea took her gloves off and removed her equipment from my hands and then turned me to look at her. "You okay?" she asked.

"What… what did we just see?" came out of my mouth. She shook her head. It was then I noticed her eyes. They were wide and she looked almost in shock. I felt ill and she wasn't thinking. I placed my hands on her shoulders. She took it as an invitation and came to lean against me. I let my arms wrap loosely around her and her own arms gripped me about the chest. I didn't want to let her go. Having her there, physically, solid, touching me was a dose of reality that my mind needed. And yet I could not help myself – I turned my head to look at the house. Against my chest I felt Anthea move until she was doing the same thing.

Then she moved away. I let my arms drop from her and she almost succeeded in smiling at me before she shrugged and pulled her phone out of her pocket. She scrolled through the numbers until she found the one she clearly wanted. Then she tapped the screen and held it to her ear, her other hand reaching across until it found mine. She needed the reality as much as I did. "Hello, yes, this is Anthea Bowman." She looked at me and her brow furrowed. "Yes, that's the one. You gave me your number at the Haviland house this…" She stopped and her grip on my hand tightened. "Nothing?" she asked after a reasonable length of time. She shook her head. "Well, look, I've got bad news then." The pause this time was much shorter. "Yes, another. Fifteen Creek Road, Wills Creek. The deceased is a Mrs Robertson." She closed her eyes and let go of me to rub her forehead. "Yes, we'll wait. Thanks, Inspector. See you when you get here." She rammed it into her pocket and scowled at the sky.

"Bad news?" I ventured.

"Sorry, Bray, but we're stuck here until they can get here. Again." She let out a long breath and shook her head. "Some dancing partner I turned out to be, huh?" The smile that crossed her face at that was genuine and even a little cheeky.

I slid an arm around her waist and took her hand with my other before I started to move as if doing a waltz. She followed along, her eyes not leaving mine. We made motions that could have been dancing for a few moments before I let go of her body and twirled her under my arm. "You're still a good dance partner," I said with a nod and she giggled. I let her go and we both leant back against the car. "So, what did the Inspector say?" I asked.

"Oh, that." Her good mood was dampened by my question, bringing her back to where we were. "There was no trace of anything in the blood of either man. No poisons, nothing. There was no residual acid on their skin, there was no cause for what we've seen. They have no idea what we're facing." She indicated the house with a nod of her head. "And now there's another one, and we've *seen* something happen, but…" She shook her head. "I'm a herpetologist, you're a teacher. This is way above our pay grade, I'm afraid."

I rested a hand on her leg. She covered it with her own as soon as I touched her. "Okay, let's play detective," I said.

"Go on." She cast me a glance out of the corners of her eyes.

"Both times you were called out, so there were snakes there," I said, letting the words come out as they came to mind.

She nodded, and her expression became thoughtful. "The same injuries on all three, even though they were on different parts of their bodies, so we'd have to assume the same thing got them all," she went on for me.

"So, what was the same about them?" I asked. "We had a farm in the middle of nowhere and a coastal town. Different landscapes. The farm's – what? – eight kilometers inland and…" I did a quick mental calculation. "…and that'd be in pretty much a straight line from here. Wow."

"All of them were inside," she suggested. I nodded; that was a good point. "And they looked like they were taken by surprise."

"How so?"

"Well, Keith might have been a drinker, but he would never let his face get that close to something. Mr Haviland had a lower leg injury, like something hit him down low. And Mrs Robertson had just used her gun and picked… picked up…"

"The snakes," we said together.

"Can't be." She shook her head firmly. "I have never seen a snake bite do that to a person, have never read about it, nothing. What does that is a spider, like the white-tip, and even then, it doesn't eat away a whole arm. And the parasites and bacteria don't work that fast. I mean, this is nothing I've read about or anything." She sighed. "Besides, the strange snake at the farm was outside, these were inside. It just doesn't fit."

We fell silent for a little while, both staring at the house and its unseen, deceased occupants. "So that's all we've got. Coincidence," I finally murmured.

"Coincidence, and we're part of it," she replied. "I'm sorry for dragging you into this shit, Bray. Look, you can go if you want. I'll wait, they'll give me a lift back to town…"

I placed a finger over her lips. "I was there both times as well," I said. "Besides, I can't leave you here alone."

"Leroy did."

I looked at her in surprise. "What?" I managed. "You mean the divorce? But that's…"

She shook her head and then gazed up at the sky. "I was pregnant with Emma. Seven months, I think, so I was really showing," she said, her voice sounding like it was coming from a dream. "I had a guy called Milo working for me back then, but it was summer and there were snakes everywhere. So, he was down the coast somewhere and I get called to Price. I had to go, I wasn't feeling the best, so Leroy drove me. Well, when we got there, the guy was dead and the snake was on his face. It took me a little bit with my belly to get it into the bag, and then I called the police. Leroy decided if they were coming, he wasn't staying, and he went back home. Guy died of a heart attack, but I didn't get back for hours. He left me there, alone, in summer, pregnant." I searched her face, but all I could see was anger; there were no tears, no sadness, just that fury.

"Sorry, but I'm not Leroy," I said. "I couldn't do that. I… no, I couldn't do that."

She let out a long breath. "No," she murmured, "you're not Leroy." Her hand moved towards me, but then fell back to her side. I let it be. We stayed there in silence, leaning against the car, for too long. It felt awkward and not right, but I wasn't sure what to do about it.

I looked at her again. Her face looked like it was set in stone. I reached across and grabbed her hand. "Come on," I said.

"What? Where?"

"The police won't be here for a while yet. Let's go for a walk, just get away from here."

She sighed and let me drag her away from the house. Our hands fell apart as we made our way along Creek Road, looking out over the calm waters of the Gulf St Vincent.

"Thank you, by the way," I said.

"What for?" She looked at me with an expression bordering on suspicion.

"For what you did at the hotel. I mean it. It made me feel good to see Lynda and Ross squirm a little." I was about to go on, saying how I knew it didn't mean anything, but that cheeky grin that crossed her face made the words catch in my throat.

"That was all?" she asked. I smiled but didn't say anything. "Bray?" she pushed.

I shook my head and muttered, "I don't think I should…"

"Go on. Your turn to talk. Look, you've let me put everything on you. Your go."

I hesitated. "I felt good going somewhere again and not being alone," I said.

Her hand took mine. "Yeah, it did, didn't it?" she replied. And, our hands staying together, we walked the length of the road in silence, then made our way back, reaching the house less than a minute after the first police car. And then it was on…

Chapter 9

It was very late in the afternoon when I finally pulled up in front of Anthea's place. Apparently, the police are loathe to believe in coincidences, and our presence at both unexplained scenes of death had very quickly raised eyebrows. I was question three times, but it was Anthea they really went after. At one point she disappeared for well over an hour and when she came back to the car she looked like a kid who'd just spent that time with the principal. Once we were allowed to leave, the drive was quiet. She put on the radio and we listened to some sporting event that neither of us were interested in, but we didn't say anything.

I helped unload the stuff from my car and then looked at the sun as it hovered near the horizon. "Thank you for an interesting day," I said.

"You're going?" she asked.

"Well, I don't want to intrude," I replied. "You could probably do with a rest, and…"

"You came here after the gym, you didn't get lunch, I'm guessing you haven't eaten all day. Right?" she stated, sounding like her mother a little more than I felt comfortable with.

"Well, no," I returned, "but I've got eggs and bacon in the fridge at home and that'll do me."

"Then what?"

I felt like I was back with the police at Wills Creek. "Sit down, see what's on TV, I guess." I shrugged. "Don't think I can face lesson plans tonight."

"And you'll be alone."

"Alone," I agreed.

"Instead of coming in and sharing a pizza with me and watching some crappy 80s DVD." Her eyes bored into me. I snorted to stop myself from laughing. "Well?"

"Okay, yes, that does sound a whole lot better," I sighed.

"Good. Come on, then." And with that she led me inside. I let her order whatever pizza she liked – there actually is a delivery place out in that part of the Peninsula, weekends only, based out on a farm, and they are fantastic – and she then made me choose the DVD from her rather impressive collection while she took a bottle of wine out of the fridge. I was sitting on the couch when she returned, the opening menu splash panel telling her we were about to watch *The Breakfast Club*. She poured two glasses out and lifted hers. I followed suit. "To no more days like this one," she said.

"Definitely," I stated and we clinked the glasses together. With that we settled down to watch the film. Half an hour in, and there came a solid knock at the door. Anthea almost jumped up to get it, and emerged a few minutes later, already biting into a slice of the pizza. She placed it on the table in front of me and then went to get another bottle. It was then I noticed the first was empty; I was still on my first glass. She topped mine up, filled her own, and the movie resumed. The pizza and garlic bread were finished before Judd Nelson punched the air after detention was over, as was the second bottle of wine, a third already opened beside it.

"What now?" I asked.

"Do you mind if I pick?" she asked.

"Your house – go for it." She smiled and stumbled to the DVD collection. She giggled as she knelt down and pored through. I shook my head. She was well on her way to being drunk. Finally, she pulled one out and changed disks in the player, then came and fell down next to me, leaning against me heavily. She made no attempt to move. "So, what am I being subjected to?" I groaned.

She responded by pressing play on the remote control. The menu for *E.T. The Extra Terrestrial* came onto the screen. "Seriously?" I laughed.

"You don't like *E.T.*?"

"No, it's fine," I sighed, then smiled at her. She returned it and snuggled in a little closer to me. I felt slightly uncomfortable and enclosed, so I moved my arm out of her grip and placed it around her shoulders. And there we stayed as a rubber alien tried to get home. Drew Barrymore screaming made Anthea jump a little, and when she relaxed after that, she was somehow even closer to me, her arms wrapped around my waist from the front and behind. When it looked like the little alien was going to die, she sniffed and wiped her nose with her sleeve. I moved my hand and rubbed the back of her hair, that short lock that covered the nape of her neck.

She moved into my fingers as I did that, then she looked up at me, her eyes a little red from the gentle tears and I returned her gaze. She craned her neck up and placed her lips on mine. She tasted like wine. The kiss was wet and sloppy. I let it continue, though. She finally stopped and smiled at me, then nestled herself once more on my body. I continued to stroke her hair. Her grip about me loosened, and her breathing became deeper, louder. I stayed where I was until the credits rolled and I turned the film off. She did not respond at all. I sighed and sat her up, then stood and scooped her up in my arms, making sure her head was resting against my shoulder.

I carried her to her bedroom and placed her on the bed. I took her shoes off, then covered her with the blanket. Her arms reached up and gripped me about the neck, her mouth seeking mine. I let her kiss me briefly, then disengaged myself and placed a final kiss on the tip of her nose. She smiled, though her eyes did not open. "You coming to bed?" she asked, her words slurred enough to be noticeable.

"I'm one of the good ones," I whispered in her ear.

"One of the good ones," she repeated dreamily, a little smile settling on her lips. I watched her for a few seconds, then left the room, shutting the door behind me. I hunted through a linen closet and found a blanket and a pillow, made myself a cup of tea, found a *Die Hard* movie in her collection and settled down on the couch to watch Bruce Willis kill bad guys while things blew up. I guess I could have gone home, but it didn't feel right abandoning her after the really crappy few days she'd had.

I managed to get some sleep – the couch was not that uncomfortable – and woke up with the sun streaming in through the windows of the living room. I glanced back in the direction of the bedroom. The door was still closed, so I got myself up and went to the kitchen to make myself a strong coffee. While the kettle was boiling, I went out to the car and found my overnight bag under the back seat, something I had been carrying in my various cars since university. Spare underwear, deodorant, toothbrush and paste and, in this one, a clean t-shirt as well. I used a flannel to wash myself and got changed in the bathroom; by the time I returned to the kitchen, the electric kettle had switched off. I then settled back on the couch and switched on the television to watch an early morning sports show.

A knock came at the door. I looked back at the other end of the house, then heaved a sigh and went to the front door. I opened it carefully to be greeted by two men in suits. I recognized them both from the previous day. One held up an open wallet, confirming that he was a member of the South

Australian Police. "I'm Inspector Johann Wallace. Is Ms Anthea Bowman at home?"

I looked over my shoulder. "We, uhh, had too much to drink last night," I said. "As far as I'm aware, she's still asleep."

"You stayed the night?" he asked.

I felt the hackles on my neck rise a little. "On the couch. I was too drunk to drive. Now, would you like me to go and wake her up?" I knew I was a little short with him, but suddenly I didn't care. There was something about his attitude that was just negative from the word go.

"No. Please get her to call me when she can," he stated. "She has my number." He started to turn, then looked at me. "Did you get another call-out to catch a snake yesterday evening?" he asked.

"Her phone did not ring once." I hesitated, then the question came out, "Was there another one?"

"I am not at liberty to discuss that," he said, keeping all emotion out of his voice.

"Where didn't this happen?" I tried. He gave me a look that asked me silently if I was serious. I smiled. "Oh well, small communities, I'm a teacher. I'll find out tomorrow, if the media doesn't get hold of it first."

"That won't be happening any time soon," the other mumbled.

"Sorry?" I took what he had said as a threat and felt myself tense up automatically.

Wallace held his hand up. "Nothing to do with you." He looked at his partner, whose gaze dropped to his feet. "All right, I have a question for you. Have you had anything to do with a Mr Adam Lynch?"

I scowled. "The reporter," I growled. "He bailed us up at the Ardrossan Hotel, but we got away from him."

"What did you tell him?"

"That we'd been called out to that farm to catch a brown snake." He looked at the other officer, who jogged to a car parked behind mine. He returned a few moments later with a plastic bag containing two notebooks, several pens, a pencil, a smartphone and a couple of screwed up pieces of paper. Wallace put a pair of those thin disposable rubber gloves on and then opened the bag and took out one of the notebooks. He went through it briefly, then stopped.

"Here. 'Found AB and' – question marks, so I guess that's you – 'at hotel. Said they were called to catch a brown snake. He pushed past me. Know something.' And here, 'Man is Brayden Kincaid, a school teacher here. Why is he snake hunting?'" He flipped the pages slowly, looking at each, then shrugged and replaced it in the bag. The other officer took the bag away and he peeled his gloves off. "So, I guess the question is: why are you snake hunting?"

"I'm not. I'm her chauffeur. Her car broke down. And one of the guys at that farm was her off-sider. She needed a hand, I was available." I tried to sound casual, but I could feel the anger in my tone emerge too easily.

He looked at me, but clearly decided against forcing anything. "That's fine, Mr Kincaid. If you could get her to call me," were his parting words. I closed the door before they'd reached their car.

I took a deep breath to calm myself and then made my way back to the kitchen. Anthea was standing there, staring at me. "Anyone important?" she muttered. Her voice sounded thick and her eyes were ringed with darkness.

"Some Inspector Wallace wants you to call him when you're feeling up to it," I said, walking across to her. She fell against my chest, her arms hanging down. "Go have a shower, clean yourself up. I'll make us some breakfast."

"I couldn't eat a thing," she slurred.

I kissed the top of her head without thinking what I was doing. "I'm still going to make you something," I said. She hugged me briefly, then stumbled back to her room without saying anything else.

By the time she emerged from the bathroom I had an omelette waiting for her and a large mug of strong coffee. She almost fell into a chair, looking at the food doubtfully. I sat down opposite her. Her first bite was tiny, the second a bit larger, and then she was eating with gusto. "What did that cop want?" she finally asked between mouthfuls.

My expression must have said a lot before my mouth could form the words. "Let me guess, another one, right?" she muttered.

"I think it was that reporter who hassled us outside the hotel." She stared at me and leant back on her chair. "They didn't come out and tell me, but that was what I could gather. Sorry."

"No, no.." she mumbled. It took her a few moments before she resumed eating, much slower this time. I finished and watched her, but her pace slowed right down until she was staring at a hunk of yellow on the end of her fork.

"You not feeling well?" I ventured.

She didn't look at me. "I did something stupid last night, didn't I?" she whispered.

I shrugged. "I wouldn't say stupid," I said. "Look, you were drunk. You fell asleep. I put you to bed. I decided to stay here because I didn't want you waking up alone… and to, be honest, I didn't feel like being alone, either. Don't worry – I slept on the couch," I added quickly.

"Thank you." Her voice was virtually no more than a breath.

I reached a hand across to her, but she moved away

from me. "Nothing happened," I said. "Honest."

She sighed and put the fork down. "I know," she murmured. She looked at me, her face flushed red. "You're one of the good ones."

"Anthea, it's been a shithouse weekend. I'm not about to make it worse for you."

"Worse," she echoed, her smile rueful. She drained the rest of her coffee, more to give her something to do than because she wanted it.

"What time's Emma coming home?" I asked suddenly.

"After netball, and so probably after lunch. Mid-afternoon, I guess. Why?" That suspicion was back.

"Well, let's see – you're going to ring this Inspector. I'm going to guess he's going to want to see you, but you can put it off. Then you're going to ring – Donna, is it? – anyway, her and tell her you're taking today off. There's at least one more outfit doing snakes over in Balaklava, and I'm sure there's one further south on the peninsula, and that's just what I know about, let them deal with it for one day. You can't do it all, you'll work yourself into the ground, so I am going to take you somewhere where you can get away from all the shit and just relax." I finished my speech and tried to give her my best teacher smile.

She greeted me with a stony face. "And where would this wonderful place of relaxation be?" she asked, her voice even.

"No fucking idea," I returned with exaggerated cheer. She continued to stare at me, but the smile broke through and she dropped her eyes and shook her head. "No?" I said.

"Well, you've got until I've made two phone calls to work out just where this place of relaxation might be," she said, getting up from the table and grabbing her phone from the counter. She looked at me for a few moments longer, the grin faltering. "One of the good ones," she sighed and disappeared to the other end of the house.

Chapter 10

I still had no idea where I was going to take Anthea; I didn't actually know her well enough to select something that fast that I thought she was going to enjoy. But I did manage to buy some time by stopping at my place in Port Clinton. She followed me into my house-for-one, and smirked at the way I had everything sorted – piles everywhere. I darted into my bedroom to change my pants and came out to find her going through my compact disc collection. "Disgusted?" I asked, sidling up next to her.

"How many do you have?" she asked, indicating the shelves of discs.

I shrugged. "Dunno. You buy videos, I buy music."

She took one out and looked at the back of it. "Oh, wow, I haven't heard some of these songs in years," she laughed. She looked along the rows of CDs in a series of bookcases I'd made just for them. "I could spend days just listening to the stuff you've got here."

"Well, any time you want, feel free to come over and…" I started.

She turned and faced me. "Let's do it."

"What?" I was lost.

"Let's not go anywhere special. Let's just stay here and we can play music and chill." The look in her eyes told me that she was serious. She really wanted to relax and not do anything. I couldn't blame her.

"Sure," I said. "Why not? But I haven't really got much to eat or drink. I'll just dart down the road to the shops and grab something. Anything in particular?"

"No, I'll come along," she said. "You can show me

your town." She shook her head. "I think I've only been to the Club for a meal here. I don't think I've really seen the rest of the place."

Now, Port Clinton is not big. Maybe three hundred residents, it's got a caravan park, the Club, a decent general store, a few small businesses, but very little else. The walk from my house to the store takes about ten minutes, but by the time I'd shown Anthea the sights, so to speak, a good half an hour had passed. We entered the store and grabbed a bag of chips and bottle of Diet Coke. Old Gwen was waiting at the counter. "How are you, young Brayden?" she asked, her raspy voice sounding a little worse than usual.

"I'm fine, thanks. You?"

"Oh, not good, not good," she muttered and I readied myself for a list of her ailments. But instead, what I got was, "Did you hear what happened at Wills Creek?" Her voice was a conspiratorial whisper.

"No," I said slowly. I cast Anthea a quick glance; she was hiding her face as well as she could.

"Two dead people," she stated with a firm nod.

"Two?" The shock in my tone was not put on.

"Well, first they found one of the old timers dead in her house, then they found some young man dead in her shed. Rhonda Jessop's sister lives up the road and said police were there late last night. Apparently, the neighbor heard something and called them, but when they got there, he was dead." She finished this with a slow nod.

"Stop the gossip, Gwen," the woman behind the counter ordered. She looked at me and rolled her eyes and I managed a smile in return. Gwen shuffled off and I stepped forward. "All gossip," the woman said.

"Well, we'll just grab this lot, thanks. Oh, and a paper." I forced false cheer onto myself.

She rang it up, we chatted a bit about the weather, then I bid her farewell and Anthea led me outside. "That reporter was at Wills Creek?" she asked.

"We don't know for sure," I said. "I mean, it is just gossip." We started to head back to my place. "The only people I know in Wills Creek are a few students. I can't very well go ringing them and asking about dead people."

"And the only person I know is" – her tongue seemed to catch in her throat momentarily – "Leroy's sister. I am not going to ring her, and besides which, her property's half a K or so out of town."

"Wonder if it was there they found him."

"It makes sense, though," Anthea mused. "He tracked us down at the pub."

"And when he got nothing from us, he went to the next place where the police were, started poking around and…"

"Yeah. *And.*" She fell silent and remained that way until we were back at my place. I grabbed some glasses and something to put the chips in while she selected a few CDs and put them in my CD player.

I sat myself on the couch; she sat so there was a distinct gap between us. She hit 'PLAY' on the remote control, then forwarded through a few songs before she stopped. Within moments Billy Idol was singing about dancing with himself, and finally a smile returned to her lips. She sang along, word-perfect, and then forwarded through another few songs until she found another one she wanted, which she also sang along to. I let her go. She seemed to be enjoying herself. The CDs changed over to the next one in line and the first song was 'Could've Been' by Tiffany. She cast me a sideways glance, and then stood up and held out her hands. "What?" I asked stupidly.

"We never got to finish the dance on Friday night," she said.

I let myself be dragged to my feet and, as we had done in that Community Room, we swayed back and forth while she sang along to the track. This time we got all the way through to the end. I started to move back towards the couch, but she didn't let go. The next song started, another slow one, and our actions remained the same – that slight swaying done by non-dancers when they try to keep in time to a ballad. She nestled her head against my shoulder. It felt comfortable, having her there like that. I tightened my grip on her and she returned the favor. The previous night flashed through my mind and I risked placing a kiss on top of her head.

She looked at me curiously, then craned her neck up towards me. I let her lips press against mine, but my response was muted. She broke off and gazed at me. There was hurt in her eyes. "What's wrong?" she asked, her voice choking a little.

"Are you sure?" I asked. She just stared at me, and all ardor had evaporated from her in that instant. I felt I had to explain. "With all the shit this weekend, with the Leroy thing, are you sure?"

She stared at me and then, quite suddenly, rested her hand against my cheek. "I'm not Lynda," she said simply. She understood.

"I…" I couldn't find the words. The more time I spent with her, the more I found myself wanting to spend even more time with her. I was becoming attracted to her, but the doubts about everything just would not leave me. I kissed the tip of her nose. "I know, but…"

Her smile was a little sad. "I do understand," she whispered. I couldn't think of anything else to say, so I grabbed her and held her close. She returned the embrace with force and I didn't want to let her go. This was comfortable. This was starting to feel like what I'd been missing, what had been missing between Lynda and I for the last portion of our relationship. This was…

And that was when her phone rang out in that default tone.

"Shit," she growled and broke off from me to reach into her front pocket. She looked at the number, rolled her eyes, and then jammed the phone against her ear. "What is it, mum?" she asked with undisguised weariness.

I went across and turned the music down. She smiled awkwardly at me, but didn't say anything. I could now hear the steady prattle of Mrs Bowman as a mosquito-like buzzing. Then the color drained from Anthea's face. "Don't you dare," she hissed. Then, "I don't care if he is. Mum, he wants to take her away. Do not let him." Brief words from the other end. "No, take her. With him. As in, go away. Leave here." Longer this time. "That's right." A single sentence. "Of course you can't let him." She looked at me and then said, "I'll be there in twenty minutes." I nodded. But she did not move as Mrs Bowman started up again. "He what?" Another little speech. "All right, fine. We'll meet there. *You* bring Emma." Something else was said and Anthea's jaw tightened. "I don't give a shit what he wants. You take Emma and wait for me. Okay?" A single sound response. "Okay, I'll see when we all get there." She disconnected the call and looked at me. Her face was red and she looked like she could punch something or someone, but her eyes were welling up rapidly.

"Come here," I said and offered an arm to her. She just came to me and wrapped her arms around my chest. She wasn't sobbing, but I was sure I could feel her crying. I played with that short lock of hair on her neck again until I heard a large sniff and she shifted away from me. "So, what do you need me to do?" I asked.

She shook her head. "Bray, this is…"

"I'm going to have to drive you, anyway. So where, and am I allowed to ask what's going on?"

She wiped her face and the sadness seemed to be replaced by anger with that one simple motion. "Leroy turned up at mum's," she said shortly. "Wanted to have some time with Emma. I said no. He told mum he just wanted to take her to his sister's house, so she could spend some time with those cousins. I said only if mum went. We're going to meet them there and sort this out once and for all."

"No lawyers?" I asked.

"Not if I can help it," she growled.

I reached across and took her hand for a second. "Get yourself cleaned up and we'll go as soon as you're ready," I said.

She stared at me for a long time, then placed a kiss on my cheek. "I told you I'm not Lynda," she whispered. "Well, you are definitely not Leroy." And with that she headed for the bathroom. I took it as a compliment.

Chapter 11

Mrs Bowman and I went down to the edge of the town of Wills Creek itself, me making sure we were as far away as we could be from the house I'd been to twice in the previous two days, and sat on a long seat at the top of the cliffs overlooking the foreshore, watching the waves. Neither of us said anything for a while. I guess we were both thinking about what was going on some distance out of town. Leroy's brother-in-law was a mechanic by trade, and he made his living working mainly on farm machinery. Their property was a large one, once the second house on an expansive farm, but now dominated by sheds and parts and the remains of tractors and utilities and large vehicles, as well as a few cars in various states of repair.

Once Anthea and I had arrived there, the tension in the air became thick. That was when Mrs Bowman stepped in. She told Anthea and Leroy to talk things over. Emma had wanted to stay with them. Leroy's sister took her two teenagers off to Ardrossan and that was when Mrs Bowman and I decided to make ourselves scarce as well. I thought the two of us, having worked together at one stage, would find something to talk about, but it felt as uncomfortable between us as between Leroy and Anthea. Then, quite suddenly, out of nowhere, Mrs Bowman asked, "What's going on between you and my daughter?" There was accusation there, what I thought was a hint of anger and actual, genuine curiosity.

"Friends," I said. "She needed one this weekend, and that's me."

"What about her girlfriends?" The anger was gone.

"They had an argument on Friday night, I think. It'll

sort itself out. It always does," I replied, keeping my tone oh so casual.

"And so you and her are friends," she repeated. She finally looked at me. "Where did you sleep last night?"

"The couch." I made sure my response was quick, not thinking about what was behind the query.

She continued to stare at me. "Friends," she muttered after what felt like a good minute or so, shaking her head.

"Friends," I agreed.

"You know she likes you, don't you?" That accusation was also gone now. "I mean, really likes you?"

"She told you that?" I returned before I could think.

She smiled, something I had seen only rarely. "Like she'd tell me anything," she snorted. "I can just tell. Trust me."

"We've spent one weekend together, and…"

"…and I can tell already, yes," she finished. Her smile became a little wider and maybe a little sadder. "Maybe you should do something about it, hmm?"

I sighed and didn't respond at all. I just returned my gaze to the ocean in front of me and the choppy waves forcing their way onto the rocky shore somewhere beneath us. Silence once more descended upon us. We stayed there for a little while longer before she stood and stated, "I need to walk, stretch these old legs. Coming?"

"Sure," I replied and also climbed to my feet. "Where to?"

"Don't care. Just need to walk." We headed off away from the town. "And how's your class this year?" she asked. That was the conversation I'd been waiting for.

"Remember Gregory Higham?"

"Who could forget him?" she sneered. Not a pleasant memory for either of us.

"Got his brother Trevor this year. Talk about chalk

and cheese!" Her laugh was genuine and the conversation flowed from then on. No more talk of Anthea and me, just the students at the school she'd left, and her telling me about her new work at the Lutheran school in Maitland two days a week, and her new passion of indoor bowls.

We were on our way back when her phone rang. She looked at the screen. "Anthea," she declared and I moved away to give her some privacy.

I didn't hear any of the conversation, but it was short, sharp and shiny. "She wants us to go back," she stated.

"Well, let's get getting," I smiled.

She didn't return it. "She didn't sound too good, Bray," she said.

Emma and Anthea were waiting out the front on the road when Mrs Bowman pulled up. Anthea came up to us and simply said, "Mum, can you take Emma back to your place, please? Bray and I need to talk."

"Of course, dear," was the very careful reply. "Is everything all right?"

"Please, mum." There was no emotion in her tone at all. Mrs Bowman obviously recognized whatever that was, and soon Emma was bundled into her car, not protesting at all; in fact, I would say she looked rather shell-shocked by something. That was not the Emma I was used to.

We stayed there until the car drove off. "All right," Anthea muttered. "Our turn." She led me across to my car. "Let's go down to the beach," she said as I started the engine. Back to Wills Creek we went until we reached the same spot where Mrs Bowman had been parked not that long before.

Anthea's eyes drifted in the direction of number fifteen Creek Street. I went to get out of the car, but she stopped me. "Leroy's back in town," she said. "For good, he says. His new woman dumped him. He's living here, with his sister." She paused to look down at her hands folded in her lap and to collect her thoughts. "He asked me to remarry him, to try again. He made promises and… and he asked."

I didn't know what to say, so I did not say a thing. I just looked at her, waiting for the inevitable.

"Bray, you should have seen Emma's face!" she cried suddenly. "She looked like all her Christmases had come at once. It was like this was what she had been waiting for for so long." A sad smile touched her mouth. "She was so happy."

"Your call," I said simply.

"My call," she muttered. "My call," she repeated, her voice drifting off like a puff of smoke. Her hands clenched into loose fists for a moment, her eyes never leaving them. "Well, I made my call. I told him, 'No.' I'm not doing that again." A tear ran down her cheek; I resisted the urge to wipe it away. "But when I said that, Emma looked like her heart had been broken. She just went quiet and sat there. I hurt her. That's when I rang mum."

"Oh." It was all that would come out.

Her eyes lifted to stare at me. "Bray, have I done the right thing?" she begged.

I reached across and took her hands. "I can't answer that," I replied softly. "It has to be your call. But I will ask you this: Is getting back with Leroy to make Emma happy going to make you happy?"

She stared at me for a long time. The tears stopped quickly and she just took me in. "No," she finally said, "it won't." She squeezed my fingers tight. "I think I know what will make me happy."

"Anthea, please…" I muttered, but she kept her grip on my fingers.

"I know," she said softly, then reached across and kissed me gently and briefly on the mouth. "No promises, but it's… yeah." Her smile was that cheeky one I was quickly growing to find very adorable. I reached a hand up and ran it through her hair, but did not say anything. She looked at me for a few moments longer before a laugh escaped. "And he hates my haircut as well," she said.

"Then he's an idiot, because you look…" I shut up before I said too much. She did not press it, she simply smiled at me.

It had been less than one weekend, and I liked where this was going already. We stayed there for a little while longer before I settled back behind the wheel. "Where to?" I asked.

She smiled at me, but then her face took on a curious expression. "Can we go look at the place up the road?"

I knew where she meant. "Really?" I muttered.

"Really." She shrugged. "I can walk it, if you want." I wanted to ask why, and to tell her that it was a bad idea, but all I did was start the engine and go directly there. So simple. I parked on the opposite side of the road and we both climbed out to look at it. Yellow tape was strung across the front door, while blue and white checked police tape was draped across the front of the yard. But that was it. If the police had come by Anthea's place so early in the morning, I guessed they might have been here most of the night, but it still felt odd that it was deserted like this.

Anthea made her way across the street. "Why?" I groaned. She turned and looked at me, then indicated with her head I should go as well. I stared at her, so she repeated the gesture. And I followed. She stood at the head of the driveway as if that plastic tape flapping in the breeze was an impenetrable barrier. I came up beside her. Without looking at me, she said very softly, "My equipment's still in your car, right?"

I had to think, but eventually I replied in the same

tone of voice, "Yeah. I didn't take it out last night."

"Neither did I."

"Anthea, we shouldn't go in there. It's a crime scene and what if… what if…" I could now see what she saw.

It was as long as the one I had seen up at the farm, but its upper body was thicker, giving it a definite torso-like appearance. It was at the far end of the drive, near a garage that was surrounded by even more tape, basking in the early afternoon sun. Its black skin seemed to absorb the light, not allowing us to see any real details from that distance. But its size and shape were more than enough for us. It was spread out, as though daring anyone to approach. It was not a corpse stretched there; it was most definitely alive and there it was.

"You want to catch it?" I sounded as scared as I felt.

"Of course," she muttered, her eyes remaining fixed on the motionless reptile.

"I…" I had no words. What could I say? This was what she did, and my fears were only going to hold her back. If this was a species of snake that should not be there, then it made sense to get rid of them. "Of course," I repeated.

She finally looked at me and her smile was sly. "Are you scared of a little snake?" she goaded.

"First, it's not little, and second, yes, I am," I replied. My eyes drifted back to the snake, still in that same position. "I am fucking terrified," was what came out of my mouth before I could think about it.

Her hand found mine and she squeezed my fingers. I forced myself to look at her and she smiled at me. It was a genuine smile, not condescending, not putting me down, just an acknowledgement of what I was feeling, and an acceptance. "All I am going to ask you to do is to watch and make sure it all looks above board. Okay?"

"Are you sure about this?"

She glanced at the reposing animal. "No," she said simply, then kissed my cheek and headed back to the car. I followed dutifully behind. She put those incredible gloves on and grabbed her hook and bag. "Please keep an eye out for anything," she said, and she was very serious.

"Like that hawk up there?" I asked, pointing at the sky above us. She followed my finger and scowled. Silhouetted against the clouds, it was circling slowly, riding a current with ease, each pass bringing it lower and lower. Neither of us moved from the car. It was soon obvious that I was wrong – it was not a hawk, but a wedge-tailed eagle, and a decent-sized one at that. And I, at least, had no doubts what it had set its eyes on. "Don't often see them around people and especially towns," I muttered. Being a teacher, especially in a rural area, you learn a little bit about many varied subjects, and local raptors was something that I had some basic knowledge of.

And, it turned out, Anthea had quite a deal of knowledge. "That's right," she muttered, "so there can be only one thing it's going after." I saw a strange expression cross her face. "I'm torn," she said suddenly, as if just saying her thoughts out loud. "On the one hand, I don't really want an eagle to take this thing away where it might let it go and so that snake could end up anywhere. On the other hand, I want to see what happens. I mean, that's a damn big snake there and I don't think I've seen an eagle take anything that size before." She seemed to be chewing the inside of her cheek as she contemplated the situation.

"So… what do we do?" I asked, amazed at just how pathetic I sounded.

She chose to ignore my tone of voice. "I reckon we let nature take its course," she finally said, but she sounded like it was not a decision she had come to easily, nor one she was overly happy with. I started to return to the house, but she held me back and shook her head. "Wait," was all she said. I obeyed. Instead she edged us sideways, giving the bird more room to approach.

The eagle sailed above the town of Wills Creek lazily, riding wind currents we could not feel down at ground level. The closer it came, the more it looked like something prehistoric, with its stocky legs held horizontal, its sharp beak looking like the deadliest of weapons. We froze, allowing it to think it was safe. I guess we were just lucky no other cars came by, or no residents came out, but Wills Creek was not that sort of a town. Traffic was a rarity at the best of times, and in the middle of a Sunday not during any tourist season, when most of the older people would be relaxing after attending church at Ardrossan that morning and the younger people – what few lived there – would be at various sporting events or hanging out somewhere not Wills Creek, my car was probably a complete anomaly.

And then the bird swept out over the sea, wheeled around and came gliding in, the legs lowering like the wheels on a landing fighter aircraft, sharp and large talons pointing forward, its eyes on one target and one target only. It swept past us, maybe only a meter above the top of my head, and getting lower all the time, the wings angled ready for a quick up-flight, ready to escape with its prize.

And then…

"Shi-i-it," Anthea groaned; I was struck completely dumb.

The snake was fast, so incredibly fast. Just before the talons could hook under the centre of that long, pythonic body, the crocodilian head snapped around, lifting up like the pictures of cobras I'd seen from India, locking onto the neck of the attacking bird. It whipped itself around and dragged the eagle straight down to the ground. The wings flapped once, and then fell still. The snake, however, did not let go, its jaws clamped about the feathered throat with a grip that looked like it was trying to decapitate its prey.

Feathers drifted from the body and fell to the ground. One wing, already hanging limp, dropped away. The chest cavity was revealed. We couldn't make out the finer details, but it was not skin we were seeing. The whole upper body of the bird was growing progressively thinner, and still the snake did not let go. A shudder ran through me, like an earth tremor, as realisation struck. The body drooped down; the only thing holding it up now was the reptile. "Oh, fuck," I groaned.

"What?" Anthea asked, her voice rising a little louder than either of us would have liked.

"That's what happened to, to, to everyone," I whimpered.

"What?"

"The snakes. They… Oh, shit. Anthea…"

"I can see it." She grabbed my hand. "Run!" she screamed.

I didn't need to be told twice. The snake had let go of the remains of the poor eagle and its yellow eyes – now clearly visible – had fixed onto us. It raised its head again, and then it launched itself forward.

We were back at the car when it reached the end of the driveway, a black guided missile, eyes glaring at us the whole while. Anthea threw herself into the back seat while I jumped in behind the steering wheel and fumbled with the keys in my pocket.

The thud that rocked the car was solid and made me cry out and drop the keys into the footwell. "Bray…" Anthea's voice was slow and drawn out and quiet. I sat up and turned my head.

That very unsnake-like head was staring at me

through the glass of the window. It opened its mouth, those long fangs coming out of their little mouth pockets, purple glistening on the tip of each, something black discoloring them. Slowly I pushed the key into the ignition. It moved its head a little, as if watching my actions.

"Get moving," Anthea rumbled from behind me.

I turned the key and depressed the accelerator, then dropped the parking brake and screeched up the road. There was a bumping jerk but I did not care. The snake had started to recoil as soon as the engine had roared into life, but then the head had dropped away the moment I took off. I looked in the rear-view mirror but Anthea was on her knees, peering through the back window, blocking my view.

"Stop," she ordered.

"What? Are you crazy?" Panic was getting a very good foothold on me.

"Stop!" she repeated, louder and more firmly. I shook my head, but pulled over. "Reverse," she then commanded. I had to actually force myself to drop the gearstick and slowly made my way back the way we'd come. Very slowly. But that seemed to suit Anthea. "Okay, stop," she finally said. I didn't need to be told that twice. She turned around and carefully opened the door.

"What are you doing?" I whimpered.

"Don't worry," she said, but her tone lacked that firmness that would have given me some confidence. I waited for her to leave the vehicle and then I also climbed out. I looked where she was going and recoiled. The snake was writhing on the road, but not moving away from her approach. I took a few paces forward before I saw what had happened – it had not been fast enough and I had driven over it. The centre of the serpentine body was flattened where, probably, my rear wheel had squashed it into nothing.

But it was alive and I didn't need to be an expert to see that it was beyond angry. Now, I know that it's not right to attribute human emotions to animals – anthropomorphising, it's called, and it's the stuff of fairy tales and fantasy books, really. But, looking at that creature, it was angry. Furious, even. And Anthea was approaching it, wearing thick gloves, holding a hook and a material bag on a pole, and looking like she was stalking it.

I stayed right where I was; she didn't need me to interrupt what she was doing… and I was petrified. I had never felt that scared before.

She hooked the snake and lifted it from the bitumen. The back half dropped back to the ground, thrashing around as if was an entity all of its own. The head half seemed to fall limp as she lifted it and edged the bag towards it.

Its strike happened in the blink of an eye. Its head lifted and just latched onto the hand holding the bag. But it fell back straight away and dropped to the ground, out of the hook, even as Anthea dropped everything and stumbled backwards herself. The spell on me was broken. I ran to her side and she let me hold her around the waist from behind. The top half of the snake tried to lunge at us, but it had nothing to give it the momentum and so that fanged mouth snapped at nothing.

Anthea looked down at her hand. The metal covering on her glove was dented and a drop of purple sat in the depression, like a drop of thick oil. Her eyes lifted to the snake, blood flowing from the end of its sliced body in a steady stream, its movements growing less and less vigorous. The tail end had also started to slow in its motions. The yellow eyes suddenly latched onto us and, I swear, the mouth sneered.

We stayed where we were for a few long minutes until all movement had ceased. Anthea removed herself from my arms and went to the side of the road. She returned quickly with a rock that she struggled to carry a little. She strode right past me and stood over the creature. The eyes moved to gaze at her. That was all she needed. She simply dropped the rock, crushing the head into oblivion, sending red spraying out like a stylistic flower pattern. She backed away from it until she bumped into me again. I let my arms enfold her once more and she placed her hands over mine.

"Fuck," she finally whispered, but I struggled to hear her over the sound of my heart hammering away in my throat.

Chapter 12

Mrs Bowman and Emma were waiting for us when we got back to Anthea's place. I made a brief foray into the house, then said I really had to get going because I did have work to do. Anthea followed me out to the car. We did not say anything about what we had seen and what had happened in Wills Creek. She simply thanked me for being there for her over the weekend, and I added I hoped we could do it again sometime, but maybe without the snakes. She laughed and our kiss was short and almost passionate before she let me go. She watched me until I was on the road.

I was half-inclined to call her that night, but I got lost in making sure I had everything ready for the week, and decided she probably needed some time alone with Emma. That and I really wanted to try and not think about the whole snake thing… or maybe not think about Anthea in general. It somehow felt safer that way.

I skipped the gym on Monday morning and went straight in to work. The talk of the staffroom was Friday night and the fundraiser. Of course. Photos were plastered everywhere, and I noticed more than a few of me, mostly on the dance floor. I had a feeling I wouldn't be living that down in a hurry. But it was all good-natured, and it ended up raising a decent amount of money to help the junior sports teams with equipment and other things. However, there was another discussion that seemed to bypass me. Conversations changed abruptly and some of the other teachers took to smiling at me a little too wide and for a little too long. It wasn't until I heard Anthea's name that I realized what was going on – of course, we had been seen at the hotel. I mean, being seen was part of the point, but now…

This week was starting off really well. I hurried back to my class and waited for the bell. The children were excited; about half had been at the Friday night function and even amongst them it was quite the topic of conversation. Yes, my turns on the dance floor got a few mentions, but at least the seven and eight-year-olds in my class didn't care if I'd had a drink in a hotel with someone. And held their hand. And kissed their nose.

The morning went by in its usual Monday routine – literacy, with new word lists for the week, then numeracy, finishing with a bit of "sharing time" – what was called "show and tell" when my parents were kids. I stayed in the room through the recess break to set up for the big science block we always did between recess and lunch on a Monday, thus avoiding my colleagues. Science went off without a hitch, and that brought about lunchtime. I had yard duty on the oval for the first half, so off I went, with hat and bag and everything else a dutiful teacher needed.

So far, normal.

I was wandering near the back fence when one of the students approached me. It did not take long for me to realize it was Emma. "Can we talk, Mr Kincaid?" she asked quietly. I knew that tone of voice and readied myself to offer another sort of counselling session; after all, her mother had rejected her father's offer of a reconciliation right in front of her.

"Of course," I said. We walked around the boundary of the oval. A few groups were playing football, but there were not many children at this end of the school, so we were essentially alone, and yet she remained quiet. "What's up, Emma?"

"Did you stay with my mum all weekend?"

To say I hadn't been ready for that question was an

understatement. But I knew better than to be evasive here. "Yes," I replied simply.

"Why?"

"She needed a friend." So far, so good.

We walked on in silence for a little while longer. "Mum said you're a special friend," came next.

"I'm glad she thinks so."

"She likes you," Emma said, her voice somehow sounding like I was being berated. Then she stopped to look at me carefully. I returned the gaze. "I like you, too," she said.

I smiled. "I'm glad."

"Are you going to hurt mum like dad did?" And now the truth of the matter came out. I was not sure what Anthea had told her, but there was a seriousness about the question that was so much older than her ten years indicated it should have been.

"Emma," I said, "I will try my hardest not to hurt your mum at all." I was about to add *I promise* but, like Anthea, I knew better than to say that. "I like her." I touched Emma's head. "I like you, too. I don't want to hurt you, either."

She looked at me for a few uncomfortable moments, then decided she had all the answers she needed and simply walked away. I had the strangest feeling that I had just been interrogated by a child, and that things had ended up okay.

But that was not quite the way the school day ended.

I liked to finish Mondays with art. The rest of the day is reasonably full-on, so I find doing something creative is always a good release. The bell went, I dismissed everyone and then set myself to the task of cleaning the leftover mess that was always there. I knew we had cleaners, but a sense of guilt always made me get at the worst of it before they came in. I was on my hands and knees trying to get some glue out of the carpet before it set when a cough attracted my attention.

I looked up and felt my heart sink. I recognized Inspector Johann Wallace straight away, his unnamed offsider behind him like an obedient lapdog. "Mr Kincaid, do you have time to talk?" he asked, his tone indicating he was not going to accept any answer except 'yes'.

"Sure, if you don't mind me finishing this while we do," I replied, bending once more to the task I'd set myself.

I heard them enter and could feel it as they came close, though not too close. There was a creak as one of them sat on the edge of one of the tables. I finally got the globule of glue up and dumped it on a piece of newspaper. I stood and went to the bin. I think they were waiting for me to say something.

"You went to Wills Creek again yesterday." Wallace finally broke the impasse. Not a question, but a statement.

"Yep. Went to visit Anthea's sort of family, then had a look at the house." He'd know which one.

"See anything out of the ordinary?"

"No. But we killed a snake." I finally looked at him and saw that his mouth was set into a thin line. He was struggling to control himself.

"That all?"

"Yep." I sat down behind my desk, which I knew gave me that power pose so many in authority hate when it's not them. "Look, we went to look at the house, that's all. After everything we'd seen there, it was sort of like just making sure it wasn't a bad dream. We didn't cross the police tape, we didn't trample on any evidence, we saw a poisonous snake and it was killed."

I saw his eye twitch. I think everything I'd just said was probably confirmed by whichever witness in Wills Creek reported our presence.

"My turn," I said suddenly. "What do you think we

did?"

"I think that's all the questions we have for now," Wallace said suddenly, standing with a jerk of his body.

I smiled and leant forward. "Inspector, that's not good enough. What's going on?"

"Your presence was noted, so we investigated. Do you know what we found at the property?"

"A dead snake on the road, cut in two, its head caved in by a rock?"

He actually smiled. "Yes, we did find that. Messy. But, no – what we found was a dead eagle, its body in a state similar to that of the" – he inhaled deeply – "the bodies you have already seen."

My face must have told him just how shocked I was because his face relaxed, the line becoming an actual mouth again. "What in the hell did that?" I asked hoarsely. I knew it was the snake, of course, but that was not the 'what' I had meant.

He didn't know that.

"That's the problem," he said and sat down again. "Look, did you see anything out of the ordinary, anything at all, no matter how insignificant?"

"We saw snakes, that's it," I replied. His expression told me he believed me completely. But I hadn't lied; I had just not told the whole truth. "Inspector, what's going on?"

"We don't know." He looked at his partner. "I should not be telling you any of this. Toxicology reports have indicated nothing. I mean, there is no reason for what happened to those bodies. Do you know what necrosis is?"

I nodded. "But I thought necrosis was caused by parasites or a poison like from a white-tipped spider," I said, reciting Anthea's explanation to me.

"That's correct. But everything came back negative,

nothing in the bodies, just the damaged tissue."

I considered this, then asked, "So, what did kill them? Do you know yet?"

"Cardiac paralysis." I shook my head. "Something made their hearts simply stop. There are drugs that can do that, some poisons, but none of those were in the systems of any of the victims."

I shuddered. And yet, despite listening to him and what he was divulging to me, I did not think about telling him what we had seen with the eagle, or these strange snakes. There was a part of me that did not feel it was my place, but another part, I think, that still did not believe what I'd seen, or maybe I was still in shock. Yet, I had been given the perfect opportunity to pass the buck to someone else, and I did not take it. Stupid, possibly, but that was the way it was.

Another image hit me. That snake at the Haviland farm, looming over me, readying itself to strike, almost taunting me…

"Are you okay?" Wallace asked suddenly. I didn't realize that my thoughts were writ so large on my face.

"Yeah, it's just that…" I shook my head. "We were there. Whatever did it to them could have…" I didn't need to finish.

"Yes," he said simply. "Well, if we have any further questions, we'll be in touch, but at this stage, I don't think you…"

"Can I ask something first?"

"Depends what it is," he replied with a huge degree of caution.

"Was there any link between Mrs Robertson and Mr Haviland?"

The two officers exchanged a glance. "It's not exactly a secret," Wallace finally said. "Haviland was her son-in-law.

Her daughter died a few years ago and he helps look after her place – gardening, heavy cleaning, things like that. Though looking at that back yard he didn't do much at all. Why?" Suspicion again.

"Curious," I muttered.

His eyes did not leave me for a long time. "Please do not play private investigator," he said. "This isn't the movies, this isn't a joke and you could get yourself into trouble. And," he continued before I could say anything, "if I have a hint you are withholding information, I will have you arrested in front of your entire class. Understand?"

I returned his gaze. He had been doing well until that final threat and he knew it. He'd overstepped the line, which told me two things. First, he was already frustrated, even after less than two days. And second, he liked to be the one in charge of everything, and did not mind what he said or did to maintain that. My feelings towards this man were now almost completely negative. "Oh, I understand," I replied, but I think my own tone of voice betrayed how I was now feeling.

"Right. Good day, Mr Kincaid."

I said nothing as the two of them left the room. I leant back on my chair and closed my eyes to calm myself, but it was not working. I turned to my computer and opened the 'My Music' folder. Within moments, Pink Floyd's 'Shine On You Crazy Diamond' was filling my head as well as the rest of the room and probably the two neighboring rooms as well. I closed my eyes and let David Gilmour's guitar carry my mind to a more pleasant place.

"Relaxation music?"

I turned quickly, almost falling off my chair, and could not help but smile. Anthea and Emma were standing in the doorway. "Yeah, I just…" I shrugged.

"We saw them in here," Anthea said. "I've had

enough of them for one day." I didn't ask what that meant; I guessed I'd find out if she wanted me to know.

"We hid in the toilets until they went away," Emma added, her voice very serious.

I laughed. "Well, I'm glad to see friendly faces." They entered the room and I turned down the volume. "So, what brings you by?"

"Can you stop by our place when you're finished here?" Anthea asked. "Mum's coming over to watch Em when she's finished at Maitland, so no rush."

I looked at Emma and received a glare I could only describe as stern. "I'd love to," I said. "What's the occasion?"

Anthea's face screwed up a little in embarrassment as she muttered, "I need your help in the snake room."

"Wonderful." My voice dripped with sarcasm and both of them laughed at me. "Well, I've got a literacy meeting, so I doubt I'll get out of here before four, maybe four-thirty."

Anthea nodded, and then looked at me with the hint of that cheeky grin on her face. "I'll make it worth your while," she said.

I looked down at Emma, then back at her. "Oh?" I asked.

"Join us for dinner."

"Please, Mr Kincaid," Emma added before I could say anything.

I did hesitate a little before finally nodding and replying, "Okay. Sure." I don't know if it was the thought of being in the snake room or just my own personal fears, but I was not sure I was doing the right thing. However, the die had now been cast, I was committed, and so I made myself smile at them.

Anthea came up beside me. "They're going to be in their cages. I just need some help," she said. At least I knew the reason she put on my reluctance.

"I'll be there," I returned.

"Good." She looked at Emma, then bent and kissed me on the cheek. Emma shook her head, her expression one I had seen on her grandmother many times. Anthea laughed at her, then returned to her side and pushed her towards the door. "We'll see you after work."

"We will." I watched them go – well, watched Anthea go – and gathered everything I'd need for the meeting. Just a fortnightly discussion about where we were going with our literacy lessons, and at the year levels I was teaching, it was essentially making sure they were getting a grip on spelling rules, grammar rules and encouraging creativity. But, I admit, I was distracted. Not even when I had first started dating Lynda had I found myself constantly having to draw my attention back to my work, but Anthea was on my mind.

Anthea and the fact I'd rejected her advances. But there was still a big part of me that was reluctant to let things progress too much further.

I was only just starting to get a handle on how much Lynda had actually hurt me, and how gun-shy that had made me. After the meeting I was so close to calling Anthea and making a lame excuse, but just the thought of doing that made me feel guilty. I actually found I didn't want to go, and yet, once the meeting was over, I made my way directly to her place.

Chapter 13

Mrs Bowman was already there when I arrived, sitting at the kitchen table and watching Emma do her homework. Emma greeted me cheerfully, but her grandmother tapped the page and then glared at me before, surprisingly, she smiled a little. "Anthea's in the snake room," she said. "Use the intercom. Just press the button and when the red light comes on you can talk."

"Thanks," I said, then looked at Emma, watching me through the tops of her eyes. "And you, young lady – good work." She grinned and bent her head quickly. Mrs Bowman gave me a stern look that I knew from past experience was just a front and I left them to it.

The red light came on and I said, "Anthea, it's me – Brayden."

"Hang on," she returned. I stood there for a few moments before the door opened and she let me in. She was wearing a white coat and disposable rubber gloves, but it was the head band that attracted my attention, a red and blue striped piece of material tied at the back. "What?" she asked, her mouth folding into a scowl.

I touched the headband and smiled. "Cute," I said.

She watched me for a few moments before deciding I was not making fun of her. "It's really to stop the sweat," she explained.

"Still cute." I looked around. "So, what do you want me to do?"

"You, Mr Kincaid, are going to be my cameraman," she stated grandly.

"Oh?"

"Oh." She looked at me for a few moments longer, then took my hand. "Come here." She guided me across the floor, then sat me down in front of one of the computers. She brought up her email page, then stepped back. "I want you to read the ones from today," she said.

"You sure?"

"Just do it, Bray." I shrugged and did as she asked.

Ms Bowman, Thank you for your enquiry, but we feel you have been taken in by a hoax. A picture of a creature similar to the one you have shown us was found to have been fabricated for an online Photoshop *competition. If someone has sent you this, then they are, if you'll pardon my bluntness, pulling your leg.* I stopped reading the first one and looked at her. "They didn't believe you, huh?"

"I sent a photo of the head and upper body of the one in the case over there," she muttered. I automatically looked in that direction. It was covered by a black cloth and I actually relaxed. "And that one was the nice one. Wait till you read the one from Adelaide University." I wasn't sure I really wanted to, but I made my way through three more responses to her original email. She was correct – they were not pleasant reading. She was accused of not being who she claimed, being easily fooled and, from one Dr Stockman at Adelaide University, deliberately trying to make fools of professionals and being stupid.

"I'm sorry," I said, reaching across and touching her hip. She leant against me, then sat down, squeezing onto the stool beside me, somehow sharing it with me.

"I was called over to Kadina this morning," she said. "I spent most of the morning at the police station with Inspector Wallace and Dr Guilford, the forensics expert. We went over what I'd seen. I didn't mention the eagle, though."

"That's okay, neither did I," I mumbled. "I don't know why."

"Same reason as me – we don't believe what we saw," she sighed. "But they showed me pictures. It looked like the people we'd seen, the body sort of eaten away or melted or whatever. I asked if they thought it could have been a snake, because we'd seen snakes at both sites. Dr Guilford said that it could not be the case because there was nothing in their blood or lymph systems that indicated envenomation. Besides, no known snake has a venom that can do that to living tissue. I shut up." She turned her head to look at me. Her face filled my vision, she was so close. "I heard what Wallace said to you before he left, not to play detective. Well, guess what?"

"We're about to play detective?" I tried. She smiled. "How?" was my next question.

"Okay, I am going to feed our friend in the case over there," she explained, "and you are going to film it. We need to have video evidence of what we saw with that eagle. You can get close." She paused and chewed the inside of her cheek briefly. "But you do know this is not going to be pleasant, don't you?" I would have thought she was being condescending if not for the expression on her face.

I sighed and nodded once, slowly. I did not like where this was going.

"We're going to see it up-close. Very up-close. And you'll have one shot to film it, so I can't afford to have you getting all squeamish on me," she went on.

"I'll do what I can." It was the best I could say.

"It gets worse," she finished. I just looked at her. "I'm going to feed it a rabbit. That way it should be big enough for the video to capture everything."

I was impressed; that was a very fair warning. "Look, are you sure you want me to do this?" I asked.

"You're the only one who knows what to expect.

And," she added quickly, "I trust you."

I took one large, slow breath. "Okay, let's do this," I said, sounding as far from confident as I could possibly have sounded.

Her smile was sweet and she kissed my cheek before standing up. She went across to a drawer and pulled out an old Handycam and a pile of cords. "All right. If you can sort this out while I get everything else ready," she said apologetically.

I turned the camera on. The battery was low but it looked like there was plenty of storage available in its memory. I found enough cords and cables to plug it into a wall socket, then I experimented with the zoom and focus until I felt confident with what I was doing. Only then did I take notice of Anthea. She had placed a larger container made of what looked like Perspex over the glass one still covered by the black cloth, it looked like there were strips of metal which she had threaded underneath the covered container as well, metal that ran around the new container like barrel staves. In this, hopping around nervously, was a rabbit, most likely one of those feral ones that have been a plague on the Yorke Peninsula for decades. This container also had built-in gloves, which Anthea had covered with a pair of those steel-covered ones she had worn at the house in Wills Creek. "Ready," I said.

"Cool." She slid her hands in and flexed her fingers a few times to get them all the way in. "Now I want you to focus in on the gloves," she commanded. I did so, starting to record straight away. With one hand, she grasped the rabbit by the scruff of the neck and picked it up; with the other, she slowly slid the black cloth back.

I started to shake a little, but tried to control myself so I could hold everything steady. The snake looked like it hadn't moved since the last time I had been in here. But just the fact that it was there, in front of me, so close to me was enough.

"I need you to now keep the camera on the rabbit. No matter what happens, just film the rabbit. Keep the whole thing in shot." She sounded very matter-of-fact, as though this was something she did every day. "If it moves, you go with it. Okay?"

"Yep." It was a struggle to get that word out, to be honest. My mouth had gone dry at just the thought of what was about to happen.

"Cool," she repeated, and I had the feeling that that was at least in part as much for her own benefit as it was mine.

The rabbit struggled in her strong grip, but she ignored it as she reached the other hand across and lifted the lid of the internal container a fraction. Watching through the viewscreen I saw the snake's head appear, then move down. The angry attack of the first time I had seen it was gone, replaced by caution. "Come on," Anthea whispered as she shoved the rabbit against the brim of this second container. It pressed its feet against the container, trying desperately to prevent being forced inside, but Anthea's grip on its neck was firm and with a sudden movement she shoved it forward and then pressed the lid closed.

The viewfinder caught it all. The snake waited, as if making sure this was not a trick or a trap. That was very calculating for a reptile, I thought to myself. That was showing almost a degree of intelligence. The rabbit, on the other hand, scrambled against the double thickness glass, as if trying to climb out, but Anthea had secured the lid once more.

The snake's strike was fast, a blur of darkness that latched onto the poor creature's neck. Its yellow eyes narrowed even as the rabbit's eyes closed and it fell still. Just like that, it was now just the snake that was doing anything. That was when I almost dropped the camera. There would have been a brief hiccup in the image, but I got myself back under control.

Somehow.

The flesh was melting. There was no other word for it. It was turning into a thick liquid the same color as the snake's skin and was dripping down. The snake's long fangs remained embedded in the animal, but its gullet moved continuously. I zoomed in a little more. Now what it was doing was clear – it was swallowing this liquid meal like a drink. That was how it fed. Its venom or whatever it was in those fangs liquified the flesh and whatever else of the victim, and the snake drank it up. And this snake was hungry. It was not stopping. I watched as more and more of the rabbit disappeared, including the skin, leaving stained bones and scraps of sinew. Even the internal organs were dissolving. Then the snake moved and latched itself onto the carcass a little lower, then once more it sucked up the aqueous body it was creating.

"Are you getting this?" I heard Anthea whisper as if she was a long way away.

I think I nodded, but I'm not sure. This had me completely mesmerized. The snake's ingestion of the second part of the beast's body slowed until it finally let go, letting the remains of its meal fall to the bottom of its container. Then, slowly and deliberately, it turned and looked at the camera. I watched its eyes gaze into the lens, then close slowly as the head settled down. That was it. It had finished. I let the camera run for another thirty seconds or so, but when it was obvious that was it, I stopped it and put it on the counter.

Then I ran across to a sink set in the counter and threw up.

I didn't notice Anthea beside me until I felt her hand running over my back in a wide circle. I turned the tap on and washed my face, then rinsed my mouth out before I faced her.

"Pretty gross, huh?" she said as though we'd just simply watched a horror movie.

I nodded. "Oh yeah," escaped my lips. She smiled and grabbed a towel and wiped my face for me. "Thanks," I muttered.

"You did well," she said. "I'll send that video off to… to someone and they'll see… they'll see…" Her voice trailed off and she looked back at the twin containers holding the snake. "They won't believe this either, will they?" she sighed. "They'll just think I'm some sort of weirdo, or trying to make a name for myself, or anything else."

"But we know," I said, dropping onto a stool. "We know what's going on. We know…"

"What do we know, Bray? All we have is a bunch of snakes that no one believes exists that eats in a way I've never even heard of. We don't know where they came from, how many there could be, anything. I mean, we know some things, but not enough." She shook her head. "I don't know what to do," she finished, and she sounded defeated, which was not something I associated with her.

We stayed there in silence for what seemed too long before I eventually stood. "I don't know if I can face a meal," I muttered. "Sorry."

She appeared disappointed. "Emma will not be happy," she stated. "You don't want to let her down, do you?"

I sighed and shook my head. She was good at the guilt trip as well. "Okay," I muttered. "But don't expect me to eat a lot."

She looked back at those twin containers. "Me either," she said. "Now, let's get you cleaned up properly."

With that, she took me out of the snake room and led me to the bathroom where she leant me a toothbrush. I cleaned my mouth twice; that did a surprisingly good job of making me feel better, but it also meant I really wasn't looking forward to eating now. There is nothing that tastes good after toothpaste. I scrubbed my face as well and examined myself in the mirror, then turned and looked at Anthea.

"All done," I smiled. She grabbed my face and planted her lips on mine. I couldn't respond for a few moments, but I did eventually, a little.

"Minty fresh," she giggled.

"Great, now I feel like I'm on a television advert," I groaned.

She wrapped her arms around my neck and kissed me again, lightly. "TV for one," she whispered.

"Ah-hem!" came a voice from the doorway. We parted as we turned to face the intruder. "If you're *quite* finished, dinner is ready," Emma stated.

"Sorry, Em," Anthea said, casting me a worried look as she left the bathroom. Emma took her hand, but then, to the surprise of both Anthea and myself, she took my hand as well and led the two of us back to the kitchen.

"Found them," she said to her grandmother, who had placed bowls of spaghetti bolognaise at four seats of the dining table. We all had wine glasses as well, though Emma's contained lemonade. I didn't contribute much to any discussion, and I noticed Anthea was relatively quiet as well; it was mainly Emma regaling Mrs Bowman with stories of the fundraiser on Friday night and Mrs Bowman complaining about one of the teachers she was now working with at Maitland.

I will say right now that this felt more like a family meal than any I had had since leaving home to go to Adelaide to attend university. I did not feel too much like an outsider, a stranger at their table, and the acceptance was there from the other three. I guess I'd known them all before in various guises over the years – classmate, teacher, work colleague – and that certainly helped. But it was a nice feeling, and one I thought I could get used to.

That thought did not sit well. Did I want to get used to a family where I was an interloper, or at the very least, a latecomer? This felt relaxed and fine, but my head told me it was not mine.

Maybe it was seeing a snake eat a rabbit by liquefication, maybe the whole weekend was finally swamping over me, but as the meal came to an end, I did not feel like I belonged there. Emma and Mrs Bowman cleared the dishes, leaving Anthea and I alone. She leant across to me. "You okay?" she whispered.

I looked at her. "I don't know," I replied quietly.

She reached across and took one of my hands with both of hers. "It was gross, but you did well," she said. "This whole weekend, you did so well. I couldn't have done any of this without you…"

I was already shaking my head. "No, you don't need me. I was just a driver," I said. "If your car hadn't broken down, you would have coped just as well by yourself. You're that sort of person."

She looked at me for what felt like a long time. "Maybe," she finally agreed, "but I am glad I didn't have to go through it alone. It was good having someone with me, and having you with me now." She paused and her voice dropped even lower when she continued, "Being able to share those emails was important. They might not believe me, but you do. You believe me."

"I saw it."

She smiled, but shook her head and tightened her grip on my fingers. "That's not all. I am glad it's you I'm sharing this with." I opened my mouth to speak but she lifted one of her hands and pinched my mouth shut, then giggled and gave me that cute, cheeky grin. "Don't say anything. Don't ruin this. Please." I nodded. She let go of me and we separated just as the other two came back over to us with bowls over-filled with ice-cream.

I was hit with a few questions about school and my class and I answered with care and tact, considering Emma was only two years older than some of the kids in my class. I forced myself into the kitchen to do the dishes, much to Emma's chagrin, but she dried them after I washed them, leaving Anthea and her mother to talk quietly away from us. Emma told me all about her teacher this year, how she was not as good as I had been, and how she was already starting to worry about high school. I made the right grunty noises and let her prattle on. When we finished I held my hand up. "Nice job," I said. "High five."

"No," she replied and lunged forward, grabbing me around the waist in a tight embrace that only lasted a second or so, but had more feeling in it than any hug Lynda and I had shared in the last year of our relationship.

That did not make things any easier with the doubts going through my mind.

We returned to the table and I sat beside Anthea. Her hand dropped beneath the table and fell to my thigh. "I hate to eat and leave," I stated, "but I need to get home, get some sleep, get ready for work."

"You can't hang around for a while?" Anthea asked, allowing her disappointment to be obvious.

"As much as I'd love to, sorry," I said, trying to look like I was reluctant.

"Well, okay," Anthea sighed. I stood and she did as well, staying close to me as she did so.

"Goodnight, Mr Kincaid," Emma said.

"See you at school," I smiled at her, then turned to Mrs Bowman, "And it's been good to catch up with you again as well. It's been too long."

"It has," she agreed. "Have a good night, Brayden."

"I'll see you out," Anthea said. I waved once and then headed to the front door. She followed me outside, closing the door behind her, and walked with me all the way to my car, parked behind her four-wheel drive and her mother's Mitsubishi.

"I hope it's all okay," I said to her. "The video, I mean."

"It's all okay," she said, then she grabbed me in around the chest. I responded automatically, holding her in as close to me as she was pulling me into her. I didn't think as I bent forward and kissed the top of her head. This time her reaction was instantaneous – she moved her head and her kiss was a lot firmer than any other she had given me. I let my mouth open a little, and she took the invitation immediately. I don't know how long we stood there, tasting one another like the food we had just eaten. I held her waist with one hand and ran the other through her short hair. The feel of it was so soft and only added to the sensory overload that was slowly conquering me.

I was the one who broke it off, but I kissed the tip of her nose to let her know that it wasn't just a complete stop. "I do need to go," I murmured.

"I know." Her smile was so wide. She kissed me again. "Thank you," she said. "For everything." I stepped back and our hands fell away as I went to the driver's side of the car. I gazed at her for a few more moments before I slid inside.

I smiled at her as I backed off.

I was sure I saw the curtains in the house move as I reversed.

My doubts were starting to fade. Starting to. Only starting to.

Chapter 14

I was at the gym a little earlier than usual the next morning, and pushed myself an insane amount, so much so that by the time I'd finished I could barely walk, and just collapsed to the ground, lying on one of the yoga mats, trying desperately to will my body to move. A shower would make me feel better, I knew, but it was a matter of walking up the road to the school and actually doing it that did not appeal at the moment.

A knock came at the front door. I groaned; that normally meant one of the neighbors was there to complain about the volume of the music which, I had to admit, on this morning had probably been a little louder than it should have been. I was definitely not in the mood for an argument, so I chose to ignore it. However, of course, it came again, louder and more insistent.

I rolled over and pushed myself to my feet, then froze.

I was not expecting to see a smiling face at the door, especially that smiling face. I made my way across and opened it, letting Anthea in. She greeted me with a small kiss on the cheek. "What brings you by at this hour of the morning?" I asked.

"I got a call-out," she sighed. "Not at Wills Creek, this time. Down south at Pine Point. A brown snake in a shed. But I had to show you this." She pulled out her phone and brought up the email app, then opened one and showed it to me. "It's from a guy in Scotland. I sent my email to a friend in England, and she's forwarded it on to him because he's apparently identified three new species of snake in northern Africa. Well… have a look." She was so excited, so I took it and read through.

What you have should not be in Australia. It is found in northern Germany, across into the Netherlands and even on the British Isles. You cannot approach them. They are dangerous. But they need to be killed. This is a matter of vital importance. That was it, signed off by a man proclaiming he was Dr Jeremy Boyle.

"Well?" she asked.

"And this is definitely a guy in the field?" I asked. She nodded. "It seems, I don't know, strange," I ventured.

"Go on," she said, her own enthusiasm now tempered.

"First, he doesn't say what it is. He just says to kill it. That does not sound like any animal expert I've heard of. Second, he doesn't give any indication of any of the behaviors we've seen. I don't know. It feels… wrong." I handed her phone back to her and she stared at the email. "Sorry," I offered lamely.

"No, no," she said distractedly. "You're… you're right. I was just so, so, so glad to get something from someone who didn't treat me like an idiot or someone trying to con people." She sighed and shoved the phone into her pocket. "It was just… Sorry."

"There is a good thing, though," I said.

"What?" She was struggling to see my point of view.

"If this guy says there is something in Europe, then we know where to start looking. Forget the Australian experts, we need to hit European ones." I smiled at her. "And at least then we'll know if this guy's on the level."

She was nodding slowly, then grabbed me around the chest and kissed me hard. "Thank you," she said, and reached her mouth for mine again.

"Anthea, is this what you really want?" came out of my mouth before my mind could stop it. She paused, then pulled back, staring at me.

"Is what what I want?" she asked.

"Me." Confusion crossed her face. "Is this because of the shit with Leroy you thought was coming down, and now he's back, is it the whole snake thing, is it this weekend? Please, tell me now." All night these questions had been burning at my mind, and now I had given voice to them and, looking at her face, I was sure I had done exactly the wrong thing.

"Why would it be because of that?" she asked.

I shrugged. "Is it?" I pushed.

She stepped back. "Bray, I'm not Lynda," she said. Her mouth turned down a little. "Sorry, Bray. You need to…" She shook her head. "It's not because of that, no. But you have to listen to yourself. I'm not going to put Emma through anything that'll confuse or upset her." She sighed and took another pace away from me. "Sorry, Bray. Thank you for everything. You've been good for me this weekend."

She turned and strode to the front door. "Anthea," I called, my voice croaking. She hesitated before facing me. "Your hair is definitely cute."

She managed a sort of a smile. "See you 'round, Bray," she said, going outside and disappearing around the corner in the blink of an eye.

There was a part of me that wanted to chase after her, but I stayed right where I was. I knew what it was – it was something that had been going through my mind all night. I was blaming myself for what happened with Lynda and I didn't want to do that to Anthea. I liked her, but I didn't trust myself. It was that simple.

Or was it that I didn't trust Anthea to not do what Lynda had done?

I was double-guessing myself. I was confused, that was all.

It didn't stop me feeling like I'd been hit by a truck, though. I went through the motions at school in the morning, then found myself doing yard duty at recess time in the area near the school buildings. The one student I was hoping I wouldn't see seemed to hunt me down. "Hello, Mr Kincaid," Emma said, her smile wide and coy. She was going to get the same cheeky grin as her mother when she matured.

"Hiya, kiddo," I smiled.

"Are you coming over again tonight?" She seemed excited by the prospect.

"I don't think so," I said.

"Oh." Her face fell straight away.

"I think I upset your mum this morning," I told her. "I don't think she wants much to do with me at the moment."

"She likes you," Emma stated.

"And I like her," I said, not sure why I was saying this to a ten-year-old, but she was more than a student now, I supposed. "But sometimes that's not enough."

"Why not?"

A question that could only have come from a child. And a question that I should have asked myself a few hours earlier. "I have no idea," I finally responded.

She sighed and shook her head. Suddenly she looked furtively about, and then beckoned me closer. I bowed to her. "I like you, too," she whispered in my ear, then scuttled off and out of my sight before I could think of a way to reply.

It's hardly surprising, but Emma had just made me feel that little bit worse.

And that was when the screaming started.

It came from inside the building behind me and, without thinking, I ran towards the sound. Quite a few students had also started in that direction, but they were keeping themselves well away from the source. There was something about that sound that just felt so very wrong. Having said that, a sense of duty kicked in and I forced my way to the door of the building. Not one of the students tried to follow me; that was not a good sign. They could tell by the timbre of the scream that this was not going to be good by any stretch of the imagination.

I pointed at two of the largest students gathered there. "You two," I said, keeping my voice calm, though I'm not sure how, "please make sure no one comes in except teachers. Okay?"

"Yes, Mr Kincaid," they said together. I offered them an attempt at a smile, then entered. The screaming had lessened in volume, the voice growing hoarse, but it was still a simple matter to find the source. Eddie Jessop had been a member of the teaching support staff since I had been a student at the Ardrossan school. She was one of those ladies who treated every single person – student and staff – like they were her grandchildren, and she was pretty much universally liked by everyone. So, to see her with her face screwed up and that shrill voice coming from it made me rush to her side without really thinking.

She faced me and almost collapsed. I only just caught her. I started to take her into the room she was standing in front of, but she fought me. "No…" she whimpered.

"Eddie, come on," I said.

"Not there," she managed. I shook my head. I was only concerned about her, not what had caused this, and now my attention was a little wider in its scope. The room she had been standing in front of was not actually a classroom. It had tables and benches around the edges, but no chairs, with the centre of the room kept as an empty space. It was used when two or more classes wanted to watch something or see a guest speaker together, or a class wanted somewhere to rehearse an item for assembly or the annual Christmas concert, even if a class was doing large-scale art projects. Not having a huge student base, it was one of those little luxuries a small school can boast.

Sallyanne Patressi was on the floor at the front of the room. She was another support worker, a few years older than me, a former student here, and both her children also attended the school. Her husband was a worker at the sand works. I knew them socially as well as through the school, and to see her, on the floor, her eyes open, staring at nothing, was almost too much.

What did make it too much was her arm. Like poor Mrs Robertson, it had been reduced to bone with a few lines of tissue, centred at, from what I could gather, just above the elbow. The hand was intact, though the palm discolored, while the humerus was almost completely visible, and the flesh around the shoulder was black and ragged. She had been wearing a short-sleeved top, which made the injuries all the more horrific. I just stared at the woman, unable to think, for too long.

Then realisation dawned on me. My body tightened and I felt my heart rate speed up, growing heavier. I reached in and shut the door carefully, making sure I heard it click, that it was not going to open again by accident. Eddie looked at me through wide eyes. She was going into mental shock, so I had to be quick. I was not thinking about her, or about Sallyanne; I was thinking about everyone else. "Eddie, listen to me – what was she doing in there?" I asked, staring into those wide eyes, so large I could almost see my reflection in the blue irises.

Her gaze focused on me slowly, but at least she was responding. "She had something to show the older classes," Eddie muttered, her voice dream-like and vague. "Said she caught it. Something she'd never seen before. Wouldn't let anyone else see it first. She had it in a cage and everything."

There were so many questions I wanted to ask, but one came to the forefront of my mind. "Where did she get it?"

"She lives in Wills Creek, so, I guess..." And words failed her. I'd always thought Sallyanne and Sergio lived in Price. But Wills Creek... My heartbeat became firmer and sped up even more. I looked down the corridor where one of the two children I'd placed on sentry duty was peering inside, his face a complete mask of concern.

"Go to the front office, the staffroom," I ordered. "I need teachers here. Now."

He nodded and then bolted, looking like he was glad to be doing something. The other student poked her head in. "Mr Kincaid?" she said.

"Keep the other kids out," I said, calming my voice. "You're doing well."

"O-Okay," she stammered and disappeared.

I almost dragged Eddie away from that closed door and sat her in a chair sitting in the corridor. I only had a few moments before this place would be inundated, I guessed, so I pulled out my phone. I did not think about what I was doing, I simply tapped Anthea's name on the list.

It rang for a while. "What?" That surprised me. There was almost anger there.

"I need your help," I said.

She must have picked up something in my voice, because her tone softened. "Bray, I'm at work. I can't really talk now about..."

"One of those snakes is loose in the school."

"What?" Her voice dropped low.

"I've got a dead woman and one of those snakes

loose, and any minute now a heap of staff are going to be here, and I have no idea where the snake is, or what it's going to do when there's so many…"

"Fuck." There was a sense of panic in her voice. "I can't get there. I'm still at Pine Point."

"I need to catch this thing before anyone else goes in there."

"Bray, you can't…" she started.

Noise was outside. "I've got to go. I'll call you later." I paused, then added what I assumed would be a joking, "I hope." However, even as I said it, I knew there was no humor to my words.

"Bray…" she started, but I hung up.

I had to think, and think quickly. What had I seen so far? The snake stalking me, the snakes eating an eagle and a rabbit, the snake watching, the snake attacking Anthea's hand at speed, both on the road and through the glass of the cage in her laboratory…

I peered through the door. On the floor was a large aquarium, on its side, an old beach towel next to it. That told me how she'd got it in here. And also how I was going to get it out.

Tracey Grant, one of the two deputies and my own line manager, came in. I had to think so very fast. "It's Sallyanne," I said when Tracey reached us. "She's… look, it's not good." Tracey peered through the window, saw the body and gasped. She automatically reached for the handle. I stopped her. "No," I said.

"But we need to get her…"

"There's a very angry brown snake in there," I lied. "I'm going to go in and get it, but you need to keep everyone else out until I do."

"Brayden, I can't let you do this," she stated firmly.

"I know, but we need to get Sallyanne out of there, and we can't while that snake is in there. No telling what it'll do. I called the snake catcher, but she's at another job and can't get here for a while." I was forcing myself to act calmly, putting on that teacher façade to get my point across and not increase panic.

"Brayden, what in the hell do you know about catching snakes?" she demanded. She was trying to sound angry, but that fear in her eyes gave the truth away.

"Anthea Bowman taught me." Another lie to be added to a growing list.

The thing was, after all the staffroom rumors and jokes on Monday morning, that statement was accepted. Her only comment was, "Then, for God's sake, be careful."

I offered what I hoped was a smile and carefully opened the door. I edged in and closed it behind me. Sallyanne's lifeless eyes seemed to regard me as though she was scolding me. I had two hopes here – first, that the snake was already sated, that it had eaten enough, and that it had not yet learnt what glass was all about, like the animal in the snake room. I had to force myself not to keep on gazing at Sallyanne and instead focus on what I was setting myself to do. I tiptoed across and picked up the aquarium and its glass lid from where they'd fallen.

The movement was fast, the head launching out like a guided missile from beneath one of the benches. "Fuck!" I yelped and stumbled backwards, landing on my seat, the corner of the aquarium biting into my thigh painfully as I landed. The snake retreated, but I could see those yellow eyes glaring at me, watching my every move. That impression of being stalked by one of these things was there again and it took a large mental effort to not become paralyzed by the fear. I edged around sideways, keeping the aquarium on my lap, until I had Sallyanne between me and it. Only then did I slowly climb back to my feet.

I heard a commotion outside the door, but Tracey's voice ordered people to move back and let me do what I was doing. Thank God for small mercies; however, the thought of people rushing in here and being attacked by that creature actually steeled my resolve. I kept my eyes on the snake's. It dawned on me that I should probably get the higher ground, to be able to bring the aquarium down over it, lacking any of Anthea's specialized equipment or her years of experience.

The counter it had settled beneath did not look that strong, but I had to take the chance. And do it while carrying a heavy glass container.

The yellow eyes narrowed. I took that to mean it was getting ready to strike. I darted sideways. The crocodilian head emerged, but it was merely watching my progress now. I pushed myself forward and propelled myself onto the counter. My first foot bent the chipboard top, and I was sure there was a faint crack. I teetered there on one foot before I swung my other across, pressing it against the windowsill. I pushed my body forward to regain my balance until I had most of my weight on that second foot.

I clearly heard a gasp come from the other side of the door.

Panic gripped me, but I had to fight through it. I looked over my shoulder.

The top of the snake's head was just visible at the height of the counter. It had raised itself up to gaze at me, like a cobra getting ready to strike. The yellow eyes narrowed. The mouth opened, those long fangs emerging from their mouth pockets.

I was not in a good position, but I knew I only had one shot at this.

I turned and threw the lid of the aquarium at it. The glass spun lazily, but it missed the snake by less than an inch. I started to curse myself, but I noticed its attention was distracted momentarily by the flying object. I pivoted on the foot on the counter and held the aquarium out. I watched the reptile through its base, then lunged forward.

It slammed against the top of its head. I watched it even as I fell forward, its snout striking the glass as it tried to get to me. My weight forced it downwards, but I let go before I hit the floor. My back slammed against the thin carpeting but I rolled over my shoulder quickly.

The snake was furious and agitated, writhing beneath the glass container, half of its body stretching back beneath the counter. It was wriggling itself out of the confines of the aquarium. I crawled across and leant my hands on the edges of the base. The head tried again to strike at me, but it just succeeded in hitting the glass hard enough for me to feel it.

Anger overcame me and I leant all with all my weight and strength on the glass as hard and as fast as I could.

The tail end disappeared beneath the counter once more, while the head section thrashed about wildly, blood pouring from the wound I had inflicted. My breath came in short gasps and I added a final push on the top of the container before I moved away. The snake's death throes were growing progressively weaker. I grabbed the lid and shifted the corner of the aquarium up a little. The snake tried to force its head out through the gap but I pushed it back with the top. I wormed it all the way underneath, the snake's blood smeared across everything by the time I'd finished, and then, with a single movement, flipped it over. I grabbed the beach towel and covered the whole thing, then snatched a book lying on a counter and placed that on top.

I finally fell to a sitting position and looked at the

door. I was panting as if I'd just done a full-on workout, and I indicated to the faces at the door to come in.

The only person who did was Joe McGuire, one of the high school teachers, another colleague I associated with socially. "All safe?" he asked.

"I need some tape to secure this thing, but Sallyanne..." I shook my head.

And then it was like I was caught in the middle of a storm.

Chapter 15

I managed to get the aquarium and its occupant as well as the other half of the snake out to my car, with the excuse of taking them to Anthea's place later on, before any authorities arrived. But they weren't interested in the snake. This was not anything a snake could do. What they were more interested in was the fact that Sallyanne had come from Wills Creek.

Classes were cancelled for the rest of the day, and parents arrived in a steady stream to take children away. Very few knew that someone had actually died; the term used was that there had been "an incident". However, rumors spread rapidly, so that by the time Inspector Wallace arrived from Kadina, where he was staying, some semblance of the truth was starting to circulate.

I went through it all feeling numb. It had been bad enough when I had seen people dead, but this was someone I knew, someone I genuinely liked. When Sergio came, he cast me such a pathetic, forlorn glance as he was hustled somewhere by the police and other people who had filled the place that I just wanted to go across and grab him in a hug. But he was going to have worse to face – a dead wife, and then how did he tell their children?

I could not think about that. I could not think about anything.

Wallace asked me a few questions, but he had already heard the stories of my "heroism" from the other staff members and he was surprisingly gentle. Again, his concern was the connection with Wills Creek. This time, as he put it, I really was "in the wrong place at the wrong time." He asked what I'd done with the snake, and I explained I was going to give it to Anthea to identify. He just accepted that; the snake was not their concern, but he was glad I'd prevented anyone from going in and potentially being bitten.

At least, I assume he was glad. He merely acted a little more positively towards me than he had before.

I'd stayed in the room until Sallyanne had been wheeled away, and then I was sort of taken by Joe to the staffroom where I was plied with coffee and disappeared into my own head until Wallace interrupted. It was after he had gone that I suddenly found my body waking up. I had to run to the bathroom where I threw up until the dry-retching made my whole stomach go into convulsions. Two days in a row I had thrown up, something I had not done since I was at university and had been on my last nasty beer-bender. That had been more than a decade earlier and now…

"Bray, you in here?" The voice echoed in the bathroom and I jumped at the sound.

"Yeah, Joe," I replied.

He entered slowly and came up to me. "How you feeling?"

I indicated the dirty sink. "Better now. I guess." I shook my head and looked at him. His face was red, his eyes a little puffy. "That sort of a day, huh?"

"I spoke with Sergio." He stared at the mirror. "The guy is shattered. And yet, you know what? He was more concerned about you."

"How's the kids?"

Joe just shook his head. "Jillian's with them now, all three of them." She was the school counsellor. I guessed she was going to have one hell of a week ahead of her now. "They're talking about closing the school tomorrow," he added. "Some staff'll be here for any parents or kids who need it, to run a sort of all-day out of school hours care programme."

I nodded and washed my face for the third time. The face that stared back at me from the mirror looked awful. I turned the tap on and washed the remains of my regurgitation down the sink. "Suppose I should go see Tracey, huh?" I muttered.

"Maybe, but last I saw she was pretty flat out. Everyone is. This is a mess. Hell, there's even reporters hanging around, but everyone in town is closing ranks and I don't think they'll get too far," he said as he splashed water on his own face.

The door opened. "Everyone decent?" called a female voice.

"Yeah, Tracey," I replied.

She took a solitary pace in, and looked as bad as the rest of us. "How you feeling, Bray?" she asked gently.

"Getting there," I said. "You?"

She moved her hand in a see-saw motion. "But I'm glad I found you. There's someone waiting to see you," she said.

My body felt like it suddenly weighed a tonne. I just pictured Wallace getting ready to attack me, to blame me for whatever it was that was happening. "Really?" I groaned.

She smiled a little. "I don't think it's anything bad," she said. "They said they'll wait in your classroom."

"Thanks, Tracey," I muttered.

She looked behind her, then risked coming all the way inside. She rested her hands on my shoulders. "You did really well today, Bray," she said, her voice low and calm. "Don't tell yourself anything else."

I smiled. She was using the same 'pep-talk' phrases on me she did with the students. "Thanks," I replied. She squeezed me briefly, then left, touching Joe on the arm on the way out. I watched her go. *They* could only mean one thing – police. "Suppose I'd better go face the music," I sighed.

Joe slapped me on the shoulder. "You'll be fine," he said, and returned his gaze to his reflection.

The staffroom was empty apart from a trio of middle school teachers sitting in silence around one of the tables, cups of coffee in front of all of them, the smell strong. They cast me brief glances, apologetic smiles on their faces, but none said anything. There were no children anywhere as I made my way to the classroom, and only a few teachers in their rooms. I reached the closed door to my room and stopped. I shut my eyes, took a deep breath, and then opened it, ready for anything.

I was grabbed around the chest straight away.

I hadn't realized how much I needed this sort of human contact until I had it. I wrapped my own arms around Anthea and held her. Then another set of arms gripped us both, a little lower. I looked down and saw that Emma had joined us.

I finally moved away from the two of them. "Hi," I said.

"What were you doing?" Anthea demanded.

I shrugged. "Trying to help," I murmured.

She hit me in the chest. "You could have been seriously hurt!"

"But I wasn't."

She hit me again, then a third time. "You could have been!" she repeated, louder and angrier. "Don't you dare do that to me again!"

I looked at her curiously and she turned her head a little. I placed a finger under her chin and turned her back to me. A single tear had made its way down her cheek. "Are you okay?" I asked.

"When you rang me, I knew what you were going to do. I *knew* it! And then you went and did it! I was panicking the whole way back here." A fourth punch to the chest, and there was some force behind the blow. "You bastard! Don't you ever do that to me again!"

I sighed and wiped her cheek. She flinched away from me. "I'm sorry, but I had to," I said. "They were going to go in there and… and do what they had to do and I knew what would have happened, so I… yeah." I offered a hopeful smile.

The next blow was a lot gentler. "I was so fu…" – her eyes darted to Emma, taking all of this in with interest – "damn scared. You have no idea."

"I'm sorry," I muttered.

She stared at me, cast one more glance at her daughter, then grabbed my face and kissed me hard. "You know, everyone around here's calling you a hero," she growled.

"And you just think I'm an idiot?" I tried.

She glowered at me and kissed me again. "A heroic idiot," she growled, but her anger was feigned. She shook her head and took my hands with hers. "What did you do with it?"

"It's in the boot of my car. Glass box, taped up with more duct tape than probably necessary, bleeding to death. Its tail is in a plastic bag next to it."

She nodded. "Good." She squeezed my hands, then looked at Emma, who returned her gaze evenly. "Em, I need to talk with Mr Kincaid alone. Okay?"

"Oh-kay," she grumbled and pulled an iPad out of her mother's bag. She plugged in a set of headphones and quickly the sounds of some modern beat-heavy music was slightly audible. She sat herself at a desk in the middle of the room and pulled a book out which she started to read.

"Good enough, I guess," Anthea muttered and led me away from her, across to my desk. She kept hold of my hand and stared at me. "I need to be honest with you," she stated, her voice staying low.

"Oh." That is never a good thing to hear from someone, especially someone for whom my feelings were growing, and even more after our conversation at the gym.

"This morning you asked me if this is what I really want," she said, "and all morning I asked myself that question. I wasn't sure if it was your doubts, if it was what you said that made me think I was looking for something just because you're there, or what. I didn't know." She shook her head. "I did not know. I couldn't think straight. Your reasons for me wanting to be with you made sense, but that didn't explain the way I felt." She now took my other hand again. "But when you rang, and I realized what you were going to do, and when I got here and all anyone was talking about was that someone had died and you'd caught a venomous snake, I was scared. I was really, really scared. I thought I'd lost you, and lost you before I'd really got to know you." She was fighting the tears and yet her voice became softer. "I didn't want that. I don't want that. You asked me what I really want?" Her kiss was soft, punctuated by a second, small one on the tip of my nose. "I really want you."

I didn't know how to respond. That morning, I thought I'd blown it. Now…

I reached across and kissed her as well. She took it as an open invitation and she grabbed me around the chest and returned it with a passion and fervor I had not been ready for. When we finally parted, we noticed that Emma had turned around so her back was to us, music blaring even louder, a game on the screen of the iPad. I smiled and faced Anthea again. Neither of us seemed to be able to find the words to say. I'm not saying that all my doubts had vanished, because I could feel that they were still there, lurking in the back of my mind, but my feelings of comfort about where this seemed to be heading were stronger, and my feelings for Anthea were definitely growing and gave me a sense of being, at the very least, wanted, which was something I had not felt in a long time.

I took her hand; she came right into me, leaning against me. It felt natural. I felt her sigh and she looked at me. "Now what?" she asked.

"Can we take it slow?" I returned, not sure if I was asking the right question.

But she smiled and nodded. "So long as we're taking it somewhere, yes," she replied. Our eyes held for a little while longer. "What you doing tonight?"

"Well, after dropping the… the thing in my car off at your place, I was going to go home and try to put today into some sort of order in my head." I sounded as weary as I felt. At least I wasn't feeling nauseous again.

She looked at me and then shook her head. "Nope," she stated.

"Nope?' I echoed, laughing a little in disbelief.

"Nope," she repeated. "Go home, get yourself cleaned up, grab some clothes, then come back to my place. I'll cook dinner, you stay the night."

"Anthea, I can't let you do…" I started, but she silenced me by placing her hand over my mouth, shaking her head again.

"You're not letting me, I'm offering." She glared at me, but the hint of that cute smile was there as well. "I know how you're feeling, and you will feel better having people around. Being alone is never a good way to cope with anything." Of course, I knew that what she was saying was true, but it is so easy to say these things to other people and not live it yourself.

"Where did you hear that?" I groaned.

That cheeky grin broke across her face. "My daughter's teacher told me that when I was divorcing my husband a couple of years ago," she said. I closed my eyes and shook my head, letting out a long, slow breath. I had no response; she'd well and truly got me.

Chapter 16

Dinner was nothing extravagant. After we'd finished I went to do the dishes, but Emma cornered me and asked me to listen to her reading for homework. Anthea smiled and nodded, so I did as I was told, sitting at the kitchen table as she cleared off a good chunk of her classroom-assigned reader. By the time she'd done her designated time, Anthea had rejoined us, watching us with a smile that I could only describe as sad.

Anthea took Emma up to get her ready for bed and I sat in front of the television, my laptop on my knees. I watched the story about the "mysterious death" of the teacher in Ardrossan. There was no mention of the other deaths; the media clearly had not been alerted to the similarities in them. That was a positive, I suppose. Several people I knew were interviewed, children looked upset, and that was extended to three minutes. The rest of the news was just depressing on all fronts, and I soon lost myself looking through a day's worth of emails on my phone. Then I remembered the message Anthea had received from Scotland. What was his name? Dr Jeremy Boyle, that was it. I tapped his name in and waited. Not an uncommon name, unfortunately, and even a few famous people who shared it with him. I didn't find my first hit about the good doctor until the third Google search page. But there he was, formerly of the University of Aberdeen.

He had a WordPress website which detailed his academic achievements and a reasonable list of accolades and a formidable list of published papers. But one page drew me in: 'The Truth of Mythical Creatures.' I opened it and found myself groaning. He had claims and a lot of sub-pages with what he called "evidence" of the actual existence of a number of beasts from legend and mythology. I only skim-read one of them, about the ancient Egyptian creature called an *axex*, which was a sort of wingless griffon. His explanation of the alleged beak and claws made sense from a straight-up scientific standpoint, but not from an evolutionary one. At least, that was how I saw it.

I went back to Google and now checked a site called *Dr Boyle's Beliefs*, which a quick glance at the first page told me was not favorable. In fact, the second paragraph said everything I thought I needed to know: "If you have ever seen the well-done faux documentary *The Last Dragon: A Fantasy Made Real* (2004), then you know exactly what Dr Boyle believes. In fact, it would not surprise anyone who knows him to learn that he claims this work was adapted from his own notes and research."

"Awesome," I whispered. And this was the only person who had responded positively to Anthea's email. A horrible, sinking feeling rumbled through my stomach. The logical part of me said that we should get the authorities here and show them the strange serpent in Anthea's snake room and let them deal with the problem. But there was also that part of me that said we'd been sitting on this animal's existence for four days, and in that time five people had been killed. That was not going to go down well. It seemed only the police and Anthea and I knew that the five were related, but with Sallyanne's death making the news, I supposed having kept it from them would now make it worse.

I was so lost in my own world that I didn't notice anyone coming into the room until Emma bounced on the couch beside me. I turned and smiled at her. She was dressed in a cat onesie that made her look decidedly younger than her ten years. Her long, wet hair was pulled back into a ponytail that slapped against her back and she was still glowing pink from her bath or shower or whatever it was she'd had. "Ready for bed?" I asked.

"Yep," she nodded, then she leant across and kissed me on the cheek. "See you in the morning." I cast a glance at Anthea, standing at the end of the couch and she turned away, an expression of mock innocence on her face.

"See you in the morning," I echoed and watched as she danced up the hallway towards the bedrooms. My smile froze on my face. That had felt incredibly awkward. I still saw her as a student, and now I was sort of seeing her mother and was about to spend the night at her house. I had a feeling that would not go down well at the school.

I didn't want to think about that, so I turned back to the search results about Dr Boyle. I found a few websites defending him and his beliefs, but they were all sites dedicated to cryptozoology, the belief in creatures that apparently defy science. One of these sites had a whole page dedicated to Dr Boyle that was essentially a sycophantic rehash of some of the things on Boyle's own site. My disillusionment was growing, and so was my feeling of dread.

I had a sinking feeling that was growing steadily worse.

Two arms wrapped around me from behind and soft lips were pressed against my cheek. "I don't get greeted like that anywhere near enough," I said, leaning back against Anthea. She rested her chin on the top of my head.

"What you looking at?" she asked, sliding her head down to my shoulder and looking at the images on the laptop's screen.

I sighed. "Just looking into the life and craziness of one Dr Jeremy Boyle."

"Oh?" She climbed over the back of the couch and

slid down next to me. I couldn't help but notice all she was wearing was an oversized, long-sleeved t-shirt and very little else, especially obvious as she leant against me. "I'm guessing it's not good?"

I shook my head. "Well, let me put it this way – he's a laughing stock."

She read some of the page open in front of me. "What do you think?" she ventured.

I leant back and grimaced. "Look, some of his stuff makes no sense, seems crazy, shit like that, but…" I looked at her. "Isn't that what we're dealing with here?"

She snuggled in against me and I closed the machine. I didn't need to read anything else. I was feeling like I was stuck in the eye of a storm, unsure of when I was going to be sucked up and find myself pummelled by everything surrounding me.

Anthea started to kiss my neck and slipped my arm around her shoulder. She lifted her head, her lips moving slowly across my face before finding my mouth. She moved her body across mine, her legs straddling me, her kisses raining down on me in an unending barrage.

And then her phone rang. She fell against me, shaking her head. "The timing is always perfect, isn't it?" she muttered as she climbed off and went to the dining table where she picked it up and looked at the screen before answering it. "What's up, Sarah?" she asked, her voice resigned to a long conversation. I turned to look at her and she blew me a kiss. "I can't tonight. It's too late to get a babysitter and I'm…" She waited. "I'm busy." Pause and she smiled at me. "Yes, that's the one. The one from the hotel on Saturday." She listened a little longer and then ran her hand over her hair. "I still think you went too far. And I like it." A brief pause. "Yes, he does." Longer pause. "Oh, I don't know, maybe fifteen years, maybe longer." She smiled this time. "I am serious. I've known him that long. I don't think you've met him, but I know Eloise and Tanya have." Her smile became almost cruel. "No, I'm not going to tell you his name. Now, I have to go." She rolled her eyes. "I'll talk to you later, Sarah. 'Bye." And she hung up and stared at me, then I heard the beep as she turned the phone off.

"No one I know, obviously," I laughed as she returned to her position over me.

She was about to say something, then held her tongue and rolled off, landing beside me. "Sarah's been my best friend for years," she explained. "But when I left Leroy, she didn't understand and said I was doing the wrong thing. She's been a little off since then, and I think Friday when she was just so obnoxious, I saw who she really was. Maybe."

I ran my fingers through her hair. "I'm sorry," I muttered.

She snuggled in next to me. I held her close and she curled her legs up next to her. She grabbed the remote control and pressed a few buttons before the splash panel of *Die Hard* came up on the screen, the DVD left in there from the last time I'd spent the night. I was asleep not long after the bad guys killed Ellis.

Chapter 17

I woke, alone, on the couch. I was covered by a blanket and my jeans and shoes had been removed. It was still very dark outside; a quick check of my phone told me it was not quite four o'clock. I was not one to wake up early normally, so I sat up and took in my surroundings. It could just have been that I was in a strange house, and those noises that are unique to every building got to me. But I didn't think so.

I stood and slid my pants on, then padded up to the other end of the house. Emma was asleep, one arm and one leg hanging out from beneath her bedclothes, her head buried by an avalanche of pillows and stuffed toys. As I watched her hand disappeared under the soft mountain, did something, and then reappeared again and dropped down.

I went across the hallway and looked into the master bedroom. The blanket was bunched up at one end of the bed and the pillow was on the floor, but there was no sign of Anthea anywhere. Even though I knew she would not simply go and leave her daughter here, a twinge of panic did hit me. I peered into the empty bathroom and then went to the front door and opened it to look outside. Her car was there, parked in front of mine. A hint of panic became genuine concern. I had no idea where else to look. The third bedroom? That simply looked like the junk room Anthea had told me it was. There was nowhere else…

Yes, there was. I didn't want to, but I made my way down the corridor to the door of the snake room. I pressed the buzzer on the intercom and waited. Then came a tentative, "Yes?"

"That's okay," I said. "Just wondering where you'd

got to."

"Hang on." I waited and the door buzzed, then opened. Anthea was standing there in the same clothes I had seen her in the previous night, that red and blue striped headband around her head once more. "What's up?" she asked.

"I was just…" I suddenly felt so pathetic. "I guess I got worried. Didn't know where you were."

Her smiled was accompanied by a shake of her head, then she bridged the gap between us and kissed me. "That's sweet," she said, "but everything's okay." She looked behind her, then stepped aside. "Come on in," she said.

"Look, if you're busy, I've already interrupted you and..." I started, but she placed her hand over my mouth.

"Stop talking and come on in," she said. I obeyed. One of the computers was one and she dragged a second stool over to it. I sat on it and she tapped at the keyboard. "Couldn't sleep," she said. "I kept thinking that we should have told someone earlier, that it might be too late, that maybe, if we had, then some of those people…" She let her voice trail off as she looked at me. Her smile was sad. "You, too, huh?"

"Oh, yeah," I muttered.

She placed a hand on my leg. "It's not anyone's fault," she said. "We don't know what's going on with these things." She squeezed my thigh and looked right in my eyes. "And there is no way you could have known your friend was going to take one to the school."

"I know, but…" I shrugged. She nodded. She understood. "So, you came in here?" I asked, trying to sound casual.

"Yeah." She turned the monitor a little. "I took a few screen caps from the video you took – oh, good job, by the way; I mean it" – I smiled awkwardly at her – "and did a picture recognition search. The first bunch were from photoshop sites! Can you believe it? Some people have created these out of their own imaginations?" She shook her head.

"So, nothing, huh?" I sighed.

"Not exactly. Look." She brought up a picture. It looked very similar to the creature still in its glass case under the black cloth at the other end of the counter, but it was sitting beside what looked like a river or stream. There was nothing to give a point of reference as to the size of anything, but there was no denying that it looked like the same animals we were faced with here: the black skin, the snub-nosed crocodile's head, the strange sort of torso-like thoracic region. "And this one." The next picture was a little blurred, but the head was a closer approximation to the shape of the ones we had. "And this one." The next was a photograph of a man holding what looked like a dead one. "And there's maybe ten more, and a lot of repeats of this lot. It's like these are the only ones and people just keep on using them."

"At least there's some pictures," I muttered.

"Yeah. That's a relief, right?" she said. "It means this isn't the first time this has happened. The problem is…" She brought up the website the final picture and I looked at it and grunted. It was in German. "I ran it through a translator, but it doesn't help. The best I can work out, it's a cryptozoology site and these photos were taken in Schleswig. I had to look that up – it's in northern Germany." She went down the rest of the pictures. "None of them are in English. Oh, except this one." She went to one of the final images in the very short list, a recreation of the blurred one, and brought up the site.

I looked at it. "Picture of one of the fire snakes," it read. "Note the bulbous body, which is where the fuel for the flame is contained before being expelled and burnt." I didn't bother to read any of the rest. I turned and looked at Anthea, my expression incredulous.

"Right, huh?" she said with a humorless laugh. "Bray, there's pictures, and there's, there's bullshit like this, but there is nothing I can find online to help us."

"All right, what do we do then?" I asked. "Do we go to the cops and tell them what we know?"

She grimaced and seemed to be pondering it. "We'll get into trouble, and I'm already under a threat from Wallace." She looked at me out of the corners of her eyes. "I know he threatened you as well, but he told me he was going to close down my business. I'd lose everything, Bray. And with Leroy back in town, how easy would it be for him to swoop in and take Em from me? She'd still be at the same school and everything, but with him. And he would, too, I'm sure of it, especially after rejecting him."

"So, police are out of the question," I stated. "Then do we email this Dr Boyle in Scotland and see what he has to say?"

"But you said he was crazy."

"And what we're dealing with isn't?" She shrugged. "Look, if crazy's all we've got, then we have to go with crazy." I looked at the computer screen again. "Or German," I added.

She stared at me, but the giggle she was trying to hold back escaped. "Fine, it's the crazy Scotsman," she said. She brought up Outlook and found the email he had sent to her in reply and pondered what she was going to do. Then, in a flurry of fingers, she typed merrily away for a few minutes. I read over her shoulder. She thanked him for his offer and asked what sort of advice he could give us in dealing with these things as there seemed to be quite a number of them. She then attached a video file, labelled as 'snake-eat-edit-1'; at only fifteen meg in size, it was definitely not the full recording I'd made. "Here goes," she muttered and hit the send button on the screen, then sat back as it disappeared.

"Done and done," I said. "Now I guess you wait."

"*We* wait," she corrected. "You're in this as much as I am."

"Okay." That thought did not fill me with any confidence.

We sat there in silence for a while, staring at a computer screen with a picture of some sort of snake in a tree as the wallpaper. "Bray, are we doing the right thing?" she asked.

"I'm not sure. A part of me still thinks we should call the cops," I replied nervously. "If it wasn't for Wallace, I think I might have."

"No, are *we* doing the right thing?" Her hand fell back onto my leg and she squeezed it again.

"I'm not sure," I repeated.

She massaged my leg firmly and our eyes met. "I like this honesty thing, but it can be so frustrating," she stated, her eyes narrowing.

I placed my hand on top of hers. "Well, I'm not sure" I said for a third time, "but I am feeling confident. At least, more confident than I am about" – I waved my hand at the computer – "this shit."

She set the machine to shut down. "Well, I don't think there's anything else we can do. I've looked at pictures, we've sent an email to a crazy man, and we've decided we can't trust the police. All up, a waste of an early morning." She looked at me and I couldn't tell how much of that was serious.

"We did something," I said.

"Yeah, something." She stood up and dragged me to my feet, leaning her body against mine. "But we could do something more." That cute, cheeky grin was there, her eyes not leaving mine for one instant.

"Are you sure?" I asked.

"Only if you are," was her reply.

Beside us the computer wound down, so that the only sound in the snake room was the buzz of the fluorescent lights and hum the refrigerator. She started away, but kept hold of my hand. I followed. She stopped when we reached the door. "Only if you want to," she whispered.

My response was to kiss her lightly on the tip of her nose.

She turned the lights off and made sure the door was locked. She didn't say anything else, but she didn't let go of me either as we went through the house to her room.

She closed the door behind us and took me to the bed. She stopped me at the side of it and gazed at me, her eyes wide, filled with hope, that little grin still there, but tempered with caution. "Are you sure?" she asked quietly, her thumbs running over the backs of my hands.

"Yes," I whispered.

Her smile was filled with... love? I'm not sure, but it was something very positive, and it was all directed at me.

Our kissing started there and then. She worked my top off quickly and undid my jeans so they fell to the floor. I stepped out of them as she dragged me onto the bed. My hands ran across her body beneath her top, feeling her skin, lingering on her breasts. Hers cupped my behind and pulled me in towards her.

I didn't really need any further prompting.

I wasn't sure of my feelings, but the doubts... they'd gone. Anthea filled my mind and I just wanted to make her happy. At that moment, as our naked bodies joined, all I cared about was making her happy.

Nothing else mattered.

Chapter 18

I woke with Anthea curled up beside me like a cat, her arm resting on my stomach. I ruffled her hair, placed a kiss on the top of her head and carefully disengaged myself, then made my way to the toilet, my clothes under my arm. I went from there directly to the living room. The sun was already lighting the morning sky, casting everything in a yellow and orange glow.

I could not remember the last time I had felt so good within myself.

I folded the blanket that had been placed over me and placed it on the end of the couch when I realized I was not alone. "Morning," I said to Emma, a feeling of guilt washing over me. I felt like I had intruded into a family that was struggling to settle into a way of life that was being made uncomfortable enough by Leroy's passing fancies without me adding an extra layer of complexity.

"Morning," she echoed. She still looked half asleep. She still wore the onesie, but half her hair had fallen out of the ponytail and her eyes looked not quite open. Under her arm she held a well-worn teddy bear; my limited experience told me that that was not common for a ten-year-old, though maybe I was just missing something. She trudged across and looked at what I was doing, then gazed at me. There was a question on the tip of her tongue, but it did not come out. My guilt was now compounded by embarrassment.

That was when Anthea made her appearance. Her expression matched Emma's – half-asleep and a little confused. But then she saw her daughter and hugged her from behind. "Good morning," she said, tickling her a little, waking her up with a squeal. Emma turned and hugged her tight about the neck before they let go of one another. "Sleep well?" she asked.

Emma nodded, then asked, "Can I have Coco Pops for breakfast?"

Anthea rolled her eyes. "Well, no school today, so, okay."

"Goody!" she cried and bounced off to the kitchen.

"One bowl only!" Anthea called as she came across to me. She hugged me and our kiss was gentle and yet passionate. "And did you sleep well?" she asked.

"Better than I have for a long, long time," I replied, not letting go of her. Her smile beamed at me. I ran my hands through her hair and kissed her again. Her grip about me tightened and she held me close; I felt she didn't want this to stop as much as me.

"Mu-um!" We parted instantly, like teenagers caught by a parent and looked at Emma. She was staring at us with a stern look on her face, the mirror of her grandmother. Both of us giggled and Emma's expression took on an added dimension of confusion. "What?" she demanded.

"Nothing, dear," Anthea sighed, but her hand found mine.

Emma's eyes darted between the two of us and she nodded once, to herself, then said, "Mum, I can't open the new milk."

"Okay," Anthea sighed, letting go of me and following her to the kitchen. My phone beeped, so I pulled it out and looked at the screen. A message from the school. As a non-teaching day, I was being offered the day off after everything that had happened the previous day, but the final comment said: *It would be good to see you tho. Even if for ½ the day.* I knew what that meant – come to work. I didn't bother to respond, and rammed it back into my pocket, then made my way to the kitchen.

"I like him."

I stopped at the door, knowing what I was doing was not right, but Emma's comment intrigued me.

"So do I," Anthea replied. "A lot. I hope you're going to be okay with that."

"Will I be teased at school?" That question came out so fast I had the impression she had been thinking about it for a while.

"I hope not," Anthea replied, concern in her tone.

"I'll do my best as well." I decided to make my presence known. I walked up behind Anthea and kissed the top of her head. "I like your mum as well. We're going to take it slow, but people at school don't need to know everything." Anthea looked at me, and smiled – just a little, but there was a smile there.

"Is it like our secret?" Emma whispered.

"Our big secret," I agreed.

"Do I call you Mr Kincaid still?"

I laughed. "At school, yes. But here, you can call me Bray or Brayden."

"What about when we're alone at school?"

"I'm sure you'll do the right thing."

"I will." She sounded determined and I smiled as she bent to the soggy mess her breakfast had become.

"Coffee?" I asked Anthea.

"Please," she said. By the time I'd boiled the water and poured the cups, Emma had finished her breakfast. She rinsed her bowl, then left the kitchen. I watched her go, then looked at Anthea. "Oh, she'll put her headphones on and read. She's working through *The Phantom Tollbooth* at the moment."

"Good book," I said.

She smiled and snorted a laugh. "Leroy just ignored her reading. He wouldn't know *The Phantom Tollbooth* from *Eragon*."

"Yeah, not a fan of that one." Her smile was wide. "What?"

"He'd have no idea." She reached across and we met in the middle for a quick kiss. There was a part of me that felt like a teenager with a girlfriend back in high school, and all the joys of that first fluttering of affection for someone else, and yet the very stark reality of our situations – us both having gone through nasty break-ups, Emma's presence, both being working adults – was there as well, confusing matters. This was not two people finding one another; this involved a larger cross-section of our worlds. "So, what are your plans for the day?" she asked. I took my phone out and simply showed her the message. "Ooh, a passive-aggressive demand you go to work. Nice," she said.

"Sorry," I offered.

"No need to apologize. We have to work. That's life."

"Yeah, I know." We kissed again and settled to finish our coffees. I was cleaning the few dishes when her phone sounded. She pulled it out and looked at the screen, then scowled deeply. "Problem?" I asked.

"Leroy," she snarled. I dried my hands and started to leave. "Where you going?"

"Give you some privacy."

"Uh-uh. Sit." And she hit the button to put him on speaker, then placed the phone between us.

"What is it?" She was not hiding her emotions – that was anger and resignation there.

"Hello to you, too," came a rather cheery voice from the other end. "How are you this fine morning?"

"What do you want, Leroy?" She rested her forehead

on the palm of her hand, supported by her elbow. That weariness she'd shown when she'd first appeared this morning was back in full force.

"I want to see Emma," he stated. "Louise tells me the kids have a student-free day today because someone died at the school." I tensed up a little, but said nothing; he couldn't know what had happened or who it was. Still, hearing Sallyanne's death just put forth like it was something he'd seen on TV was not easy.

"Let you see her so you can take her away, maybe back to your girlfriend wherever she is." That anger was strong.

He did not answer for a few moments, and when he did, his voice was quieter: "I told you she and I broke up."

"So you say."

"I asked you to marry me. Would I have done that if…" He stopped himself. "We split because of Emma," he suddenly stated. "When she found out I'd engaged a lawyer to get shared custody, that was when she told me that she didn't want kids. Not my kids, not our kids, no kids at all. I said I couldn't just leave Emma, and she said I had to choose – her or my daughter." There was another pause and his voice became even quieter, but now also held a touch of hope, when he spoke again: "I chose Emma. It's time I was her dad again."

Anthea did not reply straight away. I reached across and took her other hand. She squeezed my fingers and smiled at me gratefully.

"Anthea?" Leroy's voice sounded really hopeful.

Her response was done with a clipped, terse voice. "I'll see if she wants to. I'll drop her off. But I will be telling the police where she is and giving them your licence plate number, so if you do piss off, they will find you, and that…"

"You come along as well, then." Anthea did not say

anything, but looked at me. I returned her gaze, but kept my face impassive. "Come on, we can be a family again. You, me, Emma, just like…"

She squeezed my hand again. "I will drop her off," she reaffirmed.

"Come on, it'll be…"

"I said I will drop her off." She took a deep breath. "But only if Emma wants to go."

I stood. "I'll go get her," I mouthed. She smiled and let go of my hand, then held a thumb up. I made my way to her room. She was dressed in jeans and a top, so similar to Anthea's casual clothing, her hair hanging loose about her shoulders to the bottom of her ribcage, sitting in a bean bag in front of the window, sunlight surrounding her like a halo, book open in her hands, headphones on with a mellow sound coming from them. For a moment I felt I was about to deal with a teenager, not a ten-year-old. I walked up to her and tapped her on the shoulder. She jumped a little, but smiled when she saw me.

She slid the headphones – big ones, not the earbuds I was used to kids using – to her neck. "What's up?" she asked. She sounded so much like her mother I almost laughed.

"Your dad's on the phone," I said. "He wants to see you today."

Her face screwed up. "No," she said, and went to replace the headphones.

"Emma, he's your father," I said. "At least come and talk to him."

"He didn't want to talk to me when he left mum," she growled.

I squatted down in front of her. "I know, but he's your dad. No matter what, he is your dad. You need to at least talk to him. And maybe he's trying to make up for what he did." I offered her a smile. "Be the bigger person, accept his apology. I'm not saying you have to see him, but at least talk to him."

She held my gaze for a few moments, then heaved an exaggerated sigh. "Okay," she said. I helped her to her feet and, quite out of the blue, she grabbed me in a hug. I returned the gesture. She pulled away, then beckoned me to come closer. I leant to her. "I wish you were my dad," she whispered, then kissed my cheek quickly before marching up to the other end of the house. I was not sure I felt comfortable with that at all, and I followed her slowly, trying not to think about it.

By the time I stopped in the doorway of the kitchen, Emma was asking her dad what she should bring, sounding resigned to her fate like a character in a period drama. I understood she was exaggerating everything for the effect, but poor Leroy on the other end of the line was trying desperately to make sure she was going to be happy. She was playing him like a violin and I had to hide my laugh. Finally, she told him she'd be there when she got there, Anthea told him the same thing, and she hung up on him in the middle of him saying he hoped to see them soon. "I'll go get ready," Emma sighed and trudged away from the table. She paused to lean against me as she went past, then disappeared to her room.

"Thank you," Anthea said. "I don't know what you told her, but I was sure she would not go, and that would just lead to all sorts of issues I'm not in the mood to deal with."

"How do you know I said anything?" I asked innocently.

She came across to me and draped her arms around my shoulders. "Because I just do," she said before instigating a long kiss that I really didn't want to end. "And I guess I spend the day alone." There was no accusation in her voice, just resignation.

"You could spend it with Leroy," I said casually.

"I could, or I could hit myself in the face with a brick," she countered. We both smiled. "No, I'm over him. Have been for a long time. I don't need his crap, his trying to get back with me, his attempts to butter us up."

"You could come with me," I said.

"What?" she laughed. "Me turn up with you at the school? You heard Emma – she's worried enough about teasing. How would that look if we just…?"

"No. I mean it," I said. "Come in your work clothes."

She must have seen how serious I was by the look on my face. "Why?"

"I killed one," I said. "It happened to be the one I saw. I don't know what else is there. No one does. Sallyanne brought her aquarium in and no one saw what was inside. I would feel more comfortable if a professional went through the place, just looking. You'd know where to look to find anything hiding, and you have the equipment and skill to catch them." I ran my hand over her head. "As much as I admit having you there, and seeing you is an advantage, I think this is important, especially on a day when the kids who are going to be at school are all going to be in the hall and not in all the rooms."

"I just rock up," she said as though that was not going to be a good thing, though she was clearly warming to the idea.

"By the time you've dropped Emma off and got back, I'll have it all organized." I kissed her again. "I'll even make sure they pay you."

"Well, yeah, that'd be good," she muttered, then heaved a sigh and hugged me again. "So, I suppose I'd better get ready as well." She looked at me. "Thanks, Bray. Again."

"Any time," I grinned.

"I hope so," she muttered, kissed me, and disappeared into the bathroom.

I watched her go, and the memory of only a few hours before in her bed returned to me. I wanted to tell myself that this was what I wanted, but those doubts would not leave me. Could I just walk into a family like this? Would I ever be accepted? I liked Emma, and I really liked Anthea, but was that what I wanted? And Anthea and Leroy had shared a marriage for quite a few years; what if the antagonism she felt now wore off, and Emma's desire to get her parents back together overcame everything? It was Wednesday; Anthea and I had danced at that function on Friday night – that was less than a week. This was me taking it slow? Were we both going into this without thinking? Was this just some sort of infatuation borne of loneliness on both our parts?

I was talking myself out of accepting this for what it was. I was filling my head with "what if" scenarios. I knew that, I knew I was starting to sabotage things, but they would not leave me.

And yet, when Emma emerged from her room with a backpack slung over one shoulder, I plastered a smile onto my face and accepted her offered hand. She had braided her hair into a single plait and had changed her clothes to something a little less house-casual. "Ready?" I asked. She shrugged. "Come on, it'll be as fun as you make it."

Her eyes narrowed. "You used to say that in class all the time," she stated.

"And?"

She sighed in that overdone manner she had clearly adopted for dealing with adults. "Yes, it worked. But that was at school…"

"And this time there's no teachers, just you, your dad, your Aunt Louise, and your cousins."

She looked at me. "Okay," she grumbled. I smiled at her. Somehow, she returned it and squeezed my fingers, in the same manner as her mum.

"Cute." We both looked at Anthea and saw her own grin. She came up to us and gripped me about the waist. "Okay, Em, out to the car. I'll grab my stuff and be right behind you."

"Will you be here later?" she asked me.

"Well, I'll be here some time," I said. "You can't get rid of me that easy."

"Good." She was serious and made her way outside.

We watched her go, then Anthea grabbed me and kissed me tenderly. "You know, in the shower, I was thinking that maybe we…"

"…were going too fast?" I finished. She looked stunned, but nodded. "I know," I murmured.

"Well?"

"Well what?"

"Are we going too fast?"

"Probably."

"So, what does that mean?"

"I have no idea."

She stepped back but kept hold of my hands. "I like where we're going," she whispered.

"So do I."

"Are you okay with it all?"

I wanted to tell her that I was fine, that everything was cool, but I could not start lying to her now. "I don't know how I'm feeling," I replied. "But I do like you. A lot."

She gave a deep breath, and her kiss was on my cheek. "I haven't felt like this in too long," she said.

I led her towards the front door. "Neither have I," I replied, keeping my voice low.

We reached the door. This time her kiss was deeper. "Just keep being honest with me," she said.

I smiled and we left the house. Emma was already waiting in Anthea's work vehicle. Anthea and I kissed goodbye, a pleasant kiss, though with diminished passion, and we drove away for our day.

Chapter 19

By the time Anthea arrived at the Ardrossan school, I had convinced the entire administration team that not only was her visit vital, but that even if she found nothing, she should be paid. I left her to her own devices; I had to go through the rigmarole of an internal discussion about my actions of the previous day. It was not really an interrogation or anything like that, but using the term discussion indicates it was much more two-sided than it was. While what I had done was seen as praise-worthy, especially with authorities coming to get the body, it was still an unacceptable risk. Also, I learnt Edwina – Eddie – was having some stress leave, and it was strongly hinted I should follow suit or, at the very least, see a psychologist. I made all the right noises, but baulked when I was told the Education Department would be supplying the person for me to talk to. Apparently, the next day there would be a team of counsellors coming up from Adelaide to talk to all the children in the classes and to speak to any who felt they needed someone to speak to; after all, as they well knew, Sallyanne had been a popular member of staff. I ended up spending more than an hour and a half with Tracey, Kylie – the school's principal – and a high school teacher I only knew as Richard, who was the Occupational Health and Safety staff representative.

I have to say, I left the room with my head feeling quite thick. At least I knew why my presence at the school had been required. I went into the staffroom and fell into one of the chairs. "Not good, eh?" asked Clarisse, the teacher in the class next door to mine.

"Apparently, I'm naughty and so I've just been sent

to the principal," I moaned.

She smirked and shook her head. "Going overboard again," she sighed. "These rules and regulations weren't around when I started teaching."

"Didn't they still use a clay tablet and stylus when you started teaching?" I returned.

She looked at me in shock, then burst out laughing. Clarisse had been my teacher when I was six years old; joking about her age was pretty much the only way the two of us could cope with the change in my status from smart-assed student to work colleague. "Well, if you need someone to talk to Tracey or Kylie for you, there's a few of who will. Eddie reckons you were quite the hero."

I shrugged. "Someone had to," I said.

"Speaking of which," came a second voice from behind us. We turned and saw Joe pouring himself a cup of tea. "Your – partner? Is that it?" – I didn't smile; he hurried along – "well, the snake-catcher has caught three browns on school property, one in the canteen."

"Ooh, nasty," Clarisse muttered.

"Yeah, well, she's still out there hunting." He nodded at me. "Good move to bring her in, that's for sure," he admitted.

"Glad to be of service." A part of me wanted to go out and see what she was doing, but I didn't want to look like a needy boyfriend, stalking her while she was trying to work, so I held my place. I glanced at the clock on the wall; it was half past eleven. According to Tracey at the end of our meeting, I could leave at midday without a problem. That meant I just had to cool my heels for half an hour.

However, only five minutes later, Tracey herself came in. She made a beeline right for me. Clarisse and Joe watched her come, but neither made a move to leave us alone, which I think Tracey picked up straight away. Solidarity amongst staff is not something administrators often relish, but she simply sat down opposite me. "I am so sorry about that in there," she said.

"Yeah, well," was what came out of my mouth.

"Kylie is in a bind, I'm afraid," she went on. "Apparently, you were reported to the Department. We were going to just let things go, but now our hands are tied."

"Who would do that?" Clarissa demanded. "None of the staff, surely…"

Tracey was shaking her head. She looked at the door of the staffroom, then leant in closer. "I shouldn't be telling you this, but from what Kylie said, it was one of the police officers who came here to investigate," she said quietly.

"Why would the police do that?" Joe snorted.

"It's one cop," I muttered. "He's not a local – he's from Adelaide. Anthea and I found another dead body on the weekend…"

"The ones at Wills Creek?" Tracey gasped.

"Well, just one of them. But he thinks we're hiding stuff." I shook my head. "So, yeah, I believe it. It's just the sort of thing he'd do."

"What can we do?" Tracey asked.

I thought briefly, but then shrugged while shaking my head. "I don't think there's anything anyone can do," I said with a sense of resignation and maybe even dread.

"Well, he is going to have to go through every single official channel in order to do anything on school grounds," Tracey stated as she stood. "But, Bray, really, Kylie and I are proud of you, and thankful you did what you did, even if your methods were a little, well, unorthodox."

"Thanks," I replied.

"Oh, and take off whenever you want. Don't just sit

here like a bump on a log."

"I'll wait for Anthea to finish her snake hunt," I replied. "But thanks for the offer."

She tried to smile, failed, and waddled off back to her office.

"Well…" Clarisse said. I looked at her; I knew that expression dating back almost thirty years – she was not happy at all. She pushed herself to her feet. "I'm going to see if they need any help in the hall with the kids," she muttered and strode off.

"Wow," Joe whispered once she was gone. "I'd hate to be on the receiving end of her at the moment."

I smiled but said nothing. Joe soon left me alone. That was a weird sensation – being in the staffroom all by myself, with no one else present at all. I could not turn my mind off after the berating I had received, and further knowing that the police – undoubtedly Inspector Wallace – were involved. My doubts about where I was going with Anthea had been all but obliterated with this new complication to my life. Just the thought that the police had taken that sort of a dislike to me made our decision not to tell them about this strange snake species that we kept finding at the sites of all the deaths feel like it was the right one. This was me cutting off my nose to spite my face, just to give a middle finger to the cops, and I knew it, but I now simply did not care.

The silence and emptiness got to me and I stood to leave this place to itself. I went to the front office area where I was pleased to see Anthea was busy signing some paperwork. She glanced up when I entered, then looked at me properly and grinned.

"All done?" I asked.

"Just about," she said. "Once I've signed my life

away, I get a cheque and then, I guess, that's it."

"Worth every penny," said Ms Hunter, our school's main front office staff. I'd seen her yell and stare down angry fathers; she was not a person to get on the bad side of, and fortunately, it looked like Anthea had fallen on the positive side. "How many did you catch?"

"Three browns, one of them dead, and one python," she said as if it was nothing. I guess, to her, it *was* nothing, but to the rest of us, it was quite the accomplishment. I would never have guessed so many of them would have found homes on the school grounds. I had a feeling she was going to get some regular work just looking over the place from now on.

Ms Hunter shook her head. "Don't know how you can do it," she said as she took all the papers and placed them in a new manila folder. "Just looking at a picture of a snake gives me the willies."

"Yeah, she's pretty amazing," I smiled.

"This coming from you, who caught one." She shook her head. "Good match, you two." Anthea and I exchanged an embarrassed glance. She then pressed a button on the computer in front of her. The printer beside her buzzed and spat out a piece of perforated paper. Ms Hunter stood. "Back in a sec," she said. "Need a second signature."

"No problems," Anthea replied with a smile.

We watched her go. Once she was out of sight, I asked quietly, "None of the… the others?"

She shook her head. "One of the browns was a young one, and the python is not one normally found in populated areas, so I'm guessing it might have escaped from a private collection. Quite illegal to have it, so there won't be a report of it being missing. Standard snakes." She nodded. "Thank God."

"Oh, yeah," I agreed.

Ms Hunter came back in and handed the paper to Anthea. She looked at it and nodded. "Thank you," she said.

"No, thank you," Ms Hunter replied. She then turned to face me. "Keep this one," she said. "Worth her weight in gold."

"She is," I grinned. Anthea's face flushed a slight red color and I joined her. "So, you ready to go?" I asked.

"Are you?"

"Hell yeah," I growled. Ms Hunter bowed her head; she would have known what had happened in Kylie's office. "Let's get going."

"See you tomorrow," Ms Hunter called after me.

"Yep, I'll be here," I returned and we left the building. We simply walked to the parking lot where she had managed to get a spot beside my car. "Up for a bite to eat?" I asked. "I know it's early, but…"

"Shitty day, huh?" she asked.

"Like you wouldn't believe."

"Poor baby," she cooed and kissed the tip of my nose. "Let's go down to the bakery. I could do with a strong coffee."

"Let's walk," I said. "I think the exercise'll do me a world of good."

"Sure." By the time we were passing the newsagent, she was holding my hand. It felt natural and the physical contact was something my body just needed at that moment. If I thought I could have got away with it without creating fodder for every gossip in town, I would have hugged her and held her tight there and then. As it was, I was happy enough just to have her with me.

Over coffee and some really nice – not to mention fattening – baked goods, I told her about the meeting and the revelation that the police had been to blame, and she described how she had to move a refrigerator in the canteen to get the larger of the brown snakes, and how one of the ladies in there had refused to go back in even after it was safely boxed. It was a conversation about life, showing how quickly we had fallen into that pattern of comfort.

We were getting ready to leave when my phone rang. I took it out and looked at the screen. "It's from you," I said, my confusion obvious.

"Answer it, it's Em," Anthea said quickly. "I gave her my phone and told her to ring you when she was ready to come home."

"Okay." I placed it on the table and answered it, speaker on. "Hello?"

"Mr Kincaid, is mum there?" She was whispering and her voice was coming in short gasps.

"I'm here, honey. What's up?"

"There's a snake," she said. "It's black and it's got a funny head."

"Where's your dad?" Anthea's voice was filled with the same sense of dread I was feeling. So close to Wills Creek, a strange snake – that could only mean one thing as far as Anthea and I were concerned.

"I don't know," Emma sobbed, her voice growing louder. "We saw it out the back and he made me come inside and he went to the shed. Mum, I'm scared!"

"We'll be there as soon as we can." She looked at me and I nodded.

"Dad's coming back. Gotta go. Please come." And she hung up.

We did not hesitate. We jogged up the street back to the school and we both climbed into Anthea's work car. It was just accepted that I was going to go along and she sped out of town and onto the Yorke Highway. We passed every car we came up to; I couldn't see the speedometer, but I don't think I wanted to know just how fast we were going.

She pulled to a stop halfway along the driveway leading to the property. "What do you want me to do?" I asked.

She used contemplation of the question to calm herself. "Just keep behind me, and get ready to grab Emma."

"Fine." She looked at me and I returned the gaze. I had not seen panic in her face before, not like this. "It'll be okay," I said. "We'll get her."

She tried to smile, but there was no confidence in her face. We had already seen what these things could do. The thought of finding Emma like that…

She put on those super gloves and this time added wellington boots so large they fit over her shoes. She used bicycle clips to secure the tops and then handed me the hook, bag and a large plastic container. "I'll only catch it if it is going to be easy," she told me, "so I won't need you to be too close."

"Anthea, what are you planning on doing?"

She grimaced, but the look on her face was determination with more than a touch of anger. "I hate doing this," she stated, "but we've seen what these things can do. I only use this normally when I find a severely injured one." She reached under the back seat and pulled out something long and flat. It took me a few moments to realize that what she held was a long knife in a worn leather sheath. A very long knife, maybe two feet, and quite wide – a machete. She withdrew it out a little to let me see it. "This was my grandpa's," she muttered. "He told me never to use it in anger. Well, sorry, grandpa." She grabbed a rope and strung it through a loop at the back and then tied it about her waist, using the belt loops. The final thing she did was pull that red and blue headband out of her pocket.

She finally returned my incredulous stare. "What?" she snarled.

"Just remind me never to get you pissed off," I said. She actually managed a slight smile, and then led me towards the long projection of the L-shaped house. The large window at one end was covered by blinds, beside a smaller window set higher up; the other side of the building was where the front door opened onto, and that was where I would have headed, but Anthea seemed to know where she was going.

We had no idea where the snake was, or Emma or Leroy for that matter, and so we were moving blind.

And slowly.

Anthea's caution was understandable, her actions methodical. Everything that looked like it could hide something she peered at and examined carefully, and then simply continued on. I simply followed in her wake, keeping a healthy distance between us. I did not want to get in her way.

Then she stopped at the corner of the house and the large gas cylinder that was plugged into the house. She held her hand out. "Hook," she ordered. I passed it to her. She reached in and seconds later pulled out a long, thin snake. It was not happy about being disturbed and hissed at her, trying to curl its head around to strike. She glared at it, but even I could see this was not one of the animals we were after. With barely a second thought she grasped it behind the head with a gloved hand, then returned the hook to me. It wrapped its body around her arm but she merely walked across to the long grass a little way away and held her arm out. The reptile uncoiled itself and she let it go, then stepped back. It was gone in a matter of seconds. "Just a brown," she muttered as she continued on around to the rear of the house.

Already my heart was thumping way too hard in my

chest. A brown snake, and that apparently wasn't even worth worrying about.

The back of the house was a huge glass wall, enabling us to see into the expansive open-plan living room and dining room, the wall opposite us dominated by a large window covered by Venetian blinds, with the kitchen to our right separated only by a breakfast counter. That was where our gaze fell.

Emma was perched on it, her wide eyes staring at something on the floor on the dining room side. There was no sign of Leroy anywhere, and a sour lump rose in my throat. I mean, I didn't know the guy, but the thought of Emma being there with the body of her father was not anything I'd wish upon any child.

Her head turned slowly and she saw us. Somehow, she managed to smile, but otherwise she did not move a muscle.

That was not a good sign.

Anthea slid the glass door open slowly, but the sound seemed to echo everywhere, way too loud. But opening it enabled us to see very clearly what had Emma's attention.

The snake turned its head slowly to gaze in our direction.

I couldn't help but shudder. It must have been at least as long as the one I had seen on the farm, but its body was so much thicker. It had reared up so that its head was at the level of the counter on which Emma was perched, but it was still a good meter or two away from the edge, the serpentine body stretched out all the way back to the living room.

Anthea moved slowly forward, the turned her head just a little towards me. "Emma," she whispered.

I understood and I must have nodded, because she returned her attention to the snake.

Only its head moved, slowly shifting from Emma to Anthea and me, then back to Emma again. A ripple ran through its body, like a wave down the black scales, pushing it closer to Emma's position. She whimpered and edged back a little more, but her back was already against the wall, right beside the kitchen window which looked out to the front of the building. Anthea moved towards the tail end of the creature, slowly drawing the machete from its scabbard as she did so. I stayed where I was.

The snake's head lifted a little further; that appearance of a torso and neck became far more pronounced as it did so. It looked so much like a lizard that had lost its legs that it was hard to remind myself just what I was seeing. Then the snake lurched at the poor child. She squealed, her voice a pathetic high pitch, and drew her knees right up to her chest.

Anthea lunged and sliced down hard and fast, removing the end meter or so of the animal's tail in a spray of blood.

Its hiss was low and guttural and the head snapped around, the yellow eyes fixing on Anthea. A part of me wanted to simply go to her side and stand by her, but it was Emma's whimpering and pale-faced shock that forced me into action. I ran forward. Anthea saw me move and hacked down again, cutting deep into the flesh of the creature, increasing the blood flow and the anger.

I vaulted onto the bench, holding the plastic container to the side that the snake was located, almost as a shield against its mouth weapon of choice. I crawled across to the child, keeping everything in my hands between myself and the animal, but I was not the centre of its attention now. Its entire focus was on Anthea. "You okay?" I whispered.

Emma looked at me and then grasped me about the neck tight, sobbing against me, her tears flowing in rivers that

I could feel trickling down to my own chest. But that was good – it meant she was alert. Now I just had to get her out of there. I looked across at Anthea; she had moved so the glass sliding door was behind her, the snake moving slowly towards her, stalking her, wary, showing behaviors I just would not have associated with a snake at all. But that also meant that was not an option for leaving this place, and I did not know the house, so I could not hope to quickly find the front door.

"Dad…" Emma whispered in my ear.

I felt something lurch in me, but then I realized she was not addressing me. "Where is he?" I whispered. She pointed at the floor behind us. I looked over my shoulder and had to stifle a curse from escaping. Leroy was lying there, unmoving. There was a stain of red coming from the back of his head, but a quick glance at his body told me that there did not seem to be any of the necrosis we had come to associate with the bite of these strange animals. "Did the snake get him?" I forced myself to ask.

Emma shook her head. "He fell and hit his head on the stove," she whispered through her tears. "It only happened just before you got here." I was about to say that was good, but held my tongue. I wasn't sure how a comment like that would be received. But now I had to get Emma away from here.

I glanced over at Anthea. She was holding the machete in two hands, looking like the heroine of some amazing swords and sorcery story, while the snake was lifting its head to face her, just out of the reach of her weapon. If I didn't know better, I would have said the creature knew what it was doing. However, at the moment, a stalemate between them was as good as anything I could hope for, so that meant I could concentrate on getting Emma out of here.

"Stay there," I said to her and pushed her away from

me so she was against the wall again. I looked about and saw a frying pan sitting beside the stove. I crawled across, past the kitchen sink, and grabbed it. Then, placing my body between Emma and the window over the sink, I slammed the pan against the glass. It exploded everywhere, though most of the glass fell to the outside. I used the pan to clear as much glass out of the frame as possible, especially at the bottom of it, then reached across to grab Emma.

"Mr Kincaid…" she whimpered.

"Just get to the car and wait for us," I whispered in her ear as I lifted her and fed her through the opening I had created. "And watch the glass." She seemed reluctant to let go of me, but I forced her off my neck and let her drop to the ground. She cried out and I peered at her, seeing her shake her hands. She looked at me through tear-filled eyes, blood flowing from the cuts on her palms. "Go!" I cried. She sniffed and turned and simply ran.

"Bray!" I turned quickly as the snake's head rounded the corner of the bench, slithering along the ground with a speed that was frightening. Its eyes narrowed as it caught sight of me by the opening. Then its gaze fell to the floor.

Leroy was a sitting duck.

I swear that reptile smiled as its mouth opened, those fangs sliding out of the pockets, the purple droplets catching the sunlight.

I didn't think. I jumped down to the floor, swinging the frying pan as I did so. It waved its head backwards, avoiding the strike with what looked like deliberate skill, then lunged forward, this time at me.

My back swing caught it in the side of the face, slamming its head against the cupboard.

It recoiled instantly, then turned and darted in that direction.

get all the way through."

I reached an arm out and she came to me, dragging Emma with her. She reached up and kissed the tip of my nose. And there we stayed until a voice called out, "You left this behind!"

We all turned and saw Leroy coming towards us, holding the plastic box out at arm's length. Anthea sighed and let go of us to go to take it out of his hands. She opened the rear of the car and dumped it in. He came up to me. "Anthea says you might have saved my life," he muttered. "Thanks." He offered a hand.

I shook it. "That's okay." I gazed down at Emma, then back at him. "I'm Brayden Kincaid."

He accepted it and the shake was brief and perfunctory. "Leroy Jackson… hang on. Weren't you Emma's school teacher a few years ago?" I nodded. "And you and Anthea are…?"

"Yes, Leroy, we are," Anthea stated, coming up next to me and sliding her arm around my waist.

"Oh. Okay." He looked crest-fallen, but then he turned his attention to Emma. "Sorry about all that, Emma," he said.

"It's okay," she replied, but made no attempt to leave my side.

"How did you know to come?" Leroy asked.

"I gave Emma my phone. She rang us," Anthea explained. "And she said she was alone. What? A snake and you left her alone with it? What were you thinking?"

He looked at Anthea. "It killed Skipper," he said. "I heard him barking, and then – nothing. I saw it and went out to get a gun. The gun safe's in the workshop. But I couldn't find a key, so I came back in and shut the door. It was outside, I promise. But then it was inside. I don't know how it got in…"

"Skipper's doggy door," Anthea stated coldly.

"Oh. Yeah," he mumbled in embarrassment. "Anyway, I got Emma on the counter and told her to stay up there, and I tried to get up as well, but I slipped and I fell and… that was it."

"Good. Fine," Anthea said, her voice remaining emotionless. "Now, do you need a doctor?"

He touched his head and then looked at the red on his fingers. "I'll be fine," he mumbled. "Louise and her two will be back from Kadina soon. If I feel too bad, I'll get her to give me a lift."

"Can we go now?" Emma asked suddenly.

"Yes," Anthea said simply. Leroy didn't argue. We left the farm with Emma sitting curled on my lap. In the rear-view mirror I could see Leroy watching our departure. I had never seen a man look so heartbroken.

Chapter 20

We spent the afternoon watching *Grease* at Emma's insistence, sitting on the couch with the youngster between Anthea and I, her hand now bound and cleaned properly. It was as though she wanted the comfort of both of us present. She was engrossed in the film and I was only half-watching it, but Anthea was busy tapping away at her iPad. I guessed she was trying to distract herself in the best way she could. I think I had virtually drifted off, Emma's head leaning against me as her slightly off-key voice was singing along to the song 'Born To Hand Jive' very quietly when Anthea tapped me on the arm. I jerked a little, but it didn't seem to disturb Emma and her warbling. Anthea handed me her iPad.

It was open to Outlook and an email. "Ms Bowman, I am in Adelaide. I will be in Ardrossan at 7:30 tonight. Can I assume I will see you there? Dr J. Boyle."

"Serious?" I asked as I handed it back to her.

"Apparently."

"He's come here all the way from Scotland without a word of warning?" She shrugged. "Want me to go meet him?" I suggested.

She sighed. "Thanks for the offer, but I really should," she muttered. "However, if you could look after little miss here, I'd really appreciate it." Emma looked up at me and nodded eagerly.

I shrugged. "Sure," I said. "Why not?" Emma beamed at me and snuggled in even closer, like a cat trying to find warmth. Anthea smiled, then turned her attention back to the email. Her face took on a look of concentration.

"What's up?" I asked.

She shook her head. "I don't get it," she said. "I mean, if I work this out right, he would have got my email, and then, straight away, he got a ticket and he's flown halfway around the world without even a word he's going to do it, and he's catching a bus out here. I used my official email account, so the emails would have had contact details, but that's only a phone number and a post office box number. He didn't even ring me? He just saw that the post office is in Ardrossan and he's come out here? Just like that?" She looked up from the screen, facing me. "There's something about this that just doesn't feel right."

"You sure you want to go meet him?" I asked.

She actually contemplated this, then shrugged. "I think I can handle myself," she finally said. "But I won't introduce myself until I've watched him for a bit. If he looks shady, I'll come straight back here and wait for him to make contact again. Then we can go together."

"So long as you're sure," I said.

She smiled and reached across to touch my cheek. "I'm sure," she said. I had no doubt that she could handle herself, and if all else failed, her skill with that machete was certainly not that of a novice.

"So, what does that mean?" Emma asked without moving from my lap.

"It means that straight after dinner I'll put you through the shower, then Bray will put you to bed at your normal time." Anthea slipped into mother mode so easily.

"Can't I stay up an extra half an hour?" she begged.

"We've both got school tomorrow," I said. "After the day you've had, I think a good night's sleep will do you a world of good." I stroked her head. "I know it'll do me good, that's for sure."

She sat up and looked at me, then back at her mother.

"Does that mean you're staying here tonight again?" she asked.

Anthea was trying to hide her grin. "I suppose it does," I said. "I might even take you to school tomorrow."

She looked at me for a few moments, then an expression of defiance crossed her face. "Okay," she said, "but don't embarrass me in front of my friends." Anthea burst out laughing. "What?" Emma demanded.

"Look," I said, "if you think I'll embarrass you that much, we'll disguise you. Big floppy hat, dark glasses…"

"Fake moustache, maybe we'll paint you purple," Anthea joined in.

"Yeah, no one will know it's you, you'll be fine," I said.

Her eyes went from one of us to the other a few times, then she dropped down heavily and folded her arms across her chest. Anthea and I burst out laughing and she sank down a little more. "Do you want me to take you?" Anthea asked.

She didn't answer for a while, then fell across to lean against my arm. "No, I want Mr Kin… I want Bray to take me," she muttered.

"Fine," I smiled. "And we'll be getting there early. No one'll see you."

"Oh. Okay." Was that a note of disappointment in her voice? I shook my head and gazed at Anthea who returned my confusion. We went through the rest of the afternoon in relaxed nothingness. I was not sure what I was going to do with my class the next day, but decided to make it relaxed. Maybe a large day-long project. I was sure I'd come up with something, but without being able to go home and check through my resources, I'd be sort of playing it by ear. After ten years doing this job, I was sure I'd be able to find something educational and at least vaguely fun. I tried not to let it bug me too much, but I still found myself making too many notes while Anthea got Emma ready for bed.

I managed to convince Emma to go to bed at her normal time, and then sat in front of the television to wait for Anthea's return. She didn't come in until almost half past eight. She dropped everything on the dining table, then flopped next to me on the couch, curling up beside me in a manner identical to her daughter. "Bad night, huh?" I ventured.

"I don't know," she said. "He got off the bus and stood there. It was like he was just expecting me to come along. I waited for five minutes and, I swear, he didn't move. I finally went up to him and asked if he was Dr Boyle. He told me he was and demanded to see the place where the bodies were found. Just like that. No greetings, no small talk at all, just a demand. I told him that wasn't going to be possible at night, and asked if he had arranged for somewhere to stay. He looked at me as if that question was stupid, but I asked it again and he sounded unsure for the first time. So, I took him into the hotel, arranged a room for him, and then we shared a drink. He tried asking me about the bodies, but I told him that talking about it in public was not the way things were done, and eventually he told me he thought he knew what we had, and the video confirmed it. He just wants to see things for himself."

She sighed heavily and snuggled in closer. I started to stroke her hair. "In the end, I got him to go to his room. I told him to rest. He'd literally been on a plane or at airports for a day and a half, and then two and a half hours on a bus out here. He agreed pretty quickly and he tried to invite me in, but I told him I'd meet him at nine o'clock tomorrow morning. I'll take him to Wills Creek, and then bring him here and show him the live specimen. He knows about it already, so I couldn't really deny it."

I toyed with the short hair covering the nape of her neck. "Are you going to be okay with him?" I asked.

"Wait till you see him," she said. "He looks like one of those stereotypical professors on TV. He was dressed in brown and he smelt like he definitely hadn't had a shower in days." I stopped what I was doing and dropped my hand to her shoulder. "No," she whispered, "please don't stop."

My hand moved back to what it was doing and she moved to make it more comfortable for both of us. "So, a day with a Scottish professor. Sounds like fun," I said.

"English," she corrected. "He just comes from a Scottish university. But at the moment, he makes a living writing books and giving lectures."

"Books? About what?" She moved her head back into my hand a little more.

"Oh, all sorts of things. Cryptozoology mainly, but also stuff like evolution and natural history. He said he'd give me one tomorrow." She moved her head a little more and closed her eyes. "Can we stop talking about him now? Please?" she asked.

"Of course," I replied. "You just relax. It's been a pretty full-on day for you as well."

"Yeah." She moved her head a little more and stared at me. I returned the gaze. She grabbed my face and planted her lips on mine with force. I returned it. Her hand moved down between my legs without a hesitation and she parted our show of passion. "Come on," she said quietly, taking me by the hand and almost dragging me up the passageway. I closed the door behind us carefully. When I turned around, Anthea almost threw me onto the bed. She giggled as she undressed me, then, sitting over me, she slowly removed her own clothing, giving me a show from a weird angle. She leant over me to take off her panties, and her kiss was tender and sweet. And then she sat up and slid down on me and it was something I'd never experienced before and I never wanted it to end.

This night I didn't spend any time on the couch.

Chapter 21

Thursday started off strangely. Driving Emma to the school, I thought after her comments of the previous night that she'd keep a low profile, but she sat in the front seat and made sure she was watching everything out of her window, so that anyone who saw the car would have no doubt at all who she was. She even gave me a quick hug when she got out of the car before running off to wait for her friends and show off her injury.

My class happened to be the first one chosen by the counsellors who had come up from Adelaide, so the first hour of the day was spent with them rambling on about how talking was good, but not saying why they were there. No mention was made of Sallyanne at all, not even a hint of death, just if any of them felt sad, then today was the day when there were going to be lots of people who would listen to them. By half an hour in, my class was getting fidgety; seven and eight-year-olds do not need that long being told the same thing over and over without being told anything concrete. But that's what you get when people from head office who haven't been in a classroom for years, if at all, think they know best.

We spent the next half an hour going over the task I had assigned for the day – making a diorama of a scene from the book they were reading, then sharing it with the rest of the class after lunch time – and then they went to the recycling area outside the class to gather what they wanted, spread newspaper everywhere, and the class was a noisy, fun-filled place, which helped me forget everything that was going on. Kylie came by once, Tracey twice, but neither actually said anything to me, they just watched the students doing what they were doing.

At about two o'clock I received a message from Anthea asking me to take Emma home. I told her I would, but I had a quick meeting after school, and also she'd have to let the school know. Fifteen minutes later she texted me back to tell me all was sorted, and less than two minutes after that, Ms Hunter came in to confirm that permission had been given. Oh, the joys of a bureaucracy!

But, really, I felt like I was dissociated from it all, a feeling that was becoming a lot more frequent than I would have liked. I found my eyes wandering to beneath the benches, looking for the glistening of black scales or anything even vaguely reptilian. Any flash of yellow made me think of eyes glowing out at me. And a quick movement out of the corners of my eyes made me almost jump, just in case something was coming around a corner, ready.

I was glad I'd set the day up as something different, because I had a feeling in a normal instructive situation, I would have been completely useless.

Emma and I went home via the bakery where I treated her to a donut and told her not to tell her mother, though the fact her mouth ended up looking like a chocolate clown probably would have given it away if Anthea had been home. I made Emma do her homework and was listening to her reading when the front door opened. We both looked up as Anthea trudged in, followed by a man who looked like the British politician Jeremy Corbin, albeit with a thicker beard and longer hair. "Dr Boyle, this is my daughter Emma and my" – her eyes caught mine – "partner Brayden."

He barely acknowledged Emma but he did offer me his hand. "Another scientist?" he enquired.

"School teacher," I said with a smile. "Anthea's the intelligent one here." The scowl that crossed his face was not the response I had expected. I cast a quick glance at Anthea; her expression told me that she was not a fan of our international visitor.

"Well," he said suddenly, facing Anthea, "I want to see the specimen again and then you can take me back to the hotel where I can get something to eat that I hope is at least palatable."

"Sure thing," she stated coldly and led him towards the snake room. Emma and I watched them go until we heard the door close.

"I don't like him.," Emma muttered.

"You've only just met him," I countered.

She looked at me, the seriousness in her face almost laughable, and very adult. "I don't think he's one of the good ones," she declared, then went back to her book and resumed her recitation of the words that held very little interest for a girl who was reading works like *The Phantom Tollbooth.* Sometimes I wonder at the one size fits all manner of assigned 'readers' to students, but it is a part of the job, I guess.

Once Emma was finished I decided to prepare dinner and left her to her own devices with her iPad and her headphones. I was close to finishing cutting everything up when Anthea and Dr Boyle finally emerged. She poked her head into the kitchen. "Just going to drop him back at the hotel," she said. "Won't be long." Her eyes narrowed. "Are you cooking?" she asked.

"I am capable," I replied.

"Careful," she grinned, "or I might expect it all the time."

I responded by looking down my nose at her and turning my head. She laughed and left with the doctor. She was back a lot quicker than I would have thought, and she stood in the kitchen while I was cooking everything. "Well, he seemed an interesting character," I mused.

"Sexist, know-it-all, arrogant, self-righteous pig," she snapped. "He thought I was the secretary or something."

"But did he know anything about the snakes?"

She chewed her lower lip for a few moments. "I think he does, and that's the only reason I'm going to stick with him. He didn't tell me anything, but I reckon he knows. Oh, but get this. He wants me to find out if anyone had a large package delivered to Wills Creek from anywhere in Europe recently. How the hell am I supposed to find that out?" She glowered at nothing in particular. "He is impossible. It's like dealing with Leroy's father all over again." I didn't want to know, so I didn't ask. "Bray, I really do think he knows, but he's not telling me anything. I'm afraid he's going to do something stupid that is going to get me – or us – into trouble."

"That bad, huh?" I drained the vegetables, then dumped them in with the meat I was stir-frying.

"You didn't spend the day with him." She sighed heavily. "How'd things go with Em today?"

I smiled a little; changing the subject. Nice mental diversion. "Got to school fine, and she really played up the sore hand. Her teacher even came to ask me if it was genuine." I paused. "Yes, they automatically assumed I'd know."

"Well, you do know," Anthea said.

"But they shouldn't assume that." She came across and hugged me from behind. "I mean, it's only been a week, and…"

"…and that's not a real lot of time. I know." She kissed my neck. "But it feels like it's been so much longer. I like this. Us, I mean."

I leant into her a little as I moved the plastic spoon through the food. "I'm glad," I said. We stayed there for a few moments, then I continued, "Homework's all done, even reading. Last I saw her, she was on the iPad."

"Yep, she's still on it, there at the dining table." She dropped her voice a little. "I think she's happy with this as well."

"Leroy's not."

She stiffened behind me. I felt it straight away. She started to let go, but then she gripped me even tighter. "I don't care," she whispered, but I didn't believe her, not completely. I turned my head and kissed the tip of her nose. She smiled at me, returned the gesture, then went to get the bowls out of the cupboard. She finally looked over my shoulder at the mess I was creating. "Smells wonderful," she whispered, kissed me once more and disappeared.

We let Emma dominate the conversation over dinner. Apparently, she wasn't that embarrassed by being driven to school by a teacher, and she told everyone how her mum had killed a huge snake and how Mr Kincaid had made sure it didn't get her. Leroy, from what I could gather, did not even get a mention. Once the meal was over, I gathered up the dishes and headed into the kitchen. Anthea followed behind while Emma disappeared to her bedroom. "If you keep cooking like that, I am not going to let you go home ever," she smiled.

"Right," I snorted.

"Bray, I haven't seen Em have seconds of anything that had that many veggies in it. You're a hit." She draped her arms around my neck. "In more ways than one," she finished with that cheeky grin crossing her face.

Our kiss was passionate and yet tender, but I was the one who broke it off. "I can't stay the night," I muttered.

She sighed, but nodded. "I know," she said. "Clothes, lesson stuff, all that sort of thing."

"Yeah." Our arms remained around one another.

"But I have enjoyed this."

"I'm glad." Her kiss was so soft I almost caved in and offered to remain yet again. Almost.

"But now I need to ask you something," I eventually said.

"Oh?" Suspicion clouded her face.

"Yep – can you do the dishes for me?"

She looked like it was hardly a request. "Of course," she laughed. "Why ask?"

"Because I reckon I can find out about a delivery to Wills Creek."

She snatched up a towel and shooed me out of the room. "Go. The quicker I can get rid of this guy, the better. Find out!" I laughed at her and went into the living room. I scrolled through the phone until I found the number of the woman who ran the shop in Port Clinton. Telling her I had to find something out from Old Gwen, she gave me the woman's number. We chatted for a few minutes, her asking if I'd been out of town lately because my mail was building up at the shop – we don't have roadside mail delivery in Port Clinton – and me saying I was staying close to the school, and I even told her there'd been a death. That was enough for her to call the conversation to an end.

Next, I rang Gwen. If anyone was going to know, or would be able to find out for me, it would be her and her little clique of old age gossips. It took her a little while to answer. "Yeah?" she barked, her voice that familiar rasp.

"Mrs Goodrich, it's Brayden Kincaid." I tried to put on as cheery a voice as I could.

"Haven't seen you around town," she muttered suspiciously.

"No, we had a death at the school, and I'm staying close."

"Sallyanne Patressi, yes, I heard." *Of course you have*, I thought. "So, what can I do for you?"

"Look, I heard that someone in Wills Creek had a delivery from Europe somewhere," I said, careful to make the story in my head sound as believable as possible. "Do you have any idea who it might have been?"

"Why?" Suspicion clouded her voice, but also intense curiosity.

"Well, I was hoping some of the packaging will still be around, so I can show my class stamps or post-marks or something from another country. I thought it'd be something they wouldn't have seen before." I just hoped that sounded plausible to her, because as I said it out loud just did not ring true.

"Oh, that's sounds great," she enthused, her voice growing even rougher as she grew excited. "Well, I haven't heard, but I'm sure someone will know."

"Thanks, Mrs Goodrich."

"Anything to help the kiddies," she laughed and thankfully I managed to get out of the conversation before it degenerated into one huge gossip session. I think helping me was only secondary; she now just wanted to know who could have received a huge package from overseas. It was not very gallant of me, but sometimes we have to use whatever weapons we have in our arsenal.

I returned to the kitchen and watched Anthea for a few moments. Even from behind, she looked wonderful – rounded buttocks, broad shoulders, that cute hairstyle that I was growing to like more and more – and I snuck up behind her and did to her what she had done to me, wrapping my arms around her waist and kissing her neck. "How'd you go?" she asked.

"It'll take a day or so, but I'll know soon enough," I

said.

"Good." She turned in my grasp to face me and kissed me briefly. "Going to tell me how?"

"I'm going to use the power of gossip," I stated grandly. She looked at me curiously, then broke into a smile and nodded.

"Nice," she said. "There's enough of that around this place."

"And some of it's not even about us," I added. Her eyes widened and then she darted forward and this time the kiss was much more passionate. "And on that note, I might make tracks."

"Okay," she muttered, sounding more like her daughter did when she was pouting than I would have admitted to her. "When will I see you again?"

"Your call," I said. "But I do need to go home tonight."

She sighed. "I know. Tomorrow night? Is that okay?"

I smiled. "Tell you what, after you've spent your day with Dr Boyle" – I said his name with a mock, drawn-out and very bad Scottish accent and she giggled – "you decide what you want to do. I'll do whatever." I tightened my grip on her.

"Deal," she whispered. And, like teenagers again, we basically kissed one another as though it was our first time, lasting a lot longer than I would have given us credit for, before I finally managed to disengage myself from her mouth.

I went to Emma's room. "I'm off, kiddo," I said.

"Why?" she asked.

"Because I've got to go to my own home," I explained.

"There's room here," she said matter-of-factly.

Anthea's hand gripped mine. "I know," I said, "but this isn't my home." She came up to me slowly, then hugged me about the waist. "I'll see you at school tomorrow."

"Yep." She moved her head. "When have you got yard duty?"

"Recess. Asphalt area." She nodded sagely. "I promise I won't embarrass you," I grinned.

"You won't," she stated, hugged me again, and then followed us to the front door. A brief kiss from Anthea, and I was gone.

It was hard, I admit, to leave, but there was a part of me that was also glad to have some alone time. I'd grown used to being alone, even during the end of my relationship with Lynda, and I did find myself relishing living with my own thoughts. But Anthea would not leave me. I had not felt this way about anyone before, so intense and so quickly.

But those doubts… they would not leave me alone.

Chapter 22

It was just another school day, punctuated by a fight at recess time between two students who should have known better and which took up all of my time, first trying to separate them without actually touching them, and then getting details – apparently, it had something to do with a Facebook post the previous night – and finally getting them to the front office. If Emma was there, I didn't see her.

But at the end of the day, as I was packing up – unless something exceptional was happening, there were no meetings after school on Fridays, and because of Sallyanne's death, we weren't even doing a casual coffee – the door to my room opened. I smiled as Anthea entered, Emma holding her hand. "This is a surprise," I said.

"Yeah, and I hope it's not a bad one," Anthea said. She looked uneasy.

"What's wrong?" I asked.

She sighed and looked down. "I sort of agreed to catch up with Sarah and the girls tonight," she muttered.

"That's okay," I said. "They're your friends."

"Yeah, well…" She nudged Emma. "You ask. It's what you want."

The youngster's face flared bright red and she gripped Anthea's hand tighter before asking in a higher pitch than normal, "Can you look after me tonight, please?"

"You want me to be your babysitter?" I confirmed. She nodded slowly. I looked at Anthea.

"I said I'd call mum, see if she could spend the night there, maybe see her cousins tomorrow, but she said she wanted you." She shrugged. "I don't have a problem with that, by the way."

I dropped my eyes to Emma. "You sure you don't want to spend time with your grandma?" I asked carefully.

"I see her all the time," she mumbled.

"It'll probably be boring, you realize that," I warned.

"I don't care." She was becoming more defiant.

"What time will you be home?" I asked Anthea.

She smiled. "If I know who I'm coming home to, it won't be late at all." Emma missed the cheeky grin Anthea gave me as she said that; the meaning behind the comment went right over her head.

"Okay. What time?"

"Straight after school?" Emma asked, her enthusiasm picking up.

"I need to go home first," I said.

Emma pouted, but Anthea took up the conversation. "I'll feed her. I reckon the girls'll want to grab something to eat. So, say, six-ish."

"I'll be there," I said with a nod. Anthea's smile was happier than Emma's as they said their farewells and left me alone. I wasn't really sure I was doing the right thing, but what overcame everything in my mind was the thought of spending another night with Anthea. That was my driving motivation.

And so, sure enough, at about quarter to six I rocked up at Anthea's house, as if this was something that was completely natural and normal. Anthea was wearing dress pants and a shirt and more makeup than I had seen before, her hair brushed straight back. Her kiss was perfunctory; after being with Lynda for so long, I guessed it was so the lipstick was not messed up. Emma was already in her onesie and her wet hair in a low ponytail, ready for bed. Anthea gave me last minute instructions – she was letting Emma stay up half an hour past her normal bedtime, and I had to approve the film she selected to watch, no snacks, no soft drink, typical mum stuff – and then we were left alone.

The movie of choice tonight was *Shrek* which I'd seen a few times during my years as a teacher. Emma leant against me, making sure she was under my arm, making herself comfortable, so much so that I was sure a few times she'd fallen asleep. At about the point where Shrek and Donkey meet the dragon for the first time, my phone rang. Emma moved off me slowly and I smiled at her apologetically before moving away. I did not recognize the phone number.

"Hello?" I asked, nervous though I wasn't sure why.

"Brayden? It's me, Gwen," came a raspy voice I would have recognized anywhere.

"Mrs Goodrich, how are you?" I heard noise in the background and smiled. Friday night at the club at Price.

"Good, good." She sounded fine. "I thought I'd ring you while I remembered," she went on suddenly. "Rhonda Jessop's sister says that George Barker – you know the one? used to be a cleaner at your school before he retired" – I didn't know him, but made a noise of confirmation – "well, his sister died and he got some furniture from her. She still lived in England, where he's from. Anyway, the furniture he got was their mother's or something. Well, according to Rhonda, he hasn't even unpacked it. He didn't want it. It's in his shed. He's waiting to hear from his sister's kids to see if they want it or not. If not, then he'll sell it off." She was in her element, telling someone else about another person's life.

"Well, I might go and visit him tomorrow and see what he's got. Do you know where he lives?" I needed information more than I needed the extras.

"Wills Road." The sounds became muted, but I still heard her bark out, "What number does George Barker live on?" I didn't hear the answer, but she then relayed, "Number eight. It's the house with the boat in the front garden."

"That is excellent. Thank you, Mrs Goodrich," I said.

"Oh, Bray, for you, anytime," she gushed.

"I'll let you get back to the ladies," I said.

"Thank you, Bray. Goodnight."

"Goodnight, and thanks again." And that was it. I had an address. I wrote it down quickly before I forgot and shoved the piece of paper into my pocket, then returned to the couch.

Emma was laying across it, eyes closed, her breath coming in drawn-out purrs. I sighed and shook my head and sat myself at the dining table, going online on my phone to kill some time. When the film finished, I picked her up and carried her to her room. She rolled into me and was even smiling a little when I placed her under the covers. I risked kissing the top of her head and turned the light out and started to close the door. "Goodnight, Bray," she whispered, her voice seeming to float out of nowhere.

"Goodnight, Emma," I returned and shut the door on her. Now I guessed I simply had to wait for the lady of the house to return.

To my surprise, it was not even nine-thirty when Anthea walked in. I looked up from the dining table as she came in. She looked like she had been crying, but the tears had long finished. In their place was anger. I stood and went across to her, but she shrugged me off before I could get too close. "No. Please, just… no," she stated.

"Are you okay?" I tried.

She glared at me. "It was fucking awful," she growled.

"Why? What happened?"

Her eyes bored into me, then she stepped back. "They invited Leroy," she muttered. "They all ganged up on me and said I should take him back. You know who else joined in? Your Lynda. Apparently, she and Eloise have known each other for ages. They told me I should take Leroy back. I told them no way, he'd cheated on me three times. You know what Sarah told me? 'No, it was four times.' You know who he cheated with? Sarah! That was when I was pregnant with Emma! I said you'd never do that. Lynda laughed. Bray, who's Jasmine?" Wow. On top of her friends and her ex trying to get her to go back to him, Lynda was there, stirring the pot.

"A friend from university," I said slowly. "I was her best mate at her wedding." I shook my head. "Lynda wasn't invited. She thought there was something going on."

"She said you slept with her."

"Lynda is full of shit. She can't handle me being happy. She's just being a bitch." My own anger was rising; those doubts were rising again.

She stared at me for a few moments. "I want to believe you, Bray, I really do," she whispered.

"Why don't you?" I asked.

She shook her head. "I want to," she repeated.

I reached for her, but stopped myself. "Anthea, you said you're not Lynda. And I know you're not. But I'm not Leroy, either, and if you take Lynda's word..."

"Eloise said she heard it, too."

I sighed and shook my head. "They're your friends. I don't know why they're doing this, except they want you and Leroy back together. That's fine. But I can't do this game-playing, Anthea. I can't. I did it with Lynda, and not again." I sighed and went back to the table. I grabbed my keys, wallet and phone. "Emma's asleep. She was good." I stood a little distance from her, feeling every single doubt assail my mind like a barrage of artillery. "I'm sorry your night wasn't what you wanted." I smiled at her; her face looked like she was on the verge of tears again, but she was fighting them with fury. "Goodnight," I muttered when I received no response. I let my hand brush her arm as I walked past her.

"Bray..." I heard as I closed the door, but I was afraid I was going to say something that would make this somehow even worse. Why was Lynda doing what she was doing? Was she having problems with Ross? Was it something to do with Anthea's friends? And for Anthea to simply fall into the trap of believing them. Then again, Sarah was her best friend. A best friend who'd slept with her husband apparently.

I hated shit like that. It was as though some people never got out of the high school mentality. And Anthea was falling for it. Was she that insecure about us? Of course, even as I thought of that, the simple fact was we had been together for a whole week – hardly the sort of time frame that is going to lead to something deep and meaningful, I suppose.

I didn't look back. I got in my car and drove back to Port Clinton.

Sleep did not come easy that night.

Chapter 23

I woke up on top of the bed, still dressed in my clothes from the night before. From the living room came the sounds of *Rage*, the music show on ABC-TV that went all Friday night. Modern pop music; not the most pleasant way to be awoken. I dug my keys out of my pocket where they were poking into me, and found the piece of paper with the address on it. I sighed; I really should let Anthea know what I'd been told, but the thought of talking to her at that moment didn't appeal. Instead, I went and had a shower. I debated whether I should go to the gym; I'd feel better physically, but my mind would keep wandering, as it often did, so maybe that wouldn't be the best bet.

Instead I set myself on the couch and turned the volume on *Rage* down while I decided what to do. The address… I groaned and grabbed my phone. *Gwen gave me address of delivery. 8 Wills Rd. George Barker is home owner. Good luck with Doc Boyle,* was what I typed and sent to Anthea, then dropped it on the table in front of me and leant back, closing my eyes. Maybe a day trip to Adelaide, to visit a few old friends, was in order. I smiled. I hadn't seen Jasmine since before the previous Christmas. Interacting on Facebook was hardly the way a friendship should go. Maybe a visit would be good, especially with Jasmine on my mind at the moment.

My phone beeped. Without thinking I picked it up and swiped to read the message. *You not going 2 B there?* was what I read. It was from Anthea.

I grunted. I knew what I was about to get into, and I knew I should have simply phoned her, but I didn't feel like it. Maybe this was the better way to go. *Didn't think you'd want me there.* I had a feeling that was a little aggressive, but I hit 'send' before I could talk myself out of it.

There was no immediate response, so I stood and went to the kitchen. I made myself a coffee – strong, black, too many sugars – and poured it in my travel mug. By the time I got back to the living room, there was a message waiting. *Please, Bray.* And as I looked at it, a second one popped up: *I'm sorry.*

My hand hovered over the 'call' icon on the screen, but I did not go any further. Now I was the one acting childish. Instead, I typed, *Give me a time I'll meet you there.*

There was no immediate response. I went to the study and found my laptop backpack, loaded the machine up and added a few extra things I thought I might need. If I was going to meet Anthea and Dr Boyle, I might as well do something productive while they looked at the furniture that had been delivered, and getting some lesson planning done was probably going to be the best use of my time. So much for getting to Adelaide and spending a decent amount of time with some old friends, I groaned to myself.

I had almost given up on hearing from Anthea when the phone beeped again. *Mum's got Em. She's not happy. I'll get Boyle. Be at Wills Creek ½ hr.* Well, that made my decision for me, I supposed. I still could have refused, but it was not Anthea I was angry with, not really. Annoyed, maybe, for not trusting me; and I wasn't even sure I was actually angry, truth be told. I was new into this little circle, and cliques always hate changes, especially new members coming in. Leroy was what and who they knew, had been a part of their lives for years; I was someone who may have taught their children, but I had really come out of nowhere. I was the interloper.

I was now blaming myself, and I knew it.

I decided not to wait and I arrived at the house long

before Anthea was due with her esteemed guest. I went straight up to the front door and knocked loudly. It took quite a while before I heard someone approaching. The door was swung open, but the screen door between us remained firmly closed. However, the wire mesh could not prevent the cloud of cigarette smoke from wafting out. I forced a smile onto my face. "Mr Barker?" I asked.

"Yes. Who are you?" he snarled. He was really just a shape; I could not make out any details.

"My name's Brayden Kincaid. I'm a teacher from…"

"The teacher? Oh, yeah, they were talking about you at the club last night," he coughed. "You want to see the shit I got from my sister, yeah?"

"Well, more the packaging, if that's okay," I said.

He moved back a little, and I had the impression he was looking me over. Finally, he grunted, "Go 'round the side gate."

"Thank you…" I started to say, but he'd already closed the door.

I went to the driveway and the six-foot high wooden fence that had once been painted white which blocked it. I waited for a fair while before I heard a cough and then the sound of a set of keys rattling. A portion of the gate swung open and he invited me through. He was dressed in an old pair of tracksuit pants with holes in the knees, a t-shirt advertising a brand of beer that hadn't been available for over fifteen years and a dressing gown that had probably started its life colored blue. But his attire was not what my eyes drifted to. Wills Rd ran parallel to Creek Rd, and it was the house at the corner of his property that attracted my attention – well, more the police tape I could see flapping in the wind from over the fence. We were close to Mrs Robertson's place. He saw where I was staring. "Yeah, couple of dead people," he said as though he was describing the deaths of feral cats.

"What happened?" I asked.

"Who knows?" he grunted. "Old biddy always complained. Maybe she complained to the wrong person."

"Okay," I think I said.

"It's down here," he muttered, walking to a tin shed that was about the size and style to hold two family cars comfortably, and that was right near the corner of the yard where his property and Mrs Robertson's met. The front door of it was open about a foot and a half and when he pushed it the rest of the way it made a noise I was sure could be heard at the beach. A pair of decent-sized wooden crates sat right there in the front of the shed, stamped with the word 'Fragile'. They looked like something out of a 1950s movie set in the Hollywood version of Africa. "I don't think my sister ever unpacked them," he growled. "I reckon they're the same boxes our ma put them in." He looked at me. "Is old furniture crap easy to sell?"

"Hell yeah," I said. "Hipsters all over will buy. Depends on their condition, but you could probably sell them pretty easy."

He was nodding. "Tell you what," he said, "if I haven't heard from the niece and nephew in a month, I'll get in touch. You sell them for me, I'll let you have twenty percent."

I let out a short laugh and shrugged. "Sure. Why not?" I said. "Done deal."

He nodded, and for the first time a smile broke his craggy features. He reached into the pocket of his dressing gown and pulled out a packet of cigarettes and a plastic disposable lighter and, in short order, he was puffing away. "So, what you want?" he asked.

"Well, I was sort of hoping to find something about

where it came from to show the students in my class," I lied. I was telling more lies recently than I had in a very long time and I was not liking the way I was letting things go in that regard.

"Knock yourself out, but watch out for snakes," he grunted.

"You seen some, have you?" I asked, trying to sound casual.

"Reckon I might have. Can't be sure. I haven't gone into the shed since the crap was dropped off." He drew back and a good quarter of the cigarette turned to ash.

"Well, to be honest, I was already warned about that. I've got a snake-catcher meeting me here," I smiled.

He nodded. "Smart move."

"So, I might go to the front and wait for her. That is," I added quickly, "if it's okay for us to look through the shed."

"Shit, mate, nothing worth stealing. Knock yourself out." He looked around and I noticed the cigarette was now finished. He sucked at the butt before dropping it to the ground and crushing it with his heel. He instantly lit a second one, and absently placed the lighter on the nearest crate. "I'm going to go inside. Shut the shed when you're done, then let us know, will ya?"

"Done, Mr Barker," I smiled. He nodded and finally offered me his hand, the entire thing stained by nicotine. I accepted it. He pumped it once, nodded at me a second time, and then trudged back to the house while I went to wait out the front.

I'd pretty much got the lessons for Monday and Tuesday worked out when Anthea's work vehicle pulled up on the opposite side of the road. She climbed out, followed by Dr Boyle, looking like he was wearing exactly the same clothes I had last seen him in. I waited until she had prepared herself in gloves and boots and they were approaching me before I left my car. "This is the place," I said, with a sweep of my hand.

"Do we just go in or what?" the doctor demanded.

"Come with me," I said. Anthea tried to catch my eye, but I managed to avoid it. I did not want to be there, and compounding it with something that was just making me feel bad enough without adding a discussion to it was not going to make my mood any better. Instead, I took the lead, opening the shed door on its rattling railing and let them see the two boxes just sitting there.

"That?" Dr Boyle spat. "It looks like they haven't been opened in years."

"Decades, yep," I agreed. "But they are literally the only things that have come here from Europe – England, in fact – in the past year or so." I added that extra little bit of information without knowing if I was telling the truth or not, but it had its desired effect – the doctor nodded and bent to gaze at the front of the first crate.

"Have you had a look at this?" he asked, directing the question at me, as though Anthea didn't even exist.

"Nope," I replied.

"Well," he said, "this isn't from England originally. See?" He pointed at a faded stamp that read, *Danmark – Dansk København Selskab Forsendelse.* My expression must have told him what I was thinking because he scowled at me as though I was hardly worth his time. "Denmark," he translated, speaking very slowly, "Danish Copenhagen Shipping Company. I take it you at least know what that means?" He now pointed at the line beneath these words: *MCMLIV*.

"I'm guessing 1954," I said, keeping my tone impassive.

"Very good." And now he added being

condescending to his character traits. "I am going to guess that is when these crates were packed, and no one has opened them since." He stood and wiped his hands on the back of his pants. "This is a waste of time," he snarled.

"How about we let Ms Bowman have a look and see if there's any sign of the snakes first?" I suggested. I saw Anthea tense up a little as I said her name; maybe that was not a good thing to do under the circumstances, but too late now.

He considered this, then nodded and stood aside. "If you please," he said to Anthea, indicating she should enter. It was her turn to avoid looking at me as she walked past and went inside the shed. I watched as she stopped by the first crate and picked up the cigarette lighter. She shook her head and dropped it into her pocket. I had to hide a smile. She pulled a small flashlight out of her pocket and used it to illuminate the junk that had accumulated through who knew how many years George Barker had been living there. In the pale orange light, I saw boxes stacked up against the far wall and the remains of what looked like a Morris Minor – no engine or tyres on the wheels – crammed into one corner. Shelving bowed under the weight of rubbish, and I could see, even from my own limited knowledge, that there were way too many places for snakes to hide in there.

Anthea, though, did her thing quite dutifully. She very carefully examined the area surrounding the crates, then looked at the crates themselves. It was on her second passage that something attracted her attention. She squatted to have a look at it and I saw a look of concentration and curiosity appear. She grabbed and tried to move something, but to no avail. She looked closer, shining her torch at something, then once more attempted to move something. "Mr Kincaid, some help please?" she called.

I hid my grin and came carefully across to her. "Yes?"

"There's a hole here, in this one," she said. "There's something inside that does not look like it belongs there."

"And?"

She sighed. "These planks here, they're all new. See? Different wood, lighter in color." I nodded; now that she'd pointed it out, it was actually obvious. "Can you pull them off, please?"

"I'll try," I said. "But what if there's a snake in there?" Just vocalising that thought made me take a hesitant pace backwards.

"Then loosen them. I'll do the rest." Her voice was emotionless, but I still did not look her in the eyes. I merely shrugged, grabbed the end of the uppermost one and yanked hard. The nails slid out surprisingly easily and I almost fell over as it came out. "That's good," she muttered, her voice sounding distracted. The torch flashed on again and she examined the inside of the container. Then she stepped back. "Can you get the other one as well?" she asked.

I simply grabbed the second at the same end, but this time I was a little more careful in my removal. The nails protested a little more this time, but I overcame that and soon enough had this on top of the first one. I couldn't help myself – I squatted down beside her and gazed at what her torch light was showing.

The crate contained what looked like the top of one of those old roll-top desks, its lower half, including legs missing, but I quickly worked out what had attracted her attention. One side of the wooden covering had been broken, with a hole that looked like a fist had punched it in at some point standing out starkly. And inside, catching the light, were what looked like shards of purple glass. A lot of purple glass. I heard Anthea swallow hard before she stood. "Dr Boyle, I think we may have found something," she said.

He grunted something neither of us could hear and made his way to us as though this was something he did all the time. But the look on his face changed completely at his very first sight of the purple objects. "Yes, this is it," he whispered, and reached a hand out towards them.

Anthea slapped it away. "We don't know what else is in there," she growled.

"But they always leave their nest, and this is their nest," he returned, not bothering to hide his anger. He then faced me. "You tell her."

"Me?" I laughed. "She's the expert. If she says, 'No,' then no it is. Look, man, you're in Australia now. This is a hole. Yes, those snakes might have left, but another snake could have gone in, or maybe a spider. Perfect home for a red-back, and you get bitten by one of those, you'll know all about it. This isn't England with quaint little creatures, so listen to Anthea and do what she says." I let a little bit of my own frustration out on him, but it did the trick and he cowered back a bit.

I even got a, "Sorry," out of him, albeit a reluctant one.

Anthea cast me a brief, grateful look, then reached in very slowly and lifted the top. It screeched, its years of lying dormant clearly evident, but with some effort, she managed to get it up. Her gloved hand came down hard and fast, squashing a large huntsman spider into oblivion, and then she moved back. "All clear," she said.

I turned to the doctor and saw that all color had drained out of his face as he stared at the mangled remains of the arachnid. "There's no more," I stated. "Now, what is this?"

He looked like he had to force himself to approach the desk, but when he did so, that fear was replaced by wonder. He almost snatched the torch out of Anthea's grasp and reached a hand in to move the purple things around. It took me a little while, but I worked out that he was gathering the largest pieces, each shaped like a broken dish, some with high edges, some not, into one place. With what looked like the precision of someone who had done this many times in the past, he started to put these pieces together until he had built a decent collection of them, standing there. He stepped back. "What do you think?" he asked.

"If I didn't know better, I'd say they were eggs," Anthea muttered, peering closer. "But the color, that's…"

"Yes, eggs. Eleven of them. That is how many of those things are out there somewhere."

"What about if they breed?" I asked, unable to hide my nervousness. "Wouldn't there be more?"

"Larva don't breed," he sneered.

"Larva? What in the hell are you talking about?" Anthea demanded.

He stood up and looked around. "It does not matter," he said. "What matters is that we hunt them down and kill them all…"

I grabbed him by the collar. He was a little man and I did not have trouble hoisting him up so his feet were off the ground. I saw Anthea reach her hands into the crate and desk but that didn't really attract much of my attention, not while I had the doctor suspended before me. "One of my friends was killed by one of these larvae of yours," I growled. "Now, you had better tell us what you know, or else I will find the biggest nest of spiders in the shed and dump you into the middle of it."

Anthea withdrew her hands and I noticed a slight smirk on her lips. She placed something in one of the large pockets of her pants.

"Let's call them snakes," he managed to reply, maintaining his aloofness. "They do not belong in your country, they are dangerous, so we should kill them. Simple."

I looked around and saw a mass of brown webs in the front of the car. Webs like that meant they probably had not been used in quite some time, but I was going to guess that Dr Boyle did not know that. I spun around and aimed for it. He saw what I was doing and that mask of professionalism disappeared in the blink of an eye. "No one believes me!" he cried.

I stopped what I was doing. "Your shit about dragons and myths being real and crap like that?" I laughed,

"I never said any of that," he protested. "I was misrepresented. What I said was some of these creatures were based on reality." He looked over his shoulder at the cobwebs that were right there. "But some of them still exist," he blubbered. "And that's what you've got here."

I set him down, but did not let go of his collar. "You're telling me that these snakes are actually going to turn into something else."

He nodded slowly. "And before they do, we need to kill them," he whispered, "because when they change, very little on earth can stop them." I looked across at Anthea. I think my expression was mirrored on her face. We might not believe what Dr Boyle was saying, but he certainly believed it, and that was enough to make both of us take stock.

Chapter 24

Dr Boyle insisted he tell both of us what was going on, so we convened in the room he had at the hotel. The confident, self-assured doctor was gone, replaced by a fidgeting, nervous one who continually gazed out of the window, where the only view was the parking lot and the back of the pub. I went to the bottle shop and got a few drinks; he refused one, but Anthea and I both cracked open a beer. We were pretty sure we were going to need it.

But the first few minutes were spent in complete silence. Anthea and I studiously avoided looking at one another and the doctor seemed to be in a world of his own. "So," Anthea finally stated, "are we just going to watch you? Is that the way this goes?" She took a drink coaster from the table and started to play it, more to give her hands something to do, I think, than out of any great interest in the object itself.

"Sorry," he muttered. This was like a completely different person, but there was a flash of the old doctor in his eyes at being admonished by Anthea. "Well, I could tell you the history of dragons and creatures like that, but I am quite confident that is not what you want to hear. However, let me say, the fire-breathing dragon of legend is not a real creature. At least, not as far as I can ascertain. However. there was another being from Medieval legend called a wyvern. Perhaps you have heard of it?" The more he spoke, the more the old doctor came out.

"Sure," I said. "Sort of a low-rent dragon. No fire, barbed tail, maybe a scorpion's tail even, wings, claws. Standard monster."

He nodded once. "Close. Take out the scorpion and

you have it. It is a winged lizard, very poisonous, very dangerous. The last was thought to have been killed in Scotland in the fifteenth century. But there is compelling evidence they survived beyond that, into at least World War Two. And, with the advent of the Internet, I have seen more and more evidence of them as humans push into areas they previously had not."

"You've lost me," I said. "We've got snakes, and you're talking dragons."

"Not dragons!" he snapped. "Wyverns!" He calmed himself, but the anger remained on his face. "I do not know how long the eggs take to hatch, but what you have seen is what comes out. They need food to grow. The more they eat, the faster they grow. Then, when they reach a certain size, I believe around twelve to fifteen feet, they start to thicken, then they sprout hind legs, and finally wings. They become a wyvern." My mouthful of beer felt like it went down the wrong hole and I coughed a little.

"Hang on," Anthea said. "You mean to say you expect us to believe that these snakes will grow legs and wings and start flying around the place?"

"Yes," he said simply. "And if you will let me kill that one in your laboratory, I will show you the growth buds."

"No," she rumbled. She started to crush the coaster she held, shoved it onto her pocket and grabbed another.

"Growth buds?" I shook my head. This had become some sort of nightmare fantasy and I could now see why he had been discredited. This man was our only chance to know what we were up against? Seriously? Still, I couldn't help but say, "What about if we give you a dead one?"

"We are not killing…" Anthea started, but I was already shaking my head.

"It's still in the back of your car, isn't it?" I asked.

She looked at me as though I was crazy, then understanding hit her. "Yeah. I didn't take it out. Other things were on my mind," she muttered. "Stay here." And with that she left the room.

"What was that about?" Dr Boyle demanded.

"She killed one the other day," I explained.

"She killed that one but won't kill the one in her laboratory?" he snorted.

"Listen," I growled, "she saved her ex-husband and her daughter from one of those things, alone, armed with a knife. Don't you dare say anything against her. She's got more, more, more *everything* in her than anyone I've met." I leant forward. "Including you."

A cough at the door distracted our attention and Anthea entered, carrying the plastic container. She cast me a strange, awkward glance as she came across and placed it on the table; my face flared red – she'd heard everything I'd said. I tried not to think about it, but I noticed that she set herself a little closer to me than she had before. Dr Boyle, however, was engrossed in the object on the table, the inside stained with the blood of the animal, now coagulated and darkened. "Are you certain it's dead?" he asked.

"It's in three pieces," I shot back. "If it's alive, then there's a helluva lot you're not telling us."

He scowled at me and yet his caution when lifting the lid was laughable. However, there was no humor in the odor that wafted out. Two days in the back of Anthea's car, in a plastic container – not the best storage method. He looked in and poked a tentative finger at it a couple of times.

"For God's sake," Anthea growled. She grabbed a nearby newspaper and spread a few pages over the table, then grabbed the main section of torso and dumped it down. It was quite long – even that piece was over two meters in length –

but she still managed to coil it so that none of it hung over the edges. "Now, where are these growth buds?"

I crawled across as he slowly worked his hands down its back down from the head end. The head itself might have been missing, but that effect of it having a torso and neck was still clearly obvious. The underbelly was slightly lighter in color, but his hands ran across the dorsal scales. To me it looked like he was hardly making any contact, and yet he stopped only about ten centimeters down from where the chest region was formed. His fingers ran across the same patch a few times, and then he nodded. "I don't suppose you have a scalpel?" he asked.

"A pocket knife will have to do," Anthea returned, pulling a small one out of her pocket. He grunted a thanks and took it, unfolding the blade carefully out. He had to press hard to penetrate the scales, and, of course, no blood came out, but he still peeled the skin back on one side, as if he was performing an operation.

Finally, he moved back. "If you feel across this side," he said, pointing to where the scales had remained untouched, "you'll notice a slight protuberance pushing the scales upwards. On the other side, I've peeled the skin back, and you can see the bud inside. This one is already starting to form the shape of the bones that will become the wings. Though small, you can see the shapes of the humerus, the ulna and the radius."

I think as much to shut him as her general interest, Anthea moved so that she could see what he was talking about. She felt the scaled side and looked at the other very closely. She took the knife out of Dr Boyle's hand without asking and poked the tip under something in there. "Look at this," she said to me.

I went across and gazed down. She moved the point

of the blade and I whistled low. Dr Boyle had been correct. It was small, but what we were seeing looked like the bones of an arm, modified the way they were in some birds. Anthea passed the knife to me and moved her hands down the ventral side of the carcass. She stopped and nodded, then took my hand and placed it on the same spot. There was a definite lump there was well, solid and starting to form.

I looked up at Dr Boyle, who was staring at us with a smugness that rankled me straight away. "Well?" he asked.

I looked at Anthea and she returned my gaze, then, as one, we faced the doctor. "We believe you," Anthea stated. "So now you need to tell us one more thing."

"Yes?" I don't often feel like being violent – you quickly get rid of that sort of mentality being a teacher – but at that moment I so wanted to just thump that arrogant smirk off his bearded face.

"How the hell do we find them?"

The smile froze on his face. She'd stumped him. And that did not make me feel any better about this situation. But he forced that look of disdain back onto his features and he glared at her.

I stood, holding my hands up. "I'll let you two sort this out," I said. "I'm going to have a beer." And with that I left the room and strode across the parking lot to the hotel, detouring via my car to grab my backpack.

Lynda was not working, so at least that was something. It was also not quite lunch time, so the place was not yet packed. Despite that, there were a few people there I knew, but when I sat at a table by myself and just started to drink, no one came over to me. Several glances were cast in my direction and a number of conversations dropped in volume, but I really could not care less. It was as though everything Lynda had told Anthea's friends had also managed to get around to everyone else, and now I was in the eye of a gossip cyclone. So be it. I pulled out my laptop to try and work on the lesson plans I was behind on. But nothing came easily. And, this time, it was not an Anthea-shaped distraction.

The thing was, I could not get what I had just seen and heard out of my mind. That snake had really had little limbs under its skin. Whether those upper limbs would turn into wings or not, I had no idea, but the fact was they were there. I knew snakes had evolved from creatures with legs, so there was that part of me that even said that this particular species was simply a genetic throwback, that these so-called growth buds were just the remnants of the lost limbs or those same limbs beginning to come back. Both of those explanations made a hell of a lot more sense than the fact what we had was the larval form of a mythical creature.

Then the bar went quiet. It was obvious enough to snap me out of my mental musings. I refocused my eyes and felt my stomach tighten. Anthea ignored the looks and whispers as she strode directly across to my table and sat opposite me. I did not say anything; I found her expression impossible to read.

"Well, that was interesting," she finally stated.

"You buy this wyvern crap?" I whispered.

She stared at me for a long time, then shrugged. "I've never seen growths like that before," she replied. "And he sounded sincere."

"Yeah, but a lot of wackos do. They believe their own stories," I returned.

"So you think he's full of shit?"

I was about to answer, but all that came out was a long exhalation, and then I shrugged. "I don't know," I muttered. "I mean, we don't have anything else, and he seemed to know about the eggs and the growth buds before we saw them."

"That's what got me," she said. "He did know about them. There was no guessing – it was all the way he said everything. Okay, we didn't know about the eggs, but he saw the purple and put them together and, bingo – eggs."

"Are they really, though?" I asked.

She stared at me for a long time. "There weren't eleven," she said. "There were twelve. An even dozen." She reached into her pocket and when she pulled her hand out, she was holding what looked like a purple gem. It was not the shape of a bird's egg, but more a sphere that had been elongated in the middle a little. "This is the last one. I saw it at the back."

"What… what are you going to do with it?" I managed.

"Study it."

I wanted to argue with her, to tell her that that was a bad idea, but the words would not come, because there was that part of me that knew that we did need to study these things, to know more about them, because if they were here, they could be literally anywhere. I shrugged and all that came out was, "Your call."

"You're not going to try to talk me out of it?" she smiled.

"Why? None of my business."

"No. I guess not." She sounded a little disheartened by my reply. I took a mouthful of my drink as she turned and looked over the people gathered in the bar. Several heads turned away from her as she did so. "I overreacted, didn't I?" she whispered. I lifted my eyes. "Last night," she clarified.

It took me a second or so to actually work out just what she was talking about. "Look," I finally mumbled, "they are your friends. They want you and Leroy back together. And

Lynda's just being a bitch. I understand that. But what got me was that you assumed they were right. You didn't ask me what was going on. And if you had, I would have shown you this." I tapped at the keyboard and brought up a picture on the screen which I then showed her. "That's me at Jasmine's wedding," I stated. "Jazz is on the left."

"Two brides," Anthea said. "Double wedding?"

"No. They both wanted to wear their mother's wedding dresses. It looks kinda sweet, really." I turned it back around and smiled at the image. "I was Jasmine's 'best man', for want of a better term. None of her family went. Marysia's sister was her 'maid of honor', and a few members of her family did go. But it was small and pleasant." I sighed and got rid of the picture. "Lynda wasn't invited," I continued. "It pissed her off, but she doesn't like… well, she doesn't like that sort of thing."

I gazed up at Anthea and saw that her face was red. "A gay wedding?" she muttered.

"It's legal," I said with a shrug. "They love one another. I've known Jazz for years. I was happy to be there for them."

"Shit, I can't believe…" She shook her head. "Lynda said you slept with her!"

"I slept at her place the night before the wedding, and we did end up sharing a bed, yes, but nothing happened." I grinned at her. "I am totally the wrong gender."

"But Eloise said she heard you and Jasmine…" She couldn't continue.

I let my frustration come through in my tone. "Anthea, none of them would know her. I met Jazz at uni. She's a teacher at some small school in the northern suburbs of Adelaide. Your friends would've got everything from Lynda, who met her maybe three times." I could feel my anger starting to rise as well and I had to control it. It was not Anthea I was angry at; it was Lynda. With Anthea, it was more, well, disappointment. "I just wished you'd talked to me."

"I wish I had, too," she mumbled. She stared at my hands around the glass of beer. "What does this mean for us?" she finally asked. It is hard to put into words her tone. She was not being submissive, but she was not demanding things of me. She was asking as an equal, as someone who was unsure herself, as someone who really wanted to know, and was not simply asking because it was expected of her.

"Anthea," I started, then stopped myself. I had to get my thoughts into line. "Anthea," I said suddenly, "I really like you. It's been a week, and I haven't felt this way about someone before. I know we've been friends for a while, but this is not anything I was expecting. I'm still trying to wrap my head around things. So, when something like this happens, I don't know what to think. Now, I know it was one little thing," I went on quickly, "but those are your best friends, the girls you hang out with, and they are not going to accept me. And Leroy's back in the picture. The question is – can you handle us trying to be together when everything is going against us?" I indicated the direction of the hotel rooms with a wave of my hand. "Even the snakes."

That last comment brought the first hint of a smile to her face. "I heard what you said to Boyle about me," she muttered. "Did you mean it?"

"I wouldn't have said it if I didn't."

Her hand reached across and took mine. "I want this," she murmured. "I want you. You accept me in a way that no one has. You take me the way I am. I need that."

"Surely your friends…" I started, but she shook her head.

"They never understood my snake-catching. When I

didn't change my name when I got married, they were horrified." She gazed at me. "I think sometimes they're still stuck in high school. We're in our thirties, and they still carry on as though everyone has to do things their way. And Leroy's just as bad. You, though, you're different. In a good way. I knew that two years ago when you let me talk about Leroy and the divorce. And the way you let me come in after school for a chat every so often, just to get things off my chest. And you did it because you're my friend. Because you're one of the good ones. I needed a friend, a real friend, one who cared about me." Her voice dropped lower. "And I got lucky. I got you. I'm sorry, Bray. The girls got to me, and I… I'm sorry."

I didn't know how to respond. This was not something I was really comfortable with. "I'm sorry, too," finally came out.

"For what?" Her confusion was genuine.

"Not explaining myself," I muttered. "And just leaving like I did. Not exactly my finest hour." She stared at me incredulously, then shook her head. "What?"

"I'm not going to let you…" she started, but instead of finishing, her grip on my hand tightened. "Bray, I am sorry."

I managed a smile. "I know you are," I whispered. I let my fingers wrap around her hand. "But what happens now?"

She stared at me. "My friends can get fucked," she growled, then smiled at me in that cheeky way of hers. "Present company excepted, of course."

I waited a beat. "Okay."

She must have seen something in my expression. "What?" she demanded.

"They're your friends," I said simply. She started to object, then sighed and slumped down a little. She understood. "I'm not going to ask you to choose. You need to do what's best for you," I finished.

"They want me to choose, though. I know it." She smirked a little, then came over to me and sat on my lap with her back leaning against my chest. She pulled her phone out and then adjusted herself. I reached a hand up and placed it on her upper stomach. She grabbed it and moved it onto one of her breasts. I laughed and that was when she took the selfie. Without moving from me, she tapped madly at the phone until there was a beep. "Well, right now Sarah is looking at us and" – she waited a second – "I would guess about now she's calling one of the other two to ask what the hell is going on." She spun on my lap so she was straddling me. "I just made my choice."

I wanted to ask her if she was sure she'd made the right one, but looking into her eyes, I couldn't bring myself to say anything like that. She did look happy and hopeful. Instead I slipped her off so that we shared the same chair. She leant against me and we both cast our eyes over the bar. We were clearly no longer the centre of attention. I preferred that. And we relaxed in one another's arms.

Chapter 25

Much against her better judgement, Anthea decided to go back to talk to Dr Boyle again. And she insisted I go with her for moral support. It took her two beers to get the courage up and we strode back across the parking lot. She knocked firmly; there was no response. She looked at me curiously and then tried the door handle.

It opened straight away. We exchanged a wary glance and she entered slowly.

The plastic container with the dead snake was on the floor, the cut up section replaced in it, along with the newspaper it had been spread on. But that was the only thing out of place. Everything else had gone. "He's just gone back home?" I asked. She stared at me out of the corners of her eyes. "Well, he came out here and we didn't know. He never said a thing. Why not just leave when he didn't get what he came for?"

"But he did get what he came for," Anthea corrected. "These things are real, they are here, and he knows it."

"So?"

"What did he tell us we had to do?"

"We had to… we had to kill them all. Oh, shit." I looked behind me. "You think he's gone to kill the ones that are left?"

"Well, on that first day I told him that a few were already dead, plus the one I've got. Because of those eggs, he now knows there's a few more out there." She was barely keeping her anger under control. "He's gone to kill them. That idiot!"

"Well, maybe he knows something we don't…"

"Everything he knows is hearsay. He's seen a few eggshells, but the one in the snake room was the first one he said he'd ever seen in real life." She shook her head. "After you left, he told me we had to kill them before they turned into wyverns. He said once they grew their wings, they changed in other ways."

"Hang on. He's never seen them. How can he know that?" I asked.

She shook her head. "Research? An eye-witness somewhere?" She growled under her breath. "You're right – I don't know how he can know that, and he didn't tell me anything beyond that, but he sure sounded sure of himself."

"They're poisonous, really poisonous. They grow wings. They're big. He said they don't breathe fire. What could be worse than just that?" I asked.

She shrugged and shook her head. "Your guess is as good as mine," she stated, "but we need to find him before he does something stupid."

"And maybe we need to hunt some snakes."

"Well, let's see…" She did some quick mental calculations. "We know there's five dead, there's one in the snake room, that leaves five at the most out there. One's out at the Haviland farm, so I'm going to guess there's four in Wills Creek somewhere."

"Does he know about the farm?" I asked.

She contemplated this, then shook her head. "I didn't tell him."

"Then we know where he's going to go, don't we?"

She glowered at nothing, then went across and grabbed the plastic container. "We'll take both cars," she said. "I'll call mum and ask her if she can keep Emma for the rest of the weekend. I have a feeling we're going to be busy."

"Wills Creek it is, then," I sighed. We stared at one

another and she quite suddenly reached across and kissed me. It was brief, but it was tender. "Feel free to do that whenever you want," I said. "I'm going to need all the extra confidence you can give me."

"I'm going to need all the confidence I can give me," she stated and we left the empty hotel room as it was, going directly to our cars and leaving Ardrossan behind us.

I sort of wished I had argued to take one vehicle, because my mind whirled with a heap of 'what if?' scenarios as I made my way north along the Yorke Highway. What if we were too late and one or more of them had already taken on wyvern form? That thought, in turn, had come from another what if: what if Dr Boyle was correct? What if this was not just crazy bullshit? But, I reasoned, even if he was completely out of his head, these snakes were still dangerous. What if we were too late, and more people had died? Would we be blamed, would the police come down on us like a tonne of bricks because we hadn't told them what we'd found so far? Even turning up the music as loud as I could possibly stand did not stop these thoughts from intruding into the forefront of my mind.

I pulled up in front of the old church. The door was open and so I entered slowly. A buzz sounded and a short man emerged from a back room. "Hello, Mr Kincaid," he said cheerfully.

"Mr Kerslake, how are you?" I returned.

"Good, good," he nodded. "You know Ebony's getting married in December?" Ebony, his daughter, had been in one of my first classes at the Ardrossan school, and there was no hiding the pride he felt.

"No. That's great. Give her my regards," I said.

"Of course." He looked around. "What brings you by?"

"Two things. First, I need a TV set, one of those old tube ones" – that was not a lie; it was for a project I had been planning for a few months – "and second, have you had any snakes here in the shop?"

"The TV no can do, I'm afraid. Snakes, though..." He looked briefly thoughtful. "Not here. Oh, one brown, but we took care of that. But there's been a few in Jessop's." He scowled. "Problem with abandoned places, yeah?"

"Yeah." Jessop's was the common name for the general store that had not seen an owner for well over three years.

"Why this interest in snakes?" he asked curiously.

"Well, there's been a rash of sightings in the area. I'm sort of working with the AB's Serpent Service. Because I know a few people, I thought I'd do some footwork," I explained.

"You not teaching anymore?"

"Oh, I'm still teaching," I replied, but the look on his face made me feel the need to explain. "I'm sort of, well, seeing Anthea Bowman, who runs the company, and so I'm helping her out."

He showed no recognition of the name and my divulging a part of my personal life did not seem to worry him. All he cared about was that I had a reason. "Well, I'm not sure who has the key to the place," he muttered. "Probably Darren in Ardrossan."

"Darren?"

"Fischer. Real estate guy. His number's on the sign in the window, but I think he's given up ever selling it."

"Well, thanks anyway," I smiled. "And let me know if a TV comes in."

"Will do, Mr Kincaid," he smiled and watched as I left. I was going to ask if he'd seen Dr Boyle, but thought that might be pushing my luck a little. Besides which, he'd come out of the back room; a car or something like that going past was not going to attract his attention in there.

I wandered down the street. This was known as Main Road to everyone, but its official designation was Wills Creek Road, the carriageway that ran from the Yorke Highway down to the beach. Creek Road and Wills Road both ran off it, curving around with the contours of the shoreline, but this was the main one, hence the church as you came into town and the general store across from the junction where Creek Road came off. Main Road eventually made its way to the beach itself, where a tiny jetty and underused boat ramp sat. It was always a nice place to go for a walk, but today I found myself being ridiculously cautious. Every single place that looked like it could hide something made me take a wide berth; every shadow that seemed to move made me speed up a little. It was absurd, and when I got to the front of the empty store, my heart was beating a lot faster than it should have been.

The glass was filthy, but that didn't matter because large sheets of butcher's paper had been plastered over the windows from the inside anyway. A few corners had started to fall away and there was a hole in the middle of one of them, but they did not allow me to see anything beyond a general atmosphere of darkened gloom. If any place was going to be a home for the snakes we were after, this would certainly be a prime candidate.

The sound of a car pulling up behind me made me turn around with a jerk, but I relaxed straight away. It was just Anthea. She got out and came across to me, greeting me with a quick kiss on the cheek. "Get lost?" I asked casually, smiling a little.

"Stopped in to see Leroy," she replied.

"Oh." Not really a huge surprise, I supposed. "How's he coping after the other day?"

She stared at me curiously for a few moments, then shook her head. "I go visit my ex-husband, and your question is how he's doing?"

"Well, what he went through wasn't real good." I ran my hand over her hair. "And I trust you," I added.

Her smile was sweet and she snuggled into me, wrapping her arms around my chest. "Yeah, he's doing fine," she finally said. "He told Louise that Skipper was bitten by a snake and that I came and got rid of it. That was all he told her. I don't think he quite believes what happened, and having you save him has him feeling really embarrassed."

"So long as he's okay," I replied, then, quite deliberately, changed the subject. "Well, I spoke to Mr Kerslake who runs the junk shop, and he reckons this'd be the place for any snakes."

"How do we get in?" she asked.

"Well, we either go back to Ardrossan and beg Darren Fischer, the real estate guy to give us a key, or we straight out lie to him, or we go around the back and…" I let the rest of that statement hang.

She smiled and took my hand. "Around the back it is then," she said, but then stopped. "Any sign of Boyle?" she asked.

"Not that I'm aware of," I replied. "So, what do we do? Look for the good doctor or break into a deserted shop?"

"Neither's really appealing," was the response. She looked back up the Main Road. "How do you think Boyle would have got here?"

"No idea. It's not like you can just hail a cab, and the bus doesn't leave Yorketown until mid-afternoon." I thought about it, then shrugged. "I am going to guess he went to the

BP on the Highway, waited for a truck heading in this direction, and maybe even paid for passage. Maybe he got dropped off at the top of the road here and walked down. I mean, it is a good five kilometers, though."

"No, he would have got lucky," she stated. "He would have got there when people were coming back from the church up at Dowlingville, the late service. Leroy's dad used to go to that one. I'll bet one of them gave him a lift. But where to?"

I snorted a short, humorless laugh. "Only one place – the campsite. I know they have a few on-site vans, but I always assumed they were all permanent residents. Maybe not…"

"So, do we go visit him at his new digs, or do we commit a crime?" she asked. I stared at her. There was no real question what we were going to do. Anthea went back to her car and put the gloves on and tied the machete about her hips, then handed me the bag and hook and carried a plastic tub herself. If anyone saw us, they would simply assume AB's Serpent Services was on the job.

The side of the building was overgrown, the grass coming as high as my knees, but much of it was yellow, as if it had not received enough water or sunlight. Still, Anthea took the hook from me and beat a path through the vegetation. I knew that snakes would flee if given the opportunity, and that most snakes only attacked people if they were feeling threatened; however, these new snakes – or larvae, if Dr Boyle was correct – did not behave like normal snakes, and they could most definitely feed on humans, and so my fear was very much at the forefront of my mind. But we made the rear of the building without any incidents, a rabbit rushing out the only sign of anything being in there.

The rear of the shop consisted of nothing more than

a small yard, once entirely covered by gravel, but with a lot of weeds and grasses having pushed through. An old chest freezer sat by the side fence on the concrete foundations of some structure that had been square in shape but no longer existed. The opposite side of the house to the one we had come along had once been a driveway, but that had been bricked in to be used as a storage facility, so I wondered how on Earth whatever had been there had been removed. Oh, the distractions our minds latch onto to avoid the reality of our situations…

The back of the shop building looked like a tacked-on afterthought of construction; my vague memories of it was that this was where the family of the final owners lived. The windows here were boarded up with planks of wood, giving it an even more dilapidated feel than the front. Anthea tried the rear door. It moved, but was firmly locked. She cast her eyes over the whole structure and scowled. "Which one do you reckon?" she asked.

My eyes fell on a window we had already walked past, near the corner of the house. The planks of wood at the base seemed to have come away already, more because the frame they had been attached to was rotting than any attempts at illegal entry. I looked up; the guttering was rusted through, so all the water collected on the roof would have simply poured down this part of the wall before it could reach the down-pipe on the very corner. "There," I said.

Anthea walked across and gripped the lower plank. It started to move, but her gloves made for clumsy work. "If you could," she smiled.

"Ah, I knew there was a reason you liked me," I said. "I'm the hired muscle."

"Well, there has to be a reason," she mused. I cast her a glance and saw that cheeky grin plastered on her face. I shook my head and grabbed the plank. I tried it carefully, but it slid out with barely a struggle. The one above it was the same, but the third one took a little more effort. By the time I had forced the fourth one off, we had a hole large enough for us to climb through. Anthea used her gloved hands to clear the few shards of glass left in the bottom of the window frame and she entered first. I handed her all the equipment, then followed carefully, those fears hitting me again with full force as I did so.

The whole house was dark. Even the hole we'd created illuminated only the room we found ourselves in. The place was completely empty. We moved from room to room, looking carefully inside. The floor was concrete, not covered by anything, and the rooms held nothing except a few shards of broken glass in the entire back half of the place. Even the bathroom had been stripped of all fittings, leaving only blocked up pipes sticking out of the tiled walls. The toilet was still intact, but the water inside was green and smelt putrid. I wondered how often the septic tank had been emptied since the place had been abandoned, but decided I really didn't need to know.

We eventually came to the door that separated the living area from the shop area – the only door still intact we had come across.

Anthea steeled herself and pushed it open. It creaked loudly at the sudden movement, but did not resist. It revealed a corridor, at the end of which we could see the back of the serving counter. To our right was a blank wall, but to our left was another opening that had once held a door. Anthea went directly through this. I followed, my fears growing now. The room was clearly a storage area, with one wall lined with built-in shelving, the other empty, but the marks and stains on the concrete floor seemed to indicate that refrigerators or freezers had lined it at one point or another. At the far end was another door. Anthea tried this one, but it was securely locked. I guessed, judging by the position, that this would lead to the bricked-in driveway area. Anthea gave the door the once over, shrugged at me and then led me into the shop proper.

This was very open, cast in browns from the light trying to force its way through the paper covering the windows. The counter was there, separating the place into two distinct areas. Behind it, where we were, was as empty as the bathroom we had already seen, plugs in the walls showing where various things had once come out – gas and water. When I was younger, this had been the place that did the best hot dogs because they deep-fried the hot dog itself in the same oil they cooked the chips in; now that whole area was a brown and yellow stain on the floor and walls. It felt a little sad seeing it like this, a part of my childhood gone. The other side of the counter saw more stains where refrigerators had been, and several poles poking out of the concrete were all that was left of the tables where patrons would sit and eat, especially in the summer when the holiday crowd came here. However, standing out like a sore thumb, a line of gas cylinders sat by the door, against the window. There were seven of them, each about a meter and a half tall, all having uncracked plastic tops that indicated they had not been used. I wondered how much gas would be left in them after the three or so years of sitting there. And that was all there was to see, apart from a carpet of dirt and dust.

I had to shake my head. I was becoming more maudlin being in here. I tried to focus my attention on Anthea, standing in front of me. She cast her eyes around, then squatted down and tried to peer underneath the counter without getting too close. Even frustrated, as she clearly was, I found myself just watching her, smiling a little. I'm not going to pretend she looked like a model, but I found her incredibly attractive, and watching her like that, working at what she did so well, made me feel good. It was so tempting to go up to her and just grab her and kiss her.

The black missile shot out from beneath the counter and struck Anthea with force.

She stumbled backwards, falling to her seat against the back wall, but all I could see was the black writhing creature attached to her hand, the body wrapping like a constrictor around her arm. "No…" I started to whisper, but she regained her composure and snapped her other hand onto the back of the animal's head. She squeezed and pulled it backwards, the purple dripping from those elongated fangs onto the hand it had bitten.

It took me a few moments to realize that it had not been able to penetrate the glove she wore. "Are you…?" I started to ask, but she cut me off.

"Shut up and listen," she stated. "I've got it, but it is fucking strong. Come here and grab the machete. Now."

"But…"

"Bray, just fuckin' do it," she growled, her eyes narrowing as she held the gaze of the reptile in her hands. I saw the hand not holding the snake clench into a shaking fist as the body squeezed even tighter. "Bray, now!"

I swallowed hard and edged forward. I squatted down beside Anthea and reached a hand slowly towards her hip.

Those yellow eyes turned and faced me. Anthea's fist tried to open and close, but it was struggling, and now the hand holding the back of the jaws, keeping the mouth open, letting those fangs glisten in the brown light, was also starting to shake. "Bray…" There was anger there, but also a sense of increasing desperation.

I stretched my hand towards the handle of the knife.

The snake's eyes narrowed a fraction.

I gripped it and slowly started to pull it out of its sheath.

The movement was quick and caught me completely unawares. The body unwrapped itself from Anthea's arm and whipped around my wrist. I tensed up even as it squeezed tight. I have no idea if it knew what I was doing or simply saw my own actions as threatening, but it had me. I continued to slide the blade out, but the grip on me grew stronger. Anthea's hand shook a little and she tried to open and close the fist now that she had been released, getting blood flowing through the limb again.

My fingers started to tingle as the circulation was cut off, and so I moved a little faster. But then the end of the handle struck the wall. I tried to angle it, but it was already lying on the ground. I tried to move it, but the strength in my fingers was dropping noticeably. "Fuck," I growled and looked at Anthea.

She was still struggling with the head. It was pressing forward, even as its eyes shifted between her and me.

Then the head snapped forward, even with her hand still gripping it, the jaws closing barely a centimeter from her nose. The mouth opened slowly again; the next strike was not going to miss.

I slid my other hand under her buttocks and lifted. Her arm holding the snake's head fell to the side and the snake's body stretched a little between her hand and my wrist. Yet what that did was give me the room to lever the rest of the machete out of its scabbard. I swore under my breath as I realized that that hand had lost the strength to do anything but move. I dropped Anthea awkwardly and grabbed the weapon with the other hand.

Anthea saw me, shook her hand that had been

released, and then made a fist as tight as she could with the glove. She cast me a sideways glance, and I only hoped I understood what was going on. I lifted the weapon but, to my surprise, she drove the fist forward. She literally punched the snake in the side of the head. Its gaze snapped to focus on that limb. Her eyes begged me.

I guessed what I had to do.

Using my bad hand, I cut through the animal, just below the bottom of her hand. Not in one clean blow, though – I hacked through it as though cutting down a tree. Blood sprayed out, splattering against every surface around us. The second strike dug in deep and the animal hissed angrily even as Anthea squeezed even tighter. The third was stopped by something solid and its hiss changed in tone to something deeper and throatier. On the fourth blow, I finally got through the last of it, the spinal column, and almost fell onto Anthea, but managed to keep myself balanced.

The yellow of the snake's eyes dulled immediately even as the body let go of me and wriggled around the floor as though it was still seeking me out to attack me, blood flowing from the wound and staining everything. Anthea immediately tossed the head aside and collapsed back against the wall. She stared at me, panting heavily, shaking both her hands.

"Sorry," I muttered as I also tried to get blood flowing back into my hand.

She gazed at me. "For what?" she panted, and offered me a smile. I fell to the wall and slid down beside her. "We did it," she mused, her voice sounding distant.

"That was a tough one," I said, though it should have been a question.

"The strength it had," she muttered and looked across at the still moving body. Even though it was writhing everywhere, slamming into everything, it was obviously a long one, well over three meters, maybe as long as four or so, but what was really noticeable now that we weren't worried about it as much was how thick that upper body was. I had chopped my way through the top of it, missing the more slender neck by some distance, but that did not diminish the appearance. Anthea's face took on a definite look of curiosity and she crawled past me to grasp it. The tail whipped everywhere, so I moved as well and sat on it. She nodded once, then picked up the machete from where I had dropped it. Her hands ran down the scaled back, then she stopped and took the blade and sliced through the scaled skin. I saw what she was doing straight away, and leant across to watch.

They were there, two partially formed upper limbs, more defined than those on the animal in the plastic tub in Anthea's car. She removed a glove and tentatively pulled one of them out.

It was not an arm. A flap of translucent skin was stretched between the upper and lower arm bones, and then down along a very thin extra growth, hard to see, which, like a bat, I assumed would become the equivalent of finger bones. She moved it a little, like the wing it was turning into, and then gazed at me.

For the first time I saw very real, very stark fear on her face.

"The old bastard was right," she whispered. I swallowed hard and nodded. Dr Jeremy Boyle's insanity was all too real. And we were stuck right in the middle of it.

Chapter 26

The campsite was small. We walked there holding hands like teenagers and stood by the office at the top of a low rise, giving us a full view of everything. A row of caravans was parked down one side, their wheels hidden, half of them surrounded by small gardens, shielded from the Main Road leading down to the jetty and boat ramp by a line of Norfolk Pine trees that had formed an almost impenetrable natural barrier. Another caravan was parked in the middle of the site, and a tent was set up near the ablutions block, a black Ford beside it. A Sunday in autumn, the weather was not too bad, and it still looked almost deserted. Another wave of depression washed over me, looking at it, remembering summers decades before when we'd come here as a family when we lived at Port Julia, south of Ardrossan, to visit my father's best friend – now fifteen years dead, after a heart attack while out on his boat – and seeing the campsite filled with virtually no room for anything else.

"Can we go for a walk or something?" Anthea suddenly asked.

That question dragged me back to the present, and I was actually glad for it. "Why? What's up?" I asked.

She faced me and her grip on my hand tightened. "If I face him now, feeling like I am, I think I'll deck him," she explained very simply. "I need to calm down first."

"Fair call," I smiled and led her away from the entrance to a path that ran north, away from Wills Creek and into the conservation park. After only about fifteen minutes, and with no houses or people visible, she stopped me and took me across to a low barrier, a horizontal wooden pole supported by shorter stumps. We sat on it, the cliff dropping down only a couple of meters in front of us, and looked out over the water, neither of us saying anything. "How you feeling?" I asked.

"Shit, Bray, that was close," she whispered. "It was like it knew I was struggling to keep hold of its head and when it went for my face, I could smell its breath. I could *smell* it!" She moved in as close as she could. "I have never, ever been that scared before. And then you lifted me up and my arm fell, and I thought that was going to be it – it was going to get me for sure. And then you cut it and cut it and I just squeezed as hard as I could until I felt the jaws crack, and then you killed it and… Shit, Bray!"

She forced her head into the crook of my neck and kissed the top of it. We stayed there for a little while, my arm around wrapped around her shoulder, hers around my waist, our other two hands holding onto each other as if for dear life. Then she let go and grabbed my hand that was around her and lifted it to the back of her hair. I toyed with the piece that covered the nape of her neck and heard her sigh as she moved into me a little closer. I dropped the hand back to her shoulders, but she whispered, "Don't stop." I did as I was told.

I guess we ended up spending only half an hour or so there before she kissed my cheek. "Let's get back," she muttered. "Time to confront Boyle." We stood and I took her hand without thinking. She squeezed it tight. "Thank you," she said. "Just… thank you." I was working her out a little better and so didn't say anything, just held her hand a little tighter and then kissed the side of her head.

She smiled at me and we made the rest of the journey back to Wills Creek in silence. But the good mood seemed to evaporate as we once more entered the town's limits, past those first few houses, knowing that we were going to have to confront a man neither of us particularly liked, but who seemed to have at least some of the answers. But then she stopped and dragged me across to the edge of the cliff and pointed down at the beach. "Is that him?" she asked.

I looked more closely, then let out a single chuckle. "I'll bet he's seen your car and he's hiding down there, just hoping we're going to go away when we can't find him," I laughed.

"What the hell does he think he's going to do here alone?" she demanded.

I watched him, sitting on a towel on the sand, what looked like some sort of tablet computer on his lap. "I wonder…" I mused and pulled out my phone. I tapped the Internet icon and tapped in his name. His personal website was the first hit and I opened it, then moved it so Anthea could see what I was doing.

The home page had a banner with a message: 'New Blog Post: Wyvern larva discovered.' I looked at Anthea, then tapped it. "Shit," she rumbled.

The post was date-stamped that very day, and read: "I cannot say where I am, but I have discovered a cache of Wyvern larvae. As detailed by Gøttleib (2014), they appear as snakes. I managed to kill one using a hunting knife." This was followed by a photo of the dead one in the plastic container we had left in his room. "I dissected the animal's carcass and have confirmed the theories of development Gøttleib put forth. The growth buds that can be felt on the ventral side of the animal do indeed have, growing beneath, primitive limb structures." There then followed a slightly out-of-focus picture of the winglet he had shown us. "I also looked at the growths that would become the legs, but they were indistinct and did not photograph well. My next goal will be to film one in its natural habitat."

I gazed at Anthea. "Keep going," she snarled.

I sighed and scrolled down. "There have been several deaths here, but the authorities have hushed them up as usual. However, I have discovered from a man on the inside that what we know from previous occurrences has been shown here: an instant death followed by the body tissues becoming liquid. The man who showed me around – a local school teacher with a science degree – became a believer in these theories when I explained them to him. I am sure he will be able to spread the word." And at the bottom was a location indicator that he had set to somewhere called Læsø, Danmark.

"That bastard," Anthea growled as I shut the site down.

"He's making this about himself," I said, "but that's really to be expected."

She watched him for a few more moments. "So, let me get this straight – he's come down here all alone to film these things? Seriously?" Anthea asked. "Is he crazy?"

I stared at him, working down there on whatever it was he was doing, then shifted my gaze to Anthea. "Let's go back to your car," I said.

Her eyes didn't leave me for a few seconds. "You want to check if the head section's still in there, right?" she asked.

"Great minds think alike," I said, unable to hide a slight grin.

"No," she said, her voice slow, "let's assume he's got the head. We'll confront him as if he does." Her glare fixed on the man down beneath us. "Ready?"

"Lead on," I said. We made our way down to the strip of sand between the cliffs and the water, but did not make ourselves known to him straight away. I think Anthea simply wanted to watch him for a little while. He seemed quite relaxed, doing whatever it was he was doing on that tablet. As we watched him, he packed it up and shoved it into the satchel at his side, then laid back, hands behind his head.

"Let's go," Anthea whispered. I nodded; I could understand where her anger was coming from.

He didn't notice us until we were too close for him to be able to flee easily. He sat up with a start, but quickly had himself under control. "Can I help you?" he asked.

"Where is it?" Anthea asked, her voice surprising me by its calmness.

"Where is what?" I couldn't even pick a hint that his composure had faltered.

"The snake's head that you took so you could fake some photos on your blog," she replied, deliberately shifting her gaze to the water before us.

"I didn't take…" Anthea dropped to one knee and jabbed her fist forward, connecting with Dr Boyle's jaw hard enough to send him sprawling on his back, leaving a red mark that was not going to go away in a hurry.

She opened and closed her hand a few times as she stood. "I'm going to ask again, and I want an answer that…"

"I'll call the police," he stated defiantly as he sat up once more. "Then we'll see…"

"I didn't see anything," I said, cutting him off. "And a man who'll lie on his blog site about something as simple as where he is in the world would surely lie about anything."

"I am a foreign national," he said. "My consul will protect me."

"Or you'll get deported, which will surely make the news considering your sort of fame," Anthea said. "And then your followers will know you lied as well, considering you're supposed to be in Denmark."

He opened his mouth to speak again, but the words did not come out. I squatted down in front of him and he flinched visibly. "What the hell is going on?" I asked, keeping my voice as calm as Anthea had.

The defiance started to return but Anthea clenched her fist again and let a deep scowl cross her features. I saw his eyes dart to that hand and he looked at me. "I haven't lied to you," he said. "Everything I told you was true."

"So, instead of helping us stop these creatures, you come down here, alone, to take fake photographs?" I asked.

"I spent a few hours walking the shore, looking for any sign of a lair. In Europe, they tend to be found on the seashore, in cliffs mainly," he explained. "I was hoping to film a live one in its hole."

"Are you fucking insane?" Anthea demanded. "Those things are fast and they kill in seconds."

"I wasn't getting too close and I use a telephoto lens," he countered, his old defiance starting to increase.

"So, instead of helping us, you're using this to prove yourself to a bunch of people online?" she went on.

"The whole community needs to know these things are real! Then they'll know everything I've been saying is real!"

"And if someone else dies in the meantime, that's just too bad?"

"You're hunting them. You know what we're up against…"

I held Anthea's arm back before she could strike again, something that did not go unnoticed by the doctor, causing him to cower away from her. "No, we don't," I corrected. "We want to know everything. Now."

I let Anthea go and she looked at me, then swung her fist, this time connecting with the side of his head. She then looked back at me, mouthed the word *What* and folded her arms. He climbed slowly to his feet, rubbing his face and looked at the two of us, "What else do you need to know?" he asked. "I've told you what they turn into, how big they get. You know about the poison, you know about how they eat. What else is there?"

"You said when they become wyverns, they're almost impossible to kill," I said. "What the hell does that mean?"

I saw a hint of his arrogance cross his face, but Anthea must have as well because this time both her fists clenched up. Dr Boyle saw that as well and yet he kept his cool. "I have nothing concrete, just stories I have gathered over the years," he said. "Nothing scientific…"

"We don't care. Tell us everything," I interrupted.

"The legends from northern Germany tell that the last state of the transformation process involves the wyvern shedding its snake skin. The skin underneath is scaled, but it is tough, impervious to swords and arrows. You have to kill them before they reach that stage." He said that final sentence as though he was delivering a directive.

"*We* have to?" Anthea snorted. "What about you?"

He held his hands up. "I am an academic. I don't know how to kill these things. And you have already shown yourself as more than capable…"

"You don't know?" I asked in complete disbelief.

"Well, there are not many tales about how they were killed," he mumbled. "I can only go by what I can research."

I stepped back. "Let's go," I said to Anthea. "He doesn't know anything. He wants us to think he's the expert, but I reckon you know more about these things than he does."

"Yeah," she agreed, resignation now in her voice, yet she spun back to the doctor. "Once this dickhead gives me back that snake's head."

He looked like he was about to deny everything,

however his eyes fell to her clenched fist. He slowly squatted down and reached into his satchel, then pulled out a Tupperware container that he handed over as if he was baiting an already set trap. She snatched it out of his grasp and then opened the corner of the lid. She nodded at me, shoved it into a pocket and took my hand. We walked away from the beach, leaving him alone. Neither of us said anything until we were back at the top of the path, standing by the road. "Now what?" I asked.

"Bray, I…" She stopped herself and bowed her head. "Bray, I'm sorry. I lost control down there…"

I shrugged. "He did sort of deserve it," I offered.

"Yeah, he did," she smiled. She then looked back in the doctor's direction. All humor faded from her face. "Is this up to us, now?" she asked.

"I think it is," I muttered. "There's only three left in Wills Creek, but I have no idea how we'd go about finding them."

"No. Me neither." She sighed, took my hand once more and we made our way back to the empty general store and her car.

We stood there for a few moments. "Shit," she suddenly said.

"What?" I looked around nervously.

"We left that window open back there," she groaned.

I sighed. "I'll go put everything back," I said.

"Do you mind if I go down and have a look at Mrs Robertson's place?"

"Why should I mind? Go for it. And good luck." Her smile looked weary. "Meet you back here when you're done. No rush," I said.

"Sounds like a plan." She kissed me, then got into her car and took off. I watched her go before I disappeared down the side of the house. It didn't take me long to force the wooden boards back into place and return to the front of the store. I looked around but couldn't see Anthea yet, so I wandered back up the road to my car.

A figure came out of the junk shop as I came nearer, but I didn't recognize who it was until I was almost there. I felt my heart sink a little. "Leroy, how's things?" I asked, forcing cheer into my voice.

He came right up to me. He was about my height and size, but where I went to the gym and tried to keep myself healthy, his build was starting to show the signs of what could well end up being middle-aged spread. "Where is she?" he growled.

I looked at him passively. "Who?"

"You know who." He was not even trying to be civil.

I indicated the rest of the town. "Somewhere in there," I said. "Working."

He inhaled deeply, then let the air out very slowly. "Why don't you leave her alone?" he growled, coming right up to me. I could smell the alcohol on his breath and wondered how I was going to get out of this without doing anything that would come back to bite me later.

"It's her call," I replied.

"It wouldn't be if you pissed off."

"She chose me," I said simply.

"So, you don't even want her," he sneered.

"Leroy, you're drunk. Go home, sleep it off, and we can talk about this later," I said, taking a pace away from him.

"You're destroying a family," he growled. That comment stung; it was not something that sat well with me, playing on the doubts I already had, and straight away my own emotions started to come out.

"And you sleeping with every female who smiles at

you didn't do that already?" I shot back. His face hardened and I saw his shoulders tense up. I moved back a little more.

"They're my family!" he shouted.

"I know. Emma is your daughter..."

"And she spent half the time the other day talking about how wonderful you are!" Now he took a threatening pace towards me. I could see where this was headed, and there was no way I was going to let it go there. "Why don't you leave them alone and let our family get back together?"

"Have you spoken to Anthea about this?" I tried.

"No, but Sarah and that lot will. They'll change her mind." He was goading me now. I think he believed he had the perfect leverage, that he could use Anthea's friends against us. The problem was, that was a genuine fear that I could not wipe out of my own mind, and I did not have a response for him. His smile became cruel. "You know they will. Maybe this isn't worth anything," he laughed. "Maybe Sarah will make Anthea see how wrong she's been..."

"And maybe you'll learn to keep out of my life!" Anthea had parked on the opposite side of the road, and now stormed across to Leroy.

"Oh, hi, we were just talking about..." She didn't give him a chance to finish. That punch I'd seen knock Dr Boyle backwards was delivered with such force that he was dropped instantly, blood pouring from his nose.

"And Sarah will not change my mind," she hissed, standing over him. "You can tell her that from me." She kicked him, a decent punt kick that slammed into the side of his thigh. He yelped and clutched the limb, rubbing it vigorously.

Anthea turned to me. "Are you okay?" she asked.

"He didn't touch me," I shrugged. "I was letting him vent."

She smiled at me, looked over her shoulder at Leroy, then kissed me tenderly and slowly. "Let's get back to my place," she said. "We've got work to do." She then squatted in front of her ex-husband. "Don't you dare do anything like that again," she growled, her voice low, then she stood, smiled at me and trotted back across the road.

"Sorry," I muttered to Leroy as I went around to the driver's side of my vehicle. He just watched me, not moving from where he had fallen. I pulled a U-turn, and followed Anthea up the Main Road, leaving him there. I had a feeling his timing could not have been worse. I think she had just taken her frustration at Dr Boyle out on him. I only hoped she wouldn't regret it later.

Chapter 27

Emma was under headphones, listening to something that I couldn't recognize, reading her book while lying on the couch. Anthea and I just sat at the kitchen table, me staring at my laptop, her at her iPad. "This is getting us nowhere," I sighed.

"No," she agreed, pushing the tablet away from her. "I can't find anything. Do you think he gave us a line of bullshit?"

I shook my head. "No, but I think he's taking it from folk legends. There is nothing in any reference I can find about the growth cycle of a wyvern, except on his website. And the Gøttleib reference he's got leads to a page not found error. I have no idea where he got this shit from."

"No, but the problem is – it makes sense. We've seen those growth buds. We've seen actual wings in that one from today!" She shook her head. "I don't know what to do. We need to find these last few, and we need to, well, kill them. It's that simple."

"I know." I felt like I was no help at all.

She stood and walked behind me, running her hand over my shoulders as she did so, then went to the couch. She popped Emma's headphones off and received an expectant look. "Bedtime, Em," she said.

"Okay," was the reply. No arguments, just blanket acceptance. Anthea's mother had told us that Emma had had a very full-on day with her cousins, and she looked like she had actually been forcing herself to stay awake to her actual bedtime. She let Anthea pick her up and carry her to me.

"Have a good night, kiddo," I smiled.

"You, too," she replied, then planted a wet kiss on

my cheek before burying her face against Anthea's chest. I watched them go to the other end of the house, then turned back to my machine. I opened up a cryptozoology website that proclaimed it was based at the Glasgow University, and focused on European creatures.

I started to read through it, but found I couldn't concentrate. It took me a few moments to work out what was going on – it was the thought of going to work the next morning. I sat back, my eyes closed, and tried to think about how I was going to face a Monday of students with everything else on my mind. This was insane; I had a ready-made out. I pulled my phone from my pocket and scrolled through the numbers. I found the one I needed and hit the icon.

"Michelle Elliot speaking," came a slightly bored voice.

"Michelle, this is Brayden Kincaid from Ardrossan Area School. Are you booked tomorrow?" I spoke quickly before I could talk myself out of what I was doing.

"No. I've got the whole week free," came the reply, her voice perking up immediately. I relaxed. The relief teacher pool was small on the Yorke Peninsula, and to get one on the first call was not that usual. Of course, at the end of term, it was almost impossible, but we weren't there yet.

"How do you feel about a class of year twos and threes?" I asked.

"Perfect. Any set work?"

"There's a relief teacher's pack in the top drawer of the desk. No non-instruction time on Mondays, so they're all yours."

"Sounds good. Any reason?"

I hesitated, then asked, "Did you hear about the death we had at the school?"

"Oh, yes. I am so sorry," she said.

"Yeah, well I found her and killed the snake," I said quietly. "Mental health day."

She seemed unable to speak for a few moments. Then: "You relax. And if you need me for Tuesday, I'm here."

"Thanks, Michelle."

"Have a good day."

We hung up and that simple conversation made my next call easier. It was also very quick. Tracey accepted that I needed the mental health day, and in fact sounded almost relieved that I was taking one. She knew Michelle, and said she'd make sure the class was all settled first thing in the morning. I thanked her, she told me it was all okay, and that was that.

Just doing that made me feel a little less stressed. I had never felt that way about teaching before – that not going in to work was going to make me feel this much better. I did not like the sensation, and guilt started to rear its head, countering the relieved feelings.

I had to stop overthinking it, so I went straight back to the university cryptozoology website I'd found. There was one mention of the wyvern, but that was to basically say Dr Boyle was an idiot. However, it did have a link to a pdf file that I did not think I had seen before. I opened it and found a probably quite illegal scan of a chapter of a book. I read through it and was still reading when Anthea returned. "You look lost in thought," she said, sliding an arm around my shoulders and kissing my cheek.

"Yeah, found this," I muttered, then looked at her. "And I've taken tomorrow off work."

"Why?" No accusation, just a question.

"I can't be there for the class with all this shit on my mind, so I've claimed a mental health day," I explained. "Relief is organized, Tracey knows, all cool."

She looked up the passageway. "Then you better stay in bed until I get Emma to school," she muttered. "I'll tell her you're sick, or else little kid rumors will be everywhere."

I sighed and winced; that was something I had not thought of. "Sounds like a plan," I agreed.

"So, what you got there?" She changed the subject so smoothly.

"It's all about the wyvern, taking a lot of myths from all over Europe. There's nothing about the larval form, but it says pretty much what Dr Boyle told us. But it does have how two of them were killed. One was stabbed by seven knights at the same time, but it says only one of the men survived. It doesn't say how the other six died. And one was killed when it was somehow convinced to wrap itself around a barrel that was covered in spikes, impaling itself." I shook my head. "Doesn't really say anything we can use."

She sighed and leant on me so her chin was on top of my head. "Does this mean we're going hunting tomorrow?" she asked.

"Only if you want to," I replied.

"Don't want to, but I have the strangest feeling we have to."

"What about the doctor?" I sounded a lot more tentative than I felt.

"Don't care," she grunted. "We need to find them and kill them. Let him have his little fantasy world." There was bitterness in her tone and I reached behind and ran my hands over the backs of her legs. She relaxed a little under my touch. "But the biggest problem is," she went on, "how are we going to find them?"

"We knock on every door and ask to have a look around?" I suggested.

"Unless we can find something better, that'll have to

be the plan of attack, I guess." She sighed heavily. "Or we could get the police involved."

"I think we're probably already in too deep for that," I muttered.

"Yeah." That was when her phone chose to ring. She went around to grab it from the table, looked at the screen, rolled her eyes, and slammed it to her ear. "What do you want?" she demanded. I looked at her curiously, and she mouthed, "Sarah," at me. She listened for a while, then said, "Yep. Sure did. Blood from his nose and everything." She looked at me. "I don't care," she growled. But, as she listened, she bowed her head and leant her forehead on her hand, elbow on the table. "I am still your friend, but I've got my own…" I went across to her and placed a hand on her shoulder. She didn't seem to even feel it. "I do, Sarah, I do," she groaned. A brief pause. "One day, if I think he'll be accepted." I moved my hand and curled that short lock of hair on her neck around my finger. She leant into me, closing her eyes. "No, you need to grow up. Leroy and I are through." I kept playing with her hair; a slight grin touched her mouth. "No, Sarah, stop. Emma's calling. I have to go. Call me back when you've calmed down." She hung up and stood and turned immediately, wrapping her arms around me and kissing me with as much passion as I think she had in her at that point in time.

Study ended for the night. The night was spent with the two of us initially using one another as a stress relief, then just being with one another. The change in emotions from the start of the night to the middle of the night was like chalk and cheese. The passion and intensity dropped off into a tenderness and gentleness that both of us seemed to relish so much more. It lasted a long, long time and we parted, but she stayed in my arms.

"I'm sorry," she whispered, running her fingers through the hair on my chest.

"What for?" I asked, confused and suddenly very nervous.

"For what I'm about to say." She sat up and straddled me, then lowered herself so she was using me as a mattress. I didn't push it; it did not feel like a break-up, but she was unsure of herself, then she moved her head so her chin was resting on the backs of her hands, which were still on my body chest. "Bray, I…" She reached up and kissed me softly and quickly. "I reckon I am falling in love with you." Her eyes looked into mine and they were so full of hope, but she moved one of her hands to cover my mouth. "No. Don't say anything. Please," she whispered.

I moved my hands so they cupped her buttocks and she turned her head so that she was lying on me again. Then she grabbed one of my hands and lifted it. I understood and moved it to the back of her head so I could play with that hair that covered the nape of her neck. She shifted into me comfortably and fell still. Her changing breath told me when she was asleep.

But sleep did not come as fast for me. I was stunned, and was not sure what to think, but I was not unhappy. Far from it. And my dreams, when they came, were some of the most pleasant I had had for ages.

Chapter 28

I didn't mind the lie-in the following morning. I heard Emma at one stage coughing, but Anthea's voice cut it off, telling her that she would ruin her throat and it didn't matter, she was still going to school. She even stood in the door and said goodbye to me before they left. By the time Anthea returned, I was showered and dressed and reading through the same websites I had the previous evening, hoping to find something I might have missed. She wrapped her arms around my shoulders from behind and kissed the top of my head. "What you up to?" she asked.

"Just going over this stuff again," I muttered, leaning into her. "There has to be something here…"

"How about we go find them if we can and kill them before they get to that stage?" She sounded firm and I shrugged. She was right, but I guess I was going by the concept of being prepared for the worst.

"Okay, you get ready and I'll finish up here," I replied.

She squeezed my shoulders, then went to the other end of the house. I barely noticed as I continued to read what was in front of me, linked through one of Dr Boyle's references on his WordPress site – a story about a German *Totenkopf* regiment that was killed by an unknown assailant in 1943. The residents of a nearby hamlet heard gunfire and screaming but when they investigated a few days later, they found dead Germans and the bodies of a number of snakes. There was also mention of a large, long burnt object in the centre of everything. Two survivors were found, one who died sometime later, the other who kept babbling about the

Drachenschlangevergiften, which was translated as "dragon snake poison". The problem was this story appeared only on Boyle's website, with no other corroborating evidence. It was well-written, but I found myself doubting its veracity, especially after everything else I'd seen on the site.

On a whim I typed *Drachenschlangevergiften* into Google. Eight hits; not even a disclaimer at the bottom saying similar results have been omitted. One was Boyle's site, six were citing Boyle's site, and one was completely different. I clicked on it. It was in German. I brought up a translate app and the slightly strange version of English gave me the same story as Boyle, but with some bizarre extra information: the surviving soldier spent the rest of his life hunting this creature, and because he claimed that shooting it was dangerous, he went out armed with a flame-thrower. He disappeared in 1949, and no trace of him was ever found. This had to be important, but I couldn't work out why…

"All ready?" Anthea was standing behind me. I set the laptop to shut down, then turned. She was dressed in her work top, that red and blue headband on. Her smile was slightly sad.

I smiled at her. "Whenever you are," I said. She nodded and led the way to the front door.

She stopped there, then faced me. "Did I upset you last night?" she whispered.

I looked at her carefully, then asked, "How?"

Her eyes searched my face. "What I said."

I shook my head. "No," I murmured. "I liked hearing it."

She stroked my cheek. "Well, I do feel that way. I know it's been stupidly short, but I do feel like that." She kissed the tip of my nose. "And I know you don't feel the same way, and that's okay."

"Yet," I said. Her eyes narrowed in confusion. "I really, really like you. More than I have anyone else. And more all the time."

"I don't want you to say you love me unless you really, truly mean it." She was serious. I nodded in response. "And with that in mind, let's go snake-hunting."

"You know," I muttered, "I never thought I'd be turned on by a woman saying that to me." She stared at me incredulously, then burst out laughing. The kiss she planted on my lips was brief but intense. And, in her car, we headed off to Wills Creek.

As we turned onto the Main Road, I faced her. "Are you going to check on Leroy?" I asked, feeling nervous at doing so.

"Why?" she snapped.

"Because you really did a job on his face yesterday. He was obviously upset enough to call Sarah. I wouldn't be surprised if he had a broken nose." It was actually a struggle to keep a straight face as the memory of her belting him came to my mind.

She glanced at me and must have seen something in my expression because a slight grin fought its way onto her mouth as well. "Yeah, maybe I should apologize to him," she managed. Her hand fell to my thigh. "But I'm not going to."

She didn't even slow down as we went past the property. Instead she went directly to the deserted general store and parked out the front. "Okay, serious question," I said.

"Go on."

"Do we go see Dr Boyle first and find out if he actually did find anything genuine after we left him?"

She watched me for a few seconds, then shrugged. "Don't know," she muttered, leaning forward on the steering wheel. "It sounds like it might be a good idea, but the thought of having to deal with him again, especially after I hit him as well…"

"Yeah, you're right. Maybe not, huh," I sighed, then looked across at the town sitting on the other side of the Main Road. "So, where do we start?"

"Well, let's not get people too worried," Anthea said, "so we'll only take my gloves and maybe the hook, but we'll carry that in sections. How does that sound?"

"You're the boss," I said. She smirked, shook her head, and then led the way to the back of the car. I noticed the plastic containers with the dead snakes were both still in there. I wondered if me being around was proving to be too much of a distraction. That was not what I wanted to think about. The thought I could potentially be the reason for her being injured made me start to believe that it was not good that I was here with her. And yet I simply followed her along Creek Road, towards the Robertson house. We stared at the property for a little while. "Which way?" I asked.

"Well…" She pointed to our left and the roof of Mr Barker's shed behind the neighboring house. "We know that was where the snakes came from," she said. "For whatever reason, three of them chose this house to come to."

"The rats," I muttered.

"Hmm?"

"You saw how filthy this place is, how rundown it is and the overgrown backyard. Rats, feral cats, maybe foxes. These snakes need to eat to grow, right? Serpent smorgasbord." I shrugged. "Wouldn't surprise me if another one was there now."

She contemplated this, then nodded. "Sounds like a plan," she stated, and simply climbed over the police tape that was still strung across the front of the property. I took a cautious look around at the surrounding properties before I followed along behind her like a loyal dog. She slowed as she reached the corner of the house. The backyard somehow seemed even worse after only one week. The junk I had seen from inside the house half-hidden by weeds and grass and other plants did not look any more recognizable now that I was closer. "They could be literally anywhere," Anthea muttered as she lifted a sheet of iron. She paused for a moment, then dropped it and faced me. "We'll need bait if we're going to find any of them out here."

"So, let's go next door and have a look there," I suggested. "We can come back here later."

"Thinking the same thing," she replied and flashed her cheeky grin at me. We carefully left the yard made our way to the next house.

I knocked on the door and we waited. There was no answer. We exchanged a quick glance and we could see that we were both thinking the same thing – Monday: people were at work. This plan was falling apart in front of us. I still went across to the front window and pressed my face against it. Nothing was on and the place seemed empty. I shook my head. "Next," Anthea sighed. I nodded and we made our way to the next house on the street.

This time the door was answered. She must have been eighty years old if she was a day, and smelt of lavender and talcum powder. "Yes?" she asked curiously.

"Hi," I said with my best friendly smile. "I'm Brayden Kincaid, a teacher at the Ardrossan school, and this is Anthea Bowman, snake expert. There have been reports of a large number of snakes being sighted in Wills Creek, and we were wondering if we could check your house."

"No charge," Anthea added over my shoulder.

"How do I know this isn't one of those scams – you

come in, see what I got, and come back later and steal it all?" she asked, her suspicion completely out in the open.

"You can call Mr Kerslake out at the second hand shop," I said. "I taught his daughter. He knows me."

"And I used to be married to Louise Piper's brother," Anthea added.

"Piper?" she sneered, then shook her head. "You're not married to him now, are you?"

Anthea placed her arm around my waist. "No, this one got me instead," she smiled.

"Good move." She looked us over. "Yeah, better choice." She stepped aside. "Come on in, see what you can find," she grunted.

I stayed by her side while we followed Anthea as she did her rounds, then we stood by the back door as Anthea went through the back yard. "Do you know Louise?" I asked quietly.

"No," she muttered, "her husband. Said he'd work on my car. Did such a good job I had to get it towed to Balaklava to get fixed properly."

"Ouch." Not the answer I had been expecting, and I really had no response. We stayed there in silence while Anthea finished what she was doing.

She finally came over to us, shaking her head, and smiled at the old lady. "All clear," she said. "You certainly keep your place in good condition."

"I might be old but I'm not decrepit," she stated, but there was the hint of a smile on her craggy features. She saw us out, wished us luck and we went to the next house. The owner of this one was also not at home, so we went to the next one, which was also the last house on the block. A road marked as Brown Street led away from the beach, while on the other side there was one more house, and then some farmland. Creek Road wound past it, continuing to follow the contours of the shore, a barrier between the farm and the sea.

I knocked again, and, like the previous property, there was no answer. However, a car sat in the driveway, so this place had a resident. I tried again, a little louder, only hoping I wasn't waking up a shift worker. That would not be a good thing, I was sure. There was still no response. So, as before, I pressed my face against the glass of the room next to the door. It looked empty, but I could see a flickering light coming from the next room along.

I made my way across to it and looked in. The large television set was showing one of those morning shows that is more about selling things than informing viewers, some inanely grinning woman filling the screen. I shifted my attention… and then stumbled back a few paces. "What is it?" Anthea asked urgently, rushing to my side. I just pointed. The words would not come. She approached and also looked through. "Shit," she hissed.

I could only nod. The man was on the couch, dressed only in underpants and a singlet, eyes closed, lying back, as if he'd merely fallen asleep. And we would have thought maybe he was just in a deep slumber except it looked like his entire lower right leg had been reduced to two sticks of bone attached to the black remnants of a foot. "What do we do?" I whispered.

"We need to get in there and catch that thing," Anthea said, sounding a lot more determined and confident than me.

"We break in?" I asked, my panic obvious in my words.

A car pulled up on the other side of the road and I turned with a start, Anthea much more calmly. But when the sole occupant stepped out a growled, "Fucking hell," escaped her lips.

Inspector Wallace crossed the street as if he owned the entire town. "And what do we have here?" he asked, his smile condescending, his attitude superior and arrogant.

"There's a dead body in there," Anthea stated, the words just coming out before, I guess, she really thought about what she was saying.

"Well, you two at the scene of another death. What are the odds?" he asked, and any hint of good humor disappeared from his visage. "Well, it looks like our information was correct."

"Information?" I looked behind him, then stood tall. "Hang on, you being here, this isn't anything legal," I said. He stopped his approach and just stared at me. "You cannot do this alone. There needs to be at least one other officer present. You're here on… No. This means someone called you directly. So, who in Wills Creek would have seen us come here and call you? Who would you have questioned in the past week?"

"Leroy," Anthea rumbled. The flicker that crossed Wallace's face was enough of a giveaway for both of us. "That bastard!" she growled.

"None of that matters," I said, placing a hand on her shoulder. I faced Wallace. "What matters is there really is a body in there."

He did not say anything as he pushed past us, making a point of bumping into me. I saw it coming and held my ground; he almost bounced off but did not let it disrupt his cocky stride. He glanced warily at us, placed one hand against the glass and pressed his face right up against it. Then he was stumbling backwards, eyes wide. However, he was quick to regain his composure and he went forward again. "Just like the others," he mused.

"Yep," I agreed.

"I need to call for back-up," he said firmly.

"And get the snake out of there," Anthea added under her breath."

But he had heard. "Snake? What snake? Did you see a snake in there?" I think we triggered some sort of fear response in him.

Anthea gave herself a second to get her thoughts in order. "Yes, I did," she lied. I understood why she didn't tell him the truth – she was protecting herself. I had even started to believe that this might all be able to be dealt with without our involvement becoming too obvious, and our prior knowledge becoming known at all.

"What sort do you think it is?" He was forcing a professional face onto himself.

She shrugged. "Couldn't tell, but judging by what we've seen so far, maybe a brown, maybe a death adder." Her face remained impassive.

He rubbed his chin and peered through the window once more. "Could a snake have done that?" he asked suddenly.

"The forensics guys said, 'No,'" Anthea stated.

He looked like he was about to ask something else, but decided against it. Maybe he was going to ask what she, as a snake expert, thought – it's what I would have done – but maybe he somehow felt that would make him lose face, and so he did not bother. Instead he said, "Okay, I'm going to check to see if the back is unlocked. I'll let myself in, and then open the front door. You come in, catch the snake, and then I'll get my people down here. How does that sound?"

"What if it attacks you?" came out of my mouth.

"I'll make lots of noise, stamping and thumping. Didn't your girlfriend here tell you that drives them away?" he sneered.

Anthea let out a long breath. "Okay, the snake's not a brown or a death adder," she said. "It's a species we don't know what we're dealing with. I reckon it's done that to that poor guy's leg. And I think you thumping around is not going to stop it attacking you."

He stared at her, and that arrogance returned in force. "So, let me get this straight," he said as if she was a teenager he'd pulled over for speeding, "there's a snake that only you know about and it does this sort of damage to people, which we've never seen before, and you know enough about it to tell me it's going to attack me even if I thump through the house. Have I got that right?"

"Why would I make that up?" she shot back.

"Good question. And one for which I don't have a good answer. Yet." He looked back into the building. "There's a reason you don't want me in there, why you want to get in first. And I'll be damned if I'm going to give you the opportunity."

"She's not lying," I said, grabbing his arm.

He snatched it out of my grip. "I could call that assault," he growled. "Now I know you're hiding something. And I don't care if you run. I know where both of you live, where you work, everything. We'll find you. And it will only make it worse for you." And with that he stormed off to the rear of the house.

"He might be an asshole," Anthea said, "but we can't let him go in there."

"No," I agreed. "But what can we do? We haven't even got your machete."

"Not even that." She pondered this, but we were distracted from our thoughts by the sound of the rear screen door banging open. "Shit," she growled, "he's inside!"

We followed his trail at a sprint, hurdling a low side fence and bolting to the open back door. Anthea simply ran in; I hesitated a second, taking in the well-kept vegetable garden first. By the time I had followed, she was looking through the drawers in the kitchen. "Here," she said, handing me a long kitchen knife while she clutched a meat cleaver.

Our pace was markedly slower as we left the kitchen. "Wallace?" Anthea called, her voice giving away some of her fear.

From a doorway a little way up his head appeared, scowling at us. "I think it's asleep," he said. "It's coiled up under the chair here." By now we were only a meter or so in front of him.

"You need to move away from it very slowly," Anthea told him, her voice quiet but forceful.

He grunted at her and squatted down, then took out his phone. "I need to get a photo," he said.

"Please, Inspector," I said, and I think I was even begging him, "just come away from it."

He looked at me as if I was a child and held the camera in front of him, arm outstretched. Anthea reached across to grab him with both hands, but the dark movement was so fast to my eyes it was nothing more than a blur. It streamed underneath the camera and latched onto Inspector Wallace's neck. Anthea stumbled backwards into me; I only just managed to catch her flight. But the snake was not interested in her now that it had its fangs into the police officer. I think Wallace tried to turn his eyes to look at us, but he did not get the opportunity as that poison paralyzed every part of him.

And then the necrosis set in. The skin turned black, riding up under his jaw and down into his suit. His tongue flopped down through the hole, hitting the snake on the top of the head, but it did not let go, and even as we watched, the tongue started to shrivel, as if being drained, turning darker as it did so. Black lines run along his lower mandible towards his ears, the skin blistering and melting, then running in a thick, black paste towards the mouth of the reptile. The eyes fell back into the head, leaving holes where we could see more blackness growing over everything. The nose collapsed before the skin was gone, leaving another hole in the face, above the visible teeth, set into a grin of death.

Anthea's strike was precise and hard, the cleaver ramming into the top of the skull of the serpent. It looked like it was struggling to let go with its fangs as the yellow eye we could see glared at the two of us. Its grip on Inspector Wallace lessened, which allowed a treacly flow of black liquid to run down what was left of his throat and over the front of his shirt. The blood from the wound in the snake's head flowed freely, but it did not seem to be overly affected by the attack. The cleaver shivered a little in the top of its skull as finally the mouth was freed from the dead man.

Anthea ripped the knife out of my hands and thrust it forward, skewering the open mouth of the animal before she withdrew her hand with a turn of speed I don't think I could have matched. "Go!" she hissed as the snake seemed to gag on the object. I didn't need to be told twice, and I turned and ran for the back door as fast as I could, not stopping until I was in front of the house, trying to catch my breath. Anthea was right behind me, but she went immediately to the window and peered inside. With some reluctance, I joined her.

The snake was thrashing about on the floor. The cleaver had been dislodged, but the knife was still stuck in its mouth. I couldn't tell if it was dying slowly or if these were those strange nervous impulses of reptiles that saw dismembered tails writhe of their own accord. It knocked into the furniture, moving the knife inside the mouth, ripping it further apart, leaving a trail of blood, not only from that but from the gash that marred the top of its crocodilian skull. And I watched that beast instead of looking at the corpse of a police officer whose lower face looked like it had simply rotted away.

It took a long time for the body to fall still. Only then did Anthea move along the house once more. "Where you going?" I asked.

"I need to look at it," she stated.

"Why?" There was only fear in my voice.

Her smile was almost sad. "Come on, I'll show you." She held her hand out as though I was a child. And I took it and went with her once more to the back door.

We made damn sure not to go near Wallace's body, but instead had a look at the dead animal. It was long, though hard to tell just how long, but what got me was the sheer girth of its upper body. It was as though it was developing pectoral and trapezius muscles like a human. Anthea squatted down and then beckoned me closer. "Look at this," she muttered. I got as close as I was able to see what she was pointing at, but it soon became obvious. There was no need to feel its back to see the growth buds – they ran in twin ridges along either side of its spine, rounded and clearly defined. She moved down to its lower half and nodded. I saw what she could see. There the growth buds had actually erupted and what looked like two fingers poked out of the skin. "We're running out of time," she muttered.

I wondered just how in the hell I'd managed to get into the middle of this…

Chapter 29

We stood by the car, trying to gather our thoughts, her shoulder leaning against my arm. It might not have been much, but that physical contact felt so important. "We should call the police, the proper cops," I said finally. "Maybe call Kyle Rivers at Ardrossan direct."

"Yeah, maybe we should," she replied. "But should we move the snake first?" I shrugged and she came in a little heavier against me. "If we leave it, maybe they'll believe us. But maybe we'll get into trouble." She turned so she was facing me. "Leroy'd use that to get Emma away from me," she whispered. "He'd say I was unfit, snakes like that in the house, hiding shit from the police. He would. And how can I defend it? They'll all know he's telling the truth! And then what if they say us not saying anything caused some of those people to be killed? And what about you as a teacher? Would anyone trust you with their kids if they thought you had anything to do with this? Our lives would be fucked…" She'd already made up her mind, and, to be honest, I was having a hard time trying to come up with a reason that would counter her argument.

"Okay, let's drive back there, remove the snake, then call Kyle and tell him what we found while we were snake-hunting," I agreed.

"And what did we find?"

"Two dead bodies. We went inside to see if they were okay, but we were too late." She was already nodding. She let a slight smile touch her mouth. "Great minds again?" I asked. She nodded. With that we climbed into her car and made our way down to the end of Creek Road. I stayed with the vehicle in case anyone came to ask us any questions, but we were left alone, enabling Anthea to come out with a large plastic tub containing the remains of the animal. She was struggling under the weight, so when she reached the corner of the house I rushed to her and took it from her. Even for me, it was a heavy load, but we soon had it in the rear of the van. That was when I called Kyle at the cop shop. I actually had his direct number from when I'd taught his twin boys a few years earlier; there was some stuff going down I never really understood, and he felt more comfortable with us being able to contact one another directly. Nothing untoward had happened, but the number had remained on my phone ever since.

I hung up and looked at Anthea, standing beside me. "He said he's on his way and he wants us to wait here," I told her.

She slid her arm around my waist. "Fair enough," she muttered. Then a laugh escaped her lips. "I somehow never thought the first dates I'd have with a new partner would involve killing snakes and seeing dead people."

"New to me, too." I squeezed her in close to me. "But I guess if we can get through this, nothing else is going to be an issue."

"Ain't that the truth," she replied. "Nothing…" Her voice faded and when she spoke again, it was hard. "Not even Leroy." She had turned her head and I looked in that direction.

Her ex was walking towards us, looking around curiously. Anthea strode towards him. I decided to follow, but keep my distance. "I thought you'd be dealing with the police," he said with fake curiosity.

Her response was the short, sharp jab I had seen already. He did not have time to react as he was sent to his rear. It was only when he was there that I realized both his eyes were ringed in black-purple bruising from the last time she had belted him. And now Anthea had added another bloody nose to his damaged face. "You called him!" she growled.

"Well, you two need to be stopped," he said. "Who knows what you're doing, and what it's doing to my daughter?"

"So, you are the one who killed the Inspector," I said suddenly. Anthea spun to face me, shock on her visage, but it was Leroy's expression that caught me more. All color drained from it and his eyes widened comically.

"K-k-killed? Wh-what?" he stammered.

"You sent him after us out of your pettiness and now he's dead," I continued. "I'm pretty sure they won't look at that favorably at all. Who knows – you might have done it deliberately to get rid of him? What did he have on you, eh?"

I noticed that Anthea had to hide a smirk before she turned back to the man on the ground. "And they'll have his phone log, so you won't be able to avoid it," she added.

He pointed a finger at us, back and forth, his actions so exaggerated it was as though he was acting. "You killed him?" he whispered.

"No," Anthea said, squatting down to look him in the eye. "The snake we were chasing killed him. The snake like the sort we saved your sorry ass from. The sort that killed Skipper. And because you sent him after us, he went in, and it killed him. How are you going to explain that?"

His lower lip quivered. "I didn't… I couldn't…" he tried to say, but words failed him.

"Well, I suppose you're going to have to… Bray! Over there!" My gaze snapped across to where she was indicating. The head was not visible, but there was no mistaking that strangely shaped black scaled body, serpentine but with a bulging torso. It was moving into the vegetation on the beach side of the road, slowly, as if trying to remain unobtrusive, heading in our direction, as if stalking us.

The problem was, the body was huge and it was longer than Anthea's four-wheel drive, even without seeing the head. That creature trying to be stealthy was ridiculous, but there was no doubt that was what it was attempting. Anthea stood and made her way slowly to the rear of her car. She reached in and pulled out the machete which she placed on the ground by her feet and slipped her hands into the gloves.

"What the fuck are you doing?" Leroy cried.

"Shut up," I growled. "Let her do her job."

"That thing's too fucking big! It'll get her!" The panic in his voice was shrill and the snake stopped moving, as if waiting once more for silence. Anthea cast him a glance filled with such fury he cowered.

"Trust her," I grumbled. "You know she can do this."

"Not that big!" He turned his attention to Anthea. "Please, honey, don't…"

Her eyes shifted to me. "What do you need me to do?" I asked.

Her smile was almost cruel. "You'll know," she said, then switched back to Leroy. "At least someone will." He was shaking his head but she just sneered and twirled the machete like Michael Dudikoff in *American Ninja* and made her way towards the head end of the snake.

"You can't let her do this," Leroy begged. "She'll be hurt!"

I shook my head and left him there as I went across to her car. The snake raised its head, those yellow eyes regarding her coldly. In the late morning sun, its scales glistened with a darkness that seemed to absorb the light. Anthea stopped what she was doing. She was there, facing the largest snake we had seen so far, armed with an ancient knife and nothing else. I was starting to feel Leroy was right, but I could not admit that. Pride makes us do stupid things at times.

Anthea moved sideways with long paces. The creature watched her, as if trying to work out what she was doing. It lowered its head; we both knew the only thing that could mean. She spun and jumped as far as she could, landing on the boot of Inspector Wallace's car, parked right there just as the snake propelled its head at her. The jaws snapped on nothing, but the head twisted around instantly, the animal's gaze falling on her, standing there, holding the blade like a sword in front of her with both hands.

Its body moved up behind it, gathering in a bunch of coils on the ground. I thought I could see what it was up to. It was getting ready to pounce upwards, to strike at her. It raised its head to be just above the level of the edge of the car. Anthea dropped to one knee and swung the weapon in her grasp. It nicked the snake, opening a cut on the front of its chest that was visible to me from where I was, but which only served to aggravate the reptile. The red line oozed blood that seemed to glow down the front of black scales. The upper body swayed backwards. And then it lunged forward. Anthea jumped back, but slashed downwards at the same time. I don't know how she missed, but it clanged against the boot and the animal recoiled instantly.

I looked in the back of Anthea's car. Everything looked to be made of plastic or to be small. About the only thing that looked heavy was the spare wheel and I was sure I didn't have time to unbolt it from the back of the door. "Come on!" I told myself as I hunted through everything.

The toolbox was buried underneath a pile of rags, red and made of metal and full. I reached in and hefted it out. It was heavy, but not enough to stop me from carrying it across the road. "What the fuck are you doing?" Leroy whined, his voice echoing like a gunshot.

The snake's attention was thus distracted and it turned it head to watch me approach. Anthea did not hesitate, and swung the machete at it. But it was just out of her reach. She teetered on the edge of the car and I felt for sure she was about to fall, right onto the snake, so I somehow increased my speed to a jog, coming at the animal from the complete opposite direction.

Anthea planted her foot with a loud bang, then hurled herself backwards so that she ended up sitting on the roof, her feet against the rear window. The snake's head now went back to her. I continued my own approach. Anthea saw me coming and what I was carrying, and once more stood, holding the machete like a Viking longsword. She swung at the snake, missing it by a long way, but the action was enough to keep its attention on her. Its head feinted a little with a forward action, but Anthea did not react and then came a larger movement. She scuttled backwards and I threw the toolbox as hard as I could. It landed on the edge of the snake, trapping two of the coils, crushing the flesh messily. The head swung around in a wide arc but I was already running away. It tried to move its body, rippling down its length, again and again, until the toolbox started to move. "Shit!" I roared and sprinted back to the car.

Anthea saw it as well and slid on her rear end to the back of the car. The snake was trying desperately to remove the heavy metal box; she had this chance.

"Watch out!" yelled Leroy. And suddenly he was moving. He hit Anthea in a dive tackle, sending them both sprawling to the grass. With a loud clang, the toolbox toppled over. Where it had landed, the reptile's body had been flattened, red meat oozing out of its side. The snake did not hesitate, and with an astonishing turn of speed, it darted into the vegetation, disappearing. I ran after it; the last I saw was the tail disappearing over the edge of the cliff. I shook my head in disbelief, then headed back to the other two.

Anthea pushed Leroy off of her. "What the fuck are you doing?" she demanded.

"It was going to attack," he returned. "I had to help you…"

"Because of you, it got away!" she screamed, an inch from his face. He flinched. "I was fine! Bray had it distracted. I could have killed it!"

"It looked like it was going to…" he started, but she slapped him. No punch, just a strong, powerful slap that echoed like a thunderclap. He was silenced instantly. He couldn't help but rub his hand against his face. I stayed where I was. This was now none of my business.

"You never took me seriously," Anthea growled. "I was just collecting snakes. And now, when I have to kill these fucking things, you stop me because you wanted to be the fucking hero. Why? Trying to make yourself look big to me? Well, you're a fucking idiot. Bray knew what to do. He was doing the right thing. Why couldn't you help him? Maybe then the snake wouldn't have got away. Now we have to find where it went!" She shook her head and I saw she was shaking as well as trying to catch her breath. She went across to where her machete had landed and picked it up, then stared right at him. "Get out of my fucking sight," she hissed.

"Anthea, I'm sorry," he whispered, "but I honestly thought I…"

"No," she interrupted. "You didn't think. If you had, then…" She couldn't finish. She strode right past him. He winced as she went, but stayed where he was. She came up to me. Her face was flushed red and sweat was dripping down her face.

"You okay?" I asked quietly.

"No," she said, "but we've got to get that damn snake."

"It went over the edge of the cliff."

"Shit!" She turned to face Leroy again. "You fuckhead!" she screamed. He recoiled as if she'd hit him again. "And we have to wait here for the cops, so we can't even go after it," she muttered.

"No, but maybe we can both calm down a little, get our heads in the game, and think what we can do next," I suggested.

"Yeah. Yeah, you're right." I went to the toolbox, threw the few errant tools back into it, and followed Anthea back to her car where I replaced it where I had found it. She smiled at me and hugged me tight. "Nice work with that," she said.

"All I could find."

"Would have worked, too, if it hadn't been for…" She couldn't continue.

I didn't know what to say, so I sat on the back bumper. She joined me, placing one of her hands on my thigh. And we stayed there until the police car turned into Creek Road at the Main Road end. I noticed Leroy finally emerge from behind Wallace's car, wiping his hands on his pants as he did so. He stayed on the opposite side of the road and watched as Kyle, along with a young female officer I didn't recognize, pulled up in front of us. He was very professional, but also had an air about him that was comforting. That's one of the many advantages of living in a rural area – the police are part of your community, not just workers who do what they have to. Anthea explained that I was helping her look for snakes because there had been a large number of reports from the town, and that was how we found the bodies. He asked if we knew why Wallace was there; we said we didn't. When Kyle mentioned phone logs, we both saw that Leroy, who was keeping his distance, blanched noticeably.

We admitted going inside, said we tried not to touch the bodies, but that was all we admitted to. He nodded, asked a few more questions, then said we could go, but that he would most likely be in touch, or someone more superior, to confirm details. He suggested we get out of there before the ambulances and other officers arrived, or else we might end up parked in. We took his advice and Anthea circled to Wills Road before coming to a halt opposite the junk store. "Now what?" she asked.

"Tell you what," I said, "let's go to my place. We can stay there for a while, have a bite to eat, and work out properly what we can do next."

"Perfect," she said before restarting the car and heading up the Main Road. Not long into our journey, a car roared past, going very close to Anthea's side before speeding off ahead of us.

"That was close," I muttered.

"That was Leroy," Anthea snarled. I groaned and watched as her mouth formed a thin line, her hands gripping the steering wheel so tight her fingers turned white. I reached across and grabbed her leg. It was like a rock.

"Pull over," I said.

"What?"

"You're too tense. You need to calm down." I tried squeezing the leg again. "Let me drive."

She glared at me out of the corners of her eyes, then suddenly came to a halt. "Are you telling me what to do now?" she growled.

I simply stared at her. Her jaw was clenched tight and

her hands still gripped the steering wheel so hard her wrists were shaking. She met my eyes and then first one, then the second hand let go of the wheel. "Feeling better?" I asked, probably a lot more carefully than I had intended.

"I…" She suddenly rammed her palms against the top of the steering wheel. "What the fuck is going on here?" she yelled. "Isn't it bad enough we've got these fucking things running amok and killing people without having that dickhead trying to act the hero and, and, and…" She faced me again. "I can't get Wallace out of my head," she whispered. "We saw him, we saw that snake feed on him, we saw… Shit, Bray, we just watched a man die. Right in front of us. Dead."

"I know." My throat felt constricted and my voice was hardly a croak.

"And what did we do? We chased after a fucking snake! What is happening to us?" There was desperation in her words.

I risked placing my hand back on her leg. "We're coping," I said. "Somehow, we're coping."

She covered my hand with hers and I'm sure she could feel the shakes that were running through me like a constant earth tremor. "I think you'd be worse than me at driving at the moment," she smiled.

"Probably, but the offer still stands," I replied. She shook her head, restarted the engine, and we resumed our journey.

Leroy was standing at the front of his sister's property as we drove past. Anthea did not even cast him so much as a sideways glance, yet her hands increased their grip on the wheel momentarily. I looked behind us. He was watching us go past. I could not really read the expression on his face, but he certainly did not look happy.

Chapter 30

I made a boring lunch which we ate in silence. Neither of us finished our food; I think the image of Wallace being eaten would not leave either of us. I finally pushed my plate away and sat back. She looked up at me, moving a section of tomato absently around her plate. "What's wrong?" she asked.

I tried to smile, but it didn't really come. "Today's been pretty shitty," I muttered.

"Yeah, it has," she sighed. "I'd hate to think what it would have been like if you hadn't been there." She looked at me through the tops of her eyes.

"You wouldn't have been in that situation," I said.

"Oh, yes, I would," she corrected. "I still would have been called to that first snake, Keith still would have been dead, these call-outs still would have made me look for them and find them, Boyle still would have come out from Scotland, I probably still would have gone searching for more of those snakes. But I would have done it alone. And I wouldn't have had someone there to even think of throwing something heavy on the body of one." She reached a hand across and took mine. "I'm glad you've been with me this past week. I'm glad it's been you here with me." A smile touched the corners of her mouth and her eyes.

I squeezed her fingers. "Thank you," I said. "I mean it." I couldn't think of anything else, and judging by the look on her face, that was not a bad thing. She stood and went into the living room. I watched her go, then cleared the dishes, dumping them into the sink, food still on them. I'd sort that out later. I looked up and found her standing in the door of the kitchen.

"Come on," she said and stretched both hands out to me. I took them and she dragged me through the dining area to the living room. She took a remote control from the coffee table, hit 'PLAY' and then took hold of me.

I knew what she wanted when I heard Tiffany crooning 'Could've Been' softly out of the speakers. And we danced. My fingers slowly wrapped in the hair over her neck and she came into me. I could hear her singing the words as we moved around the floor, feeling like we were the only two people in the world. I kissed the top of her head. She gazed up at me, still singing, then her lips brushed mine.

The dancing stopped as the kissing intensified. We stood there, lost in one another, until the music stopped. Then she moved and we just stared at one another, still holding on. I kissed the tip of her nose and she smiled at me. "There's a part of me that wants to take you into the bedroom right now," she whispered, "but…" She shrugged.

"I know." I understood completely. "But." She sighed and hugged me tight, resting her head against my chest.

"We've got work to do," she muttered.

"I know." Neither of us made a move.

"We need to work out what to do."

"I know." I started to play with her hair again. She leant into it a fraction, then planted her lips on mine, the kiss the most intense she had given me yet. We parted reluctantly, but we knew we had to. It felt like the weight of the world was on both of us, and we were struggling beneath the load.

"Let's go," she said. I nodded. I felt like I had no choice. But being with her made it feel that little bit better.

We drove back to Wills Creek, neither talking, both lost in thought. "I think we should find Boyle," Anthea finally said. "See if he's actually done anything useful."

"We should also check out that cliff where the snake

disappeared," I added.

"And see if the police have left yet." She shook her head. "We've given ourselves a lot to do."

"And not much time to do it," I muttered.

"What do you mean?" There was a hint of fear in her tone that I did not like.

"You saw that one that killed Wallace and that guy in the house – it was growing legs, the growth buds or whatever they were on its back were huge. It was getting ready to transform or whatever the hell these things do."

"Yeah, I did see that," she muttered. We fell silent again. We were now simply accepting what Dr Boyle had told us – that these snakes were the larval forms of a mythical beast that we hardly knew anything about. But after everything we had seen thus far, it just seemed a natural thing to believe, I suppose. "Why are we doing this?" she asked suddenly. "I mean, really?"

I looked at her. "Can anyone else do this?" I asked. She shrugged. "We could let the police deal with it," I suggested. "Go back to your place, let these things become wyverns or whatever the hell they become, and then hope that the authorities can stop them before they cause too much damage."

She growled under her breath. "You're right," she said. "We need to do this." I snorted a laugh and reached across to squeeze her leg. She placed a hand over mine and held me there. And we stayed that way until it came time to turn down the Main Road towards Wills Creek.

We both looked at Louise's place as we went past. Leroy's car wasn't even there. Anthea shook her head and sped up again until we were driving through the town itself. "Where first?" she asked.

"Dr Boyle," I said. "Get that out the way first."

"Sounds like a plan."

We parked outside the campsite office and entered. The man behind the counter looked up from his television watching and answered our questions in a monosyllabic manner that I could see was getting Anthea a little tense. Finally, we managed to get out of him that Dr Boyle was in on-site van number six. We thanked him but he barely acknowledged it and so we made our way across to the line of vans by the trees. The number was hard to miss, painted in red on the side, and we stood there and stared at it for a few moments, neither of us really relishing the idea of going any nearer.

Finally, I walked up to the metal door and knocked loudly. There was no response. I tried the handle, but it was locked. Then, remembering the way he'd left the Ardrossan Hotel, I went to the window and looked inside. His bag was on a chair and a newspaper was opened in front of it, a charger sitting on the floor. "Well?" Anthea asked.

"He's still in town somewhere, but he's not here," I replied.

"Well, job number one done," Anthea said and I detected a hint of relief as she spoke.

"Yeah, for now," I muttered, looking behind us. Something about that did not feel right, but I could not put my finger on it. We stopped at the edge of the road and gazed down at the houses where three police cars were now parked. "So, next we go…"

That was when gunshots shattered the air. A series of them, one after the other, and then a single large explosion. We both flinched with each blast, ducking down lower and lower until the final one made us actually jump.

An eerie silence fell over the whole town. Even the insects and birds stopped. A small curl of grey smoke was visible behind the house where the police were parked. Anthea started in that direction. Despite my own misgivings, I went with her. This was not anything to do with us, surely. As we walked down the street, the residents of the houses on Creek Road came out to see what had made so much noise, shock and confusion on all their faces, but none said anything. People appeared behind us at the end of the street. None seemed willing to do what we were doing and approach the scene of what had just happened. Then a police officer appeared from the rear of the house. We were close enough now to see that it was the young female who had been with Kyle when he had arrived earlier. She did not look well, but when she saw us approaching, she actually beckoned us over. Anthea broke into a jog and reached her in time to catch her before she collapsed.

I was right there with them. "It's… it's… the snake… you… snake…" came out of her mouth. Anthea was supporting most of her weight and so she slowly lowered her to a seated position on the ground.

"What was that shooting?" I asked, knowing that I sounded as scared as she looked.

She looked at me though I don't think her eyes were actually seeing me. "They killed it," she whispered. "But… but…" Her mouth twitched and tears welled rapidly in her eyes. "Dead…" came out of her mouth before her eyes closed and the tears tracked down her face.

Anthea looked at me and I groaned. I knew what she was thinking. "Come on," she whispered and led the way, slowly and carefully back the way the poor woman had come from.

The smell of weapons having being fired hung heavily in the air as we went. Anthea stopped at the corner of the house and waited for me to catch up. That was when she peered around the edge. "Shit…" she hissed. I saw her body tense up and my own fears increased just at that sight. She looked back at me. "This is… this is not good," she whispered. And then she proceeded onward. I had to force my body to move. I was almost stuck to the spot in my terror at what could possibly be there, and yet it was Anthea striding forward that drove me to join her.

One police officer had clearly been bitten on the upper arm. The whole limb except the hand had been reduced to discolored bone, that necrosis we had not yet grown used to seeing running across his chest, staining his uniform black, but enabling us to see the outline of his ribcage beneath the pale blue shirt, the black even running up beneath his jaw. That was a larger site of rotting on one single person than we had seen thus far.

Kyle was next to him and he looked up at us. "Get help… please…" he croaked. He was pouring water from a drink bottle over his arms, which I could see were covered in what looked like weeping burns, with holes burnt into his pants and the front of his shirt as well. I went to his side, but found that I could not bring myself to touch him.

The third police officer we could see was lying face down on the ground, not moving, and a fourth was crouched near the back tap, allowing water to run over burns similar to Kyle's, only much deeper and more nasty looking. However, it was the snake lying across the body of a fifth officer which Anthea moved towards, slowly but surely. It was as long as the longest we'd seen so far, but those growth buds on its back were long ridges of what looked like muscle, while coming from the lower part of the body, the legs were clearly legs, small though they were, with hooked talons and thick musculature attaching them to the body. Half of its head was missing, and I could also see other holes in its side. But there was something not quite right about the bodily fluids leaking from the wounds. Anthea stretched a finger towards one of the holes.

"Don't!" the one by the tap cried. Anthea stopped and looked at him, then back at me, but she stayed her hand.

"Kyle, what happened?" I asked, trying very hard to keep my voice as calm as possible.

"It came out of the yard of the house at the back of this one," he said. His voice was quiet, as if he was speaking in a dream. "We just thought it was a snake, but we were careful. We knew the two of you had been chasing them here." I nodded. "It came over the fence, and then… then… Shit, Bray, it looked like it just zeroed in on Bevan. It got him right in the arm. He dropped like a sack of spuds and straight away he started… His body, it… He seemed to…" He moved his hand over his wounded arm as he struggled to find the words to describe what he'd seen."

"That's okay," I muttered. "We've seen it."

He nodded slowly. "Anyway, we started to shoot it. I put in a couple, Rick got in a few, but the blood… the blood hit us and…" he held his arms up. "It burns! Bray, this is fuckin' killing me!" With that he poured more water over himself. I noticed Anthea moved very carefully away from the snake's corpse. "It burnt through our clothes and everything. Like, like, I don't know, acid or something. And then Simon came with a shotgun." His eyes drifted to the body lying face down. "We yelled at him not to, but he let out a blast. Took half the thing's head off. But the blood splashed over his head." He shuddered violently. "Rick turned him over so we wouldn't have to look at him… Where's Julie?"

"Out the front," I whispered, guessing who Julie was. Anthea by now had joined us. "She looked okay, I think."

"She didn't shoot it, but she might have got some of

that shit on her." He looked at the body beside him and shook his head. He was in shock and he was in pain, and when the shock wore off, he would be a complete mess. "How am I going to tell Bevan's wife?" he whispered.

"I'll call an ambulance," Anthea said gently, pulling out her phone.

"What is it?" Kyle asked, looking at her.

"I really don't know," she replied. "We tried to tell Wallace, but…" She shrugged, and let that half-told lie sit there in the air between them. The thing is, it garnered an understanding nod from Kyle, coupled with a slight, sad scowl; it seemed the inspector was not popular amongst the local police either.

"Well, at least it's dead now," Kyle muttered, his eyes falling to the body of the animal, lying there like something out of a nightmare come to life. "All over."

I looked at Anthea and she gazed at the dead body.

"What?" Kyle asked, panic rising. "There's another one? Where?"

"We don't know, but there could be," I said, trying to make it out to less than it was, even as my mind told me that he had to know. Then again, how were they going to help? How was anyone going to help? Shooting released blood, blood that could be spread everywhere, and that clearly had dangerous properties that it didn't have in the younger versions. Anthea caught my eye and indicated that we should move. I stood slowly, placing a hand on Kyle's shoulder as I did so.

"Where you going?" he asked, sounding so pathetic it was hard to imagine he'd been a police officer for his entire adult life.

"To check on Julie and call an ambulance," I said, still forcing my voice to remain as calm as I was able.

He nodded and returned to running water over his arms, though I was sure he wasn't feeling it, or anything really, just then.

Anthea and I made our way back to the front of the property. Julie had decided to sit in the back of one of the police cars and it looked like she was asleep, although her body twitched and jerked at random times. I moved away from her and found Anthea staring at her phone. "Did you call anyone?" I asked.

She shook her head. "Bray, now I'm afraid to. What if we get more people here and that other snake attacks, or they just shoot it?" She pointed at the house. "Those burns were bad. But think about this – that thing didn't have wings yet. Does the blood become more potent as it gets bigger? Is this what Boyle meant by there being very little on earth that can stop it? Shooting it will create more problems. And if your friend back there was right, those first bullets seemed to have no effect, not until they blew away half its head. And what did that? A close range shotgun that splattered so much blood everywhere that it killed the man who used it. When they get bigger, become this wyvern thing, then what?" I know she was spelling it out so she could make sense of it herself, but it was not something I felt I needed to hear.

My body shivered a little. How had we managed to land ourselves in the middle of this? I chewed my lower lip. "Anthea, I have to tell you – I am scared shitless," I finally admitted.

She reached her hand across and grabbed mine. "So am I," she whispered, "but I have the horrible feeling it's up to us now."

"What's up to us?" I asked, even though I didn't really want an answer.

"Finding the next one."

"Why did I know that was what you were going to say?" I whined. Her smile was sad as she shrugged and turned around to look in the direction we had seen the one I had injured go. It struck me then – that couldn't be the one we had been working on before Leroy interfered. There was no sign of the crushed lower part of the body. Unless it had somehow managed to heal itself. No, that was something I could not let myself assume, nor believe. No matter what, it was an animal…

And I found a part of the back of my mind forming a prayer of hope…

Chapter 31

It did not take much discussion for us to decide that approaching the cliff from the top was not going to be the way to go. We did not have any equipment to climb down, and then we would be leaving ourselves open to an attack from anywhere. We simply did not know where it was hiding, or even if it was still there. We simply decided to drive down to the campsite and then we would walk along the beach like any other couple and see what we could find. The residents of Wills Creek watched us as if they were living in a dream. None made a move towards the police vehicles; none approached us even after we left Anthea's vehicle. It was like the entire town had gone into sudden and dramatic shock.

They did not concern us; we could not afford to be sidetracked now.

The cliffs loomed over us as we made our way along the sands. As a kid, on our visits to dad's friend, I'd loved climbing up as far as I could; as a teenager in the last years of high school, it was parking at the top with a girlfriend or using them to hide our activities in the water. They were just a part of the world I grew up in. And yet, walking here, holding Anthea's hand, both our palms sweating uncomfortably, the cliffs now seemed imposing and frightening. It's not like they were that high – maybe ten meters at their maximum – but on that early afternoon, they could have been the sides of the Grand Canyon for all the negativity they were creating. A bird flew out of one of the holes; I flinched while Anthea simply stopped for a few seconds. We were both on edge, and it was only getting worse.

Something caused a bush up ahead of us to rustle in

one short burst. We both froze, not daring to move, not wanting to attract any undue attention. Anthea's hand moved to her pocket, not the machete she had strapped about her waist, and she slowly took out a revolver. I stared at it, then at her. "I'm sure the police won't miss it," she explained enigmatically.

I shook my head, but was extremely glad she had taken that sort of strange initiative. However, not for the first time, she had surprised me. A lot. I reached across and took the blade out of its sheath, she nodded at me, and we dared to take a pace forward.

"It's just me!" If I'd been holding the gun, Dr Boyle would have been shot then and there, but Anthea managed to control herself as he emerged from behind a thick, wind-blown shrub. His eyes darted upwards, then he jogged across to us. "I was going to call you," he whispered once he reached us.

"Bullshit," Anthea growled, keeping the gun clearly visible.

"No, really, but then I heard all sorts of commotion up…" His gaze shifted. "What happened?"

"They killed a snake," I said, then lifted the machete just a fraction. "Why didn't you tell us about the blood?" I growled, my anger coming through way too much.

He shook his head and leant away from me. "Blood? What blood?' he managed. He was not that good an actor, and the look in his eyes was an immediate mix of confusion and interest.

"You have no idea, do you?" I asked. He shook his head. "Well, it seems their blood, once they are at or near the wyvern stage, becomes acidic."

"You saw a wyvern?" he asked in wide-eyed amazement.

"Not quite, but obviously getting close," Anthea said. Her own anger was also boiling to the surface.

To our astonishment, he pulled a small pack from his back and fished out his iPad. Within seconds, he was madly typing away. "How do you mean, acidic?" he asked.

"Burns the skin, eats through clothes, kills the grass, makes moron scientists get their faces punched in," Anthea snapped. He nodded as he typed, then stopped and stared at her. He was trying so hard to put that professorial façade back on, but Anthea's visage stopped that in a hurry.

He tapped a few more times, then seemed to read something. "There's a story of a group of German soldiers," he said carefully.

"The *Totenkopf* regiment in northern Germany, 1943, I know," I said.

He appeared shocked at my knowledge. "Yes, that is correct," he murmured. "Well, stories say that bullets did not hurt them."

"I don't follow," Anthea said.

"Well, if the blood is acidic, maybe that dissolved the bullets before…"

I was already shaking my head. "At the speed a bullet travels? You have got to be kidding. It cannot work that quickly. No way."

"But if the tough hide slows the bullet down enough," he countered.

"That tough?" And the memory of that dead snake struck me. The bullets had not stopped it; it had taken a shotgun blast to the head. A larger, more developed wyvern…

I suddenly felt like I was going crazy, just accepting all of this like it was a fact, and I did not want to think about it any longer. "So, what in the hell are you doing here?" I then asked.

He pointed up the cliff, towards a hole that looked like a long crack in the cliff-face. "I've been here all morning," he said, regaining some of his composure and, with it, his arrogance. "The stories say they come to the shore, to the sea. I do not know why, before you ask. So, I have been waiting to see them, to try and film a real one moving around. I was sure I saw the head of one snatch a seagull in mid-flight, coming out of there. It was large enough to catch the seagull, and fast enough to catch it. It could only be one of the larvae."

"Or a full-grown wyvern," Anthea said, her eyes scanning the rock.

That actually managed to shut Dr Boyle up, and his head jerked around to also scan the cliff. And the three of us stood there, staring at rocks.

That fissure in the cliff stood out starkly, almost daring us to get closer, but none of us could bring ourselves to do that. However, Anthea and I at least knew that we had to do something. The sheer devastation we had seen in the back of that house with one that was not quite finished its development had scared us but also made us determined to finish this. We felt it was up to us; maybe there was an undercurrent of guilt there as well. Could we have prevented any of this? Looking back, probably not, but at the time… Well, that was how it felt.

I don't know how long we just stared at it. Even Dr Boyle merely watched the area, his iPad at the ready to video anything we might see. The sound of a car moving along Creek Road reached us, followed by another, and another, this one's red and blue flashing lights casting their glow through the air. "Looks like the cavalry's arrived," I mumbled.

"Did you call them?" Anthea asked.

I shook my head. "I'm going to guess Julie did." I scanned the top of the cliff. "And so we'll probably get in trouble for not contacting them."

We heard a few more vehicles go past, and more flashing lights came from at least one of them. "Maybe we should go talk to them," Anthea suggested, though there was a lack of enthusiasm for the idea.

A pair of figures dressed in blue appeared at the top of the cliff. Their eyes fell on us straight away. "Oi! Down there!" called one of them, his voice sounding angry.

"Here we go," Anthea muttered before returned in a loud voice, "What?"

"We need you to come up… What the fuck?"

From our position, it looked like the whole length of the hole in the cliff came to life. The blackness within moved and shifted, oozing over the edges, and then it erupted upwards in a thick line of darkness. It streamed up and seemed to quite simply envelope this man. Only when it stopped, its huge maw latched onto the hip of the poor officer, could we see that this creature had grown even larger. The second policeman backed away even as his companion dropped down, the body looking like he was melting as that necrosis set in fast and over such a wide area. But, more than that, hanging from the back of the snake's torso were two wings, looking too small to be able to lift this animal's weight, maybe not quite yet formed. Wings. It was real. All of this was real.

Then the second officer pulled out his gun and let off three shots, one after the other, right into the body of the beast.

All he succeeded in doing was changing its focus of attention. It took a moment or two for it to disengage its long fangs. Another shot was loosed, and then the mouth engulfed the man's head completely. Other shots sounded, and it slithered further out of the hole to go after these others as well. We saw the legs, more formed than the wings, scramble over the stone, and also saw the disfigured tail section, flattened and jutting at an angle, still carrying the scar from where I had dropped the toolbox on it.

That sat with me; Anthea grabbed my arm at the same time. We were both thinking the same thing. I looked at Dr Boyle, but he was too busy filming what he was seeing on his iPad. Finally, he was vindicated and I did not want to rain on his parade, and so long as he stayed right where he was and did not try to interfere, I didn't care what he filmed or where he claimed he was in the world to his online followers. I then glanced at Anthea. She nodded. We ran.

The beach curled around to the bottom of the campsite, and then we had to go through it to reach the road. But I ran at the cliff where it started to become shallower before coming to a stop where the campsite started. Those days of doing this as a kid returned to my mind and I quickly got back into the swing of finding the fingerholds and foot-holes as I pulled myself the few meters to the top. Once there, I turned and looked behind me. Anthea was a little way behind me, struggling more than I had. I cursed my rashness, knelt down and offered her a hand. She grabbed it with both of hers and I hoisted her to the ground beside me. She did not say anything, but this time took the lead as we made our way to her four-wheel drive.

The snake was stretched across the road up ahead of us, its head raised up, the wings stretched out. Too many police officers looked like they had already been incapacitated, and yet still bullets were being pumped into it, with no apparent effect. The mouth snapped shut, just missing one, who let loose with four rounds before he fell over backwards, clutching his face where the animal's blood had sprayed over him. It then shifted its head and gazed into the window of one of the two ambulances as if regarding whatever – or whoever

– might be inside. We were running out of time.

Anthea turned the engine on and rammed the car into gear. It lurched forward, the wheels gripped the road, and then we were accelerating right down the center of the street. I braced myself against the dashboard and she grit her teeth.

Someone leapt in front of us, waving at us, but Anthea ignored him and depressed the accelerator even further. The man only just managed to get out of the way.

I saw Anthea's face scowl; I'd recognized Leroy as well. I looked over my shoulder and saw him actually chasing after us. If Anthea saw it in the rear-view mirrors, she made no indication. I reset myself.

The front of the car rammed into the torso of the animal, just behind the wings. The wheels raised up and dug into the scaled flesh as if climbing a muddy track, spinning against the skin and gouging out holes in a spray of purple that splashed against the windows. The car bounced along until the rear wheels got up and over it as well. The snake's head snapped at us, but it merely struck the side panel and ricocheted off. Anthea screeched to a halt only a few meters up from it, rammed the car into reverse, and then looked over her shoulder as she went at it again. It was like hitting a high speed bump this time, and we bounced off, the rear wheels landing on the street behind it, but the front wheels dragging over the same wounded site again. Thick purple liquid was pouring from its back; the tail thrashed wildly, the head was shaking back and forth. She stopped the car and looked at it. "Once more," I growled.

She didn't argue. It might have been a good six meters long, and the torso might have been the size of a thin teenager, but it was no match for three tonnes of metal, and the third pass ripped through its spine. Anthea skidded on the wet road, then continued on until we were well away from the carcass.

We both looked back at the carnage we had caused.

The snake had not quite been cut in two, but the head seemed to have stopped all movement, the wings sagging down, while the lower body's nervous impulses continued unabated.

"Fuck," Anthea muttered. She squeezed my hand briefly and we slowly and carefully climbed out of the vehicle. The first thing we noticed was that where the blood had hit the car, the paint was blistering and peeling, and that where its head had struck the back, the dent was impressively large. And then we took in the bigger picture.

Where the blood had sprayed out, the grass had already withered, and the leaves of the trees and shrubs were curled and brown. Everyone was keeping their distance; the fear of what its blood could do had spread through them all, and now they were simply wondering how they were going to clean things and get the wounded out of there. But no one seemed to be in a hurry. They were all staring at the snake, wondering what the hell it was and hoping that it really was dead.

I recognized the police officer who came over to us. Julie looked as pale as she had been before, and as terrified and shocked, but her eyes were clearer. "Are you okay?" she asked.

"More to the point, are you?" I returned.

She managed a slight grin. "You did it," she said. "This is unofficial, and you'll have a heap of questions to answer, but thank you."

"We didn't get any of you guys?" Anthea asked.

"Those who could had already moved behind the ambulance, even before we saw you coming. Only if anybody was behind you when you first hit it, because that was a lot of blood… What sort of blood does that?" I almost had the feeling she simply wanted to talk.

But Anthea's face lost all color. "Leroy," she whispered, and then she was off. She ran around the back of the ambulance, pushing past confused and injured police officers, and then was sprinting down the street. All I could do was watch her go. She disappeared behind one of the police cars parked there. I heard a yelp and then she stood up, holding Leroy under his arms. He fell against the side of the car.

They were talking quietly. She reached a hand for his chest, then withdrew it quickly. He turned a little and tried to walk, but stumbled. She caught him and leant him against the car again. His clothes were pockmarked with holes, but his face looked unmarred. Maybe he had simply got lucky, or maybe he had thrown himself to safety, but whatever had happened, he had managed to survive.

They bent towards one another and their foreheads touched and they stayed there.

I felt my stomach lurch and turned away. "You okay?" Julie asked.

I forced myself to smile at her. "There was someone down on the beach. I want to make sure he's okay," I replied. I looked across at the cliff edge; out of the corner of my eye I saw Leroy had placed his hands on Anthea's hips. She did nothing to move them.

Julie's attention, however, was focused solely on the animal carcass stretched across the road. "Be careful," she said, though she sounded like she was just saying the words without any feeling to them.

"I usually am," I replied. Anthea and Leroy disappeared to the other side of the car, I guessed to sit on the grass at the kerbside. "I usually am," I repeated, not really sure what I was seeing, but mentally jumping to way too many conclusions.

Julie grunted and I looked at her. She was still staring at the edge of the cliff where the snake had come from. That was the direction I walked, skirting the end of the tail and its greatly reduced spasming, keeping my eyes on the ocean spread out in front of me, avoiding seeing anything else. When I reached a place on the cliff that I thought I remembered, I simply went back to childhood and made my way down. It crumbled a few times under my weight, but it did not take long to reach the beach, now a little smaller with the tide working its way in.

Dr Boyle was still there, only now he was sitting on the ground typing feverishly away at his iPad. I noticed he had one of those plug-in keyboards and he was so engrossed in what he was doing that he didn't even notice my approach. "Happy?" I asked.

He looked up with a start. "This video is incredible!" he gushed. "The wings! The claws! It's just like the old stories described it!" Maybe he saw something in my face, or maybe he was not as self-absorbed as I believed he was. "How is everything up there?"

"Well, the animal's dead," I muttered. "So are a few people. More injured." I shook my head. "I wish we'd listened to your email," I muttered.

"How so?" The professorial tone was gone, replaced with something verging on child-like enthusiasm.

"You said they were dangerous and we should kill them…"

He looked back at his screen. "The fact you did not or could not helps me prove their existence," he said, then looked at me carefully. "But you could not," he added suddenly. "Even now, knowing they need to be hunted down, you have not been able to. They are clever creatures. I do not think you would have had any more luck. I am sorry."

I think a laugh escaped my lips. "You know, you almost sounded sympathetic there," I said.

He stared at me for what felt like a long time. "I do not like to think of people dying," he said evenly. "If I had been believed years ago, this would not have happened."

I held a hand up. "I'm not blaming you," I said. "Hell, you came halfway across the world just to see one." I looked up at that fissure in the rock. "And now you have."

"And I've seen it kill." He tapped something and I saw the screen shut down. "And I do not want to see that again." He stood, and then looked around. "Where is your lady friend?" he asked.

"Busy," I replied. "I thought I'd come and make sure you were okay."

He looked at me curiously. "Thank you, Brayden," he said, as though he had not been expecting that at all. He looked upwards again. "And it is definitely dead?"

"In two bits, thanks to being driven over."

"So it's all over," he muttered.

"Yeah," I said. "Everything's all over."

And I made my way back towards the campsite. I tried not to think about anything. I think I could have handled Anthea running to see if the father of her daughter was all right; seeing their obvious signs of affection made me feel like I had just been used. I was jumping to conclusions, and maybe I was letting heightened emotions after everything that had happened on that day get to me, but that was the dominant feeling in my mind. It didn't matter at the time; I just felt like everything was on top of me and I had to get out of there.

I reached the road and looked down. Anthea's car was gone.

I made my way to the northern end of town and the

walking trail that stretches from Port Clinton all the way down the coast to Ardrossan. It was seven kilometers from Port Clinton to Price, so I guessed an extra five kilometers to get down to Wills Creek would be about right. I pulled out my phone, tapped on the *I ♥ Radio* app and made my way through the rather pleasant countryside with a gentle background of 1960s rock tunes.

It took me a little over two hours to reach the town. I debated whether I should go straight home, but decided against it and went to the shop where I bought a Coke and spent too long talking about the football on the weekend coming up, which I really did not care about.

My phone rang, which gave me an excuse to escape the conversation, and I went outside to answer it. It was Tracey, finding out how I was; apparently word of what had gone down at Wills Creek had already reached them in Ardrossan. I admitted I'd been there, but told her I was back home now, and everything was good, and, yes, I would be fine to go back to work the next day. Then she told me, no I wouldn't, because they'd asked Michelle to do it, and so I had an extra day off. I thanked her and hung up, but the idea of spending a day brooding about everything did not seem like a good idea. And Jasmine and Marysia would be at work, so a random trip to Adelaide would not really serve any purpose either apart from getting me out of the area.

I actually wanted to go back to work. At least there I knew what was expected of me and could understand everything so much better.

I made my way back up the road to my place. I reached for my back pocket. Wallet was there, phone in the front, but no keys. I swore long and loud; they must have fallen out in Anthea's car. That meant I was going to have to call her and get her to drop them off… and my car was still at her place anyway.

This day just kept getting better and better.

I decided to take the risk and see if I had left the back door unlocked, which I had been known to do in the past. I made my way down the driveway, then stopped.

I swore I saw something moving through the side window. So now I had an intruder, just to add to everything else.

I went back to the front and tried the front door. It was not even closed properly, and swung open under my touch.

My whole body tensed up, my shoulders aching as they did so. My right hand clenched into a tight fist, straining the forearm. I entered the living area. The curtains were drawn – had I closed them after lunch? – and the house was bathed in a gloomy half-light, but a gloom that was illuminated by a single candle sitting on the coffee table, flickering and loving as I disturbed the air around it.

The CD player flashed into life.

Tiffany's voice came out of the speakers, slow and pained, her heartbreak coming through in the words about how it just *could* have been so good.

I felt my body relax before my mind fully registered what was going on. "Anthea?" I called.

She emerged from my bedroom. All she wore was that red and blue headband. Her grin was hopeful. "Hi," she said. "You didn't wait for me."

"You looked busy."

She shrugged and looked a little uncomfortable. "He was hurt. It was sort of my fault," she muttered. "I felt I had to… to do something." I shrugged, not sure what to say. Her hands moved, starting to cover her naked body. "He begged me to go back to him. He was crying, Bray." Her own tears were starting to well up. "I've hurt him more than just physically. I feel like such a bitch." She stared at me. "And then you left, and I realized I just left you there and went to him. And then you went. I was ready to tell both of you to take a hike." She wiped her wrist across her eyes and her stare was intense.

I made my way across to her. She fell against me. I was going to ask if this was a goodbye act or her making her choice. The words were right there, ready to come out, for me to make what could have been the biggest mistake I had made in a long time, but I held my tongue. Instead I reached up and toyed with that piece of hair that covered her neck. She pressed her body against mine harder, her fingers sliding down the back of my pants. I kissed the top of her head. Her hands moved up, lifting my top with them as they did so. She dropped it beside us and we went back to our embrace. I could feel her bare breasts against my skin, so tempting, as her hands once more made their way onto the flesh of my buttocks and pulled me into her. They worked their way to the front; my physical response was immediate. She lifted her chin and I placed my mouth on hers.

"I've made my choice," she whispered as we parted. "Please don't let me down."

I lifted her like Richard Gere did to Debra Winger at the end of *An Officer And A Gentleman* and carried her into the bedroom.

The bad shit was finally all over…

Chapter 32

It was dark outside when I looked at the clock beside my bed, then flopped back onto the pillow. "Don't take this the wrong way, but shouldn't you be getting home?" I asked.

"Why?" Anthea replied, curling up next to me, running her fingers through the hair on my chest.

"Emma."

She snuggled in even closer. "I arranged things while I was waiting for you. Emma went to a friend's after school, and now mum's staying at my place tonight to look after her. I told mum I was staying with you. She made out she wasn't happy, but she's doing it." Her finger ran up my neck to run through my beard. "She likes you."

My fingers wrapped themselves in her hair and she moved into them a little. "I'm glad," I said quietly. "But you took a risk. What if I hadn't responded like I did?"

She looked at me curiously, then grinned that cheeky grin. "Yeah, I took a chance." She kissed my neck. "And it paid off. What's the problem?"

"Oh, no problem," I replied, unable to help but smile. "None at all."

"Good." Her kiss was soft and tender, but so full of passion and love that I instantly grabbed her and just held her close to me. "Because I really want to see where this leads," she whispered. "I want something good in my life."

"I know just how you feel," I responded.

That was when the Samsung default ringtone sounded. Anthea looked across at her bundled clothes and collapsed onto me before rolling off and finding her phone. Her expression became one of confusion as she looked at the number on the screen. She tapped it, then tapped it again and placed it on the bed before crawling onto me. "Hello?" came a voice from the other end. She'd put it on speaker so I could hear as well.

"Hello, this is Anthea Bowman," she replied.

"Uh, I think we have a problem," came the voice. I looked at Anthea and could tell she was thinking the same thing as me: *We should know that person.*

"Sorry?"

"I notified the police, but they are in complete disarray. You are the only person I know who even understands what is going on."

"Dr Boyle?" I whispered. Anthea looked briefly thoughtful, then rolled her eyes and nodded.

"Look, I don't know what you're…" she started.

"Are you sure you killed all of the wyverns?" he whispered, and there was very real terror in his voice.

"Yes," she said. "There were eleven eggs, right? Well, there's one larva in a cage at my place, there were two killed at the Robertson house, but that was after the farm, and… and… holy shit! The farm!"

"It's here!" His voice was now a hoarse hiss.

Anthea and I were already throwing clothes on. "Get somewhere safe," she called. "We're on our way!"

"It's… it's big…" he panted. "It looks magnificent, but it's here."

"Dr Boyle, where are you?" I called.

"I, uhh…" He seemed taken aback by my voice, but quickly recovered, "I'm at the beach. They wouldn't let me near the body of the one you killed, so I came down here…"

"The police are still there?" Anthea interrupted.

"They wouldn't listen to me!" he cried. "They say everyone's seeing these things and they have to clean up and go over everything and…" The rising hysteria in his voice was suddenly replaced by terror as he once more whispered, "I can see it! It's… it's…" Words failed him, and I think that worried me more than anything else.

"We're on our way," Anthea said.

"Please hurry," he whispered, so quietly we could hardly hear him. And then he was gone.

Anthea's expression as she looked at me was more scared than I had seen on her before. "I really don't like this," she muttered.

"Maybe *we* can convince the police that it's real," I suggested.

"Uh-huh. Of course we can." She didn't bother to hide her doubts. "I think this will end up being up to us."

"So… what do we do?"

"It takes just over ten minutes to get there from here," she said. "That's how much time we've got to work that out." She kissed my cheek. "I have to say, as far as relationships go, this one has certainly been unique." She smiled at me and after I grabbed my backpack, we made our way to her car, which she'd left in the parking lot of the old school building. I pulled my laptop out and went through the websites I'd gone through before, hoping I could find something, anything to help us.

"Well?" Anthea asked as we passed the Price turn-off.

"Look, all I've got is this story of one impaling itself, and another of one being stabbed." I sighed. "Most other stories are variations on those themes. I somehow don't think either of us are going to be able to stab an animal whose blood can kill people."

"No." She scowled a little. "And that's it?"

"Apart from one story of a bunch of German soldiers

who all died while shooting one."

"That's the one Boyle and you were waffling on about?" she asked.

"Yeah, that's the one. The *Totenkopf* regiment." I brought the webpage up, and as she continued on, I read the bad translation of the page, finishing as we turned onto the Main Road towards Wills Creek. She didn't so much as glance sideways as we went past the house where Leroy was staying. I did; his car was right there, pointing out at the road as if waiting for us to reappear.

Anthea stopped in front of the deserted general store and we looked around. My first instinct was that we should head down through the campsite to the foreshore and its thin sliver of beach, and see if we couldn't find Dr Boyle. However, Anthea glanced up Creek Road. There were no red and blue lights flashing, but there was still quite obviously a great deal of activity up there. "Beach or cops?" I asked.

"Don't know," she mused, then pulled out her phone. She brought up the last number that had called her and hit the screen. She waited and waited before it finally rang out. "Not even message bank," she muttered and gazed at the campsite. "I wonder if Boyle's okay," she muttered quietly.

"So, we look for him first?" She sighed, shrugged and finally nodded. She tied her machete around her waist, hunted through the rear of the car until she found a pair of flashlights. She tried them; they seemed to be working, and so we made our way through the camping area. We automatically headed towards the area where the fissure in the rock had housed the last one we had encountered. It was dark, very little light coming from the town above, the half-moon covered by clouds. It was like walking through a land of shadows, and that made it worse. The beams of the torches merely created glowing lines, hardly illuminating the scene at all. If anything, the extra shadows they cast made things worse. Our pace slowed and my hand found hers. We gradually came to a halt. "What are we doing?" Anthea hissed.

"I have no idea," I replied pathetically.

She shook her head and looked over the blank, black wall of rock beside us. "We have a machete and we're down here, looking for a man who could be literally anywhere, and who told us that there is a creature here which we might not even be able to hurt," she said, her voice even and slow. Her hand squeezed mine. "We are fucking idiots," she growled.

"Police?" I suggested.

She paused, then nodded slowly. "Yeah," she muttered. "I do not like this one little bit. Let the cops deal with everything."

"Hang on, where's Dr Boyle?" I asked suddenly.

I heard her growl under her breath. She pulled her phone out and again hit that number that had called her. Somewhere up ahead we heard a standard ringtone. We exchanged a glance and edged our way forward, our pace ridiculously slow. She tried the phone again; we were getting closer. I cast my torch over the sands before us.

"Fuck," I groaned.

Dr Boyle's iPad was right there, on the sand, beside a mobile phone and his carry bag. I cast the torch's search wider and Anthea joined in. "There," she whispered.

My beam of light joined hers. The lower torso of a person was sitting there on the sand, propped up by a rock, the upper portion of it showing the necrosis that we had grown unfortunately used to seeing. Straight away we shone the flashlights upwards, scanning the cliff-face, hoping we wouldn't see what we knew was up there somewhere. I darted across and snatched up the iPad, which I shoved into the back of my pants, then returned to Anthea. "Let's get back," I muttered.

"His tablet?" She looked at me curiously.

"He's got the knowledge base."

"Yeah, no. That's a good idea," Anthea returned absently, her eyes not leaving the sheer barrier beside us. "We really need to tell the cops." There was no hiding the fear in her voice.

We reached the campsite in double time and were quickly at the road. And then we ran. The end of it was blocked off, and a few local residents were standing by the barriers that had been thrown up, staring at what amounted to no more than a long tent, a makeshift marquee. We stood with them and gazed over the scene. The ambulances were gone, and only a few police officers were around, along with a number of people dressed in suits and a few in what looked like Hazmat equipment. "It's still under there," I whispered.

"They have no idea what to do with it," Anthea replied, keeping her voice just as low. "I wonder if that means the blood's still potent?"

I shuddered a little at the thought, but hid that as well as I could by peering through the darkness for a police officer. One I did not recognize walked past. "Excuse me," I called.

He stopped and stared at me coldly. "I don't know anything," he said wearily, as if this was literally the thousandth time he had been forced to say it.

"Sorry," I went on, "I was just curious how Kyle and Julie are."

He stopped and looked at me, then came over. "Who?" he asked, his voice deliberately calm and emotionless.

"Kyle Rivers was the first officer on the scene. Julie was with him. He was pretty badly burnt by the acid and she looked like she was in shock," I stated, calmly and evenly.

"Hang on," he said, then hurried away and

disappeared inside the long tent that we were sure was covering the snake's corpse.

"Nicely done," Anthea muttered. I reached across and took her hand.

A man in a suit that looked quite dishevelled appeared out of the structure and strode straight across to us. "What do you know?" he muttered. No word of greeting, no checking our credentials, nothing – just a harried man who did not want to be there.

"I killed the snake that's under there," Anthea said, making sure her voice did not carry to anyone else. "And before you ask, I know it had wings, and its blood is like acid."

He could not hide the surprise on his face, then he lifted the tape and ushered us beneath it. We obeyed wordlessly and followed him into the tent. The snake was indeed still there as the people in the protective clothing struggled to encase it in what looked like very thick rubber. "What do you know about this?" the man suddenly growled, the accusation in his tone undeniable.

"It's from Europe, the man who knows about them is dead, and there's one more and it's close." The words tumbled out of my mouth like water down a rocky stream. I almost took the iPad out of the back of my pants to show him, but thought better of it.

He shook his head and tried to make sense of what I had just said, then gazed at the carcass beside him, the thin tendrils of flesh that had held the two pieces together now clearly separated. We couldn't help but do likewise. The blood that had spread across the ground held an even more prominent purple hue in the fluorescent lights that had been strung up on the framework. "How about telling me who you are?" the man suddenly said, taking out a notepad and pen.

"I'm Anthea Bowman. I run AB's Serpent Services.

That's why I was here in the first place – a call about a snake." Anthea's voice was showing more than just a hint of annoyance.

"And I'm Brayden Kincaid, a teacher at the Ardrossan school." The look he cast me told me I should explain. "Anthea and I are… are together," I added, not sure how that sounded. He didn't seem to care, but she gave me an approving nod.

He tapped the edge of the notepad with his pencil, then demanded, "Why did you leave the scene?"

"We were told you would get in touch with us," Anthea replied.

He looked confused. "Why are you here now?" he asked. "No one would have called you. We didn't even know you existed…"

"We were called by the only expert in these things," Anthea responded, her tone becoming sharper. Again, I was tempted to pull out Dr Boyle's computer tablet, but it just didn't seem like the right time to admit I'd stolen a dead man's belongings.

"And where is this so-called expert?" The man was either having a hard time believing us or was simply beyond caring about anything.

"Well," I said before Anthea could answer, "half of him is on the beach."

The man seemed to freeze. "Half?" he sneered eventually, as though he was saying what he felt he had to say.

I ran my hand across my midsection and Anthea nodded. "We told you – there is one more out there." She was letting her frustration out on this guy.

"One more?" he asked. "Where?"

"That's just it – we don't know."

"I'll organize some men to go out and…"

"And do what?" she interrupted. "Shoot it? That one there was shot and it didn't die until I ran over it three times! And if its blood flies out or drips down on anyone or anything…"

"Okay, okay, what do you suggest we do?" He was challenging her.

"First, we just have to find the damn thing."

"And where do you suggest we look?" Now he was treating her like an idiot, something that did not go unnoticed.

"Well, let's see. Dr Boyle rang us twenty-odd minutes ago. Five minutes ago we found what was left of him on the beach. He said they always return to the shore, so I would guess any cave in the side of the fucking cliff about twenty meters from where we are standing right fucking now!" He winced a little as her venom rose, but he held his ground.

"So, I should send a few of the people left here who are not injured or burnt down the side of a cliff to find a snake? You're the snake catcher; why don't you go?" To give him the benefit of the doubt, he was countering his feelings of inadequacy against Anthea's outburst by acting like an arrogant prick.

"Because I've seen what it can do, I've seen how big it is, and I am not going near the fucking thing," she returned.

He looked at me, but I held my hands up. He returned his gaze to her. "Well, I do not have the man-power to go monster-hunting," he stated.

"Then get a heap of ambulances on standby," she shot back. She grabbed my arm. "Let's go. We're wasting our time here."

"You can't go," he stated. "We need you to answer questions, we need to know what you know." He looked back at the dead snake. "We need to know what the hell that is and what we're facing."

"I am not staying here with another one of those, a full-grown one, around the place."

The façade he had kept up crumbled at that statement. "Full-grown?" he asked. "That isn't a full-grown one?"

Anthea glared at him. "Not even close," she stated.

And if the gunshots had not started right then, I am pretty sure she would have kept on going until he had been reduced to tears.

Chapter 33

The reaction of every person in that tent was instantaneous: we all rushed outside to find out just what the hell was going on.

The first thing to come out of the mouth of the man we had been having our discussion with spoke for everyone: "What the fuck is that thing?"

"That is a wyvern," I said as if I was pointing out a kangaroo to a tourist, but I wasn't sure I believed it. How could it be real? How could any of this be happening?

But it was real, and it was in the air above us, circling slowly. Including tail, it was about the length of a bus, the wingspan the same if not a little more. It was huge, the size so much larger than we could have imagined it attaining. The skin was dark and the edges melted into the night sky, but as it entered the lights from the tents and the car headlights and the street lamps, we could see that the torso had expanded to be as large around as two grown men. And that snout was still crocodilian and the eyes were still yellow and it still looked nasty… only now it was big and nasty. Another volley of shots cut through the air, hitting the side of the creature, the purple spraying out clear in the light as it passed low over the tent. "Stop shooting!" Anthea suddenly screamed. "The blood! You're making it bleed!" And, surprisingly, her words and warning tone had an instant and definite effect. Every single police officer stopped, lowered their guns and started to move away from its flight path.

It actually looked quite majestic as it soared above us all; it was hard to imagine that it was anything but a strange and glorious winged creature, oblivious to all below it. A winged creature that was a reptile. I shuddered at the realization, but I could not drag my eyes away from it.

This was something nobody had seen in decades, maybe even centuries, and I was watching it flying in the cloudy Australian skies as though it had been in this part of the world since time immemorial.

Then it dropped down, swooping in low before coming to a landing on the roof of the house where so many police officers had been killed and wounded. Its taloned feet clutched the peak of the roof and it spread its wings out wide as it leant forward, letting out a deep guttural hiss that rumbled like thunder, those yellow eyes taking in all its surrounds. Lights were turned in its direction, as if it was the star of a stage play. The mouth was wide and dripped with some of that viscous purple poison from the elongated fangs.

And then came a single explosion, a blast that tore through the air making every single person wince or cower down briefly. A hole was torn into the flesh of its upper leg, letting loose a torrent of purple, although, even from where we were, it did not look deep, merely a flesh wound. The head snapped around and the eyes narrowed, and then it was moving, with an even greater speed than these creatures had as larvae. The mouth widened beyond what seemed possible, the lower jaw seeming to dislocate. A scream was cut short and the beast flew into the air with scarcely a movement of its wings. It moved overhead, a trail of its violet blood marking its path, burning through the material of the tent.

That was when something fell from it, bouncing against the top of one of the police cars with a loud thud before tumbling to the ground.

The lower half of a person, not only bitten through, but with the signs of necrosis at the jagged ends of the wound spreading further and further along the flesh.

Just like the remains of Dr Boyle down at the beach.

That did. That piece of human being broke the spell that everyone seemed to be under. The few residents who had been watching proceedings disappeared while the police officers panicked, with many of them also running, while others loosed shot after shot at its retreating form and others just stared in dumb fascination at what could not possibly be real.

Anthea and I fell into that last category.

"Fucking hell," the man in the suit muttered before he turned to Anthea. "How the fuck do we stop this?" he demanded, but fear overcame everything else in his voice.

"I have no idea," she muttered, her voice sounding vague and distant.

The wyvern swung around in a wide arc over the ocean, and then it rocketed back towards the town. It swooped down low, and disappeared from view in the region of the campsite. A cry was carried through the air, a scream of panic, and then a repeat of that thunderous hissing before silence descended over everything.

Everyone around us had fallen still and was just watching and waiting. Then it reappeared, flying upwards slowly before darting off once more, this time inland.

"Leroy…" Anthea whispered, and suddenly she was sprinting along Creek Road, heading for her car. I took off after her and only just managed to keep up. She threw herself into the front seat and I reached her and clasped my hand over hers on the ignition. "I can't let it kill Leroy," she snarled at me. "No matter how much of a…"

"And what will you do when you get there?" I asked. She stared at me and started to snatch her hand out from beneath mine, but stopped herself. "If it has gone that far, if they are outside, what can we do? It isn't going to let us ram it with a car, if that'd even do any good this time. It'll fly away. We, both of us, need to calm down and work out what the hell we can do here."

Her arm relaxed a little and I risked letting go. She fell back in the seat. "And what can we do here?"

"I have no idea," I muttered, but an idea slowly struck me. I pulled out the iPad and turned it on. It was simply in power-saving mode and the screen booted up to a half-completed piece of writing, getting ready, I guessed, for a new blog post.

"What are you doing?" Anthea asked.

"Asking the expert," I muttered. She nodded her understanding. I scrolled through his files. They were actually named very simply, and the word document named 'wyvern' was near the bottom of the list.

It was a series of notes and observations, some links to websites, the names of other files on the computer – video and image links, mainly – and a list of words. I read through, but nothing stood out. "Anything?" Anthea asked.

"I'm not even sure what I'm looking for," I muttered.

"Why does it attack what it attacks?" she suggested.

"Hang on." I went back up the page. "Here: 'Larva attracted to movement? Must check.' Have the snakes attacked anything except moving targets?"

Anthea wracked her brain, then shrugged. "Well, we saw the eagle, that was moving, it went after you at the farm, the people on top of the cliff. Keith would have been moving towards it. It could be," she said. "Oh, and I guess it'd also attack things that attack or threaten it. Which is standard for a lot of animals."

"Well, let's assume that's it. It attacks things that move or go after it."

"But not vehicles," Anthea countered. "So maybe it

can tell the difference?"

"Sees heat signatures, thermal vision?" I offered.

"It's possible. Or maybe they are actually not stupid. I mean, they seem to learn and they do things that snakes just don't do…"

"Okay, but that means it'll only go after something alive and moving."

She leant forward. "You're talking bait, aren't you?" she asked. "Like what?"

"A cow?"

"Would it go after something that big?"

"A sheep then?"

"And where do we get one from?"

"Can we work that out later?" She sighed and shrugged. I went on, "Now, that's fine in attracting it. But how do we kill it?"

She reached a hand across and covered my mouth. "You are making the rather huge assumption that it will be us who does the killing," she said very calmly, maybe too calmly. "I catch snakes – *snakes* – for a living. You're a teacher. And you are going on as though we are going to be able to kill a thing that should not exist. Have I got that right?"

I looked at her and was about to say she was right – that was what was in my head. But as I opened my mouth, a reality check kicked in. I was at a loss for words. She removed her hand and shook her head. "We can't do this, Bray," she muttered. "This is beyond us."

A sudden, brief volley of gunshots sounded, making us both jump. We scanned the skies, but the wyvern was not hard to discern as it swooped down, once more aiming for the gathered authorities. It moved its rear limbs so the long claws tore through the top of the long tent. It wheeled around and headed upwards once again, dragging the white material with it. The lights inside fell and crashed, further increasing the darkness, and the supporting structure collapsed. The people ran in a mad panic as more gunshots sounded, including at least two louder blasts from a shotgun or the like, but the creature did not seem to pay them any attention. It dropped what it held and came down low again. It snapped its jaws shut on something we couldn't make out, then turned and spat it out. "Shit," I groaned; that looked like a head. And it hadn't eaten anything – it had simply killed a person that was too close.

It performed a tight circle and then came to rest on the ground right beside the remains of the nearly formed wyvern we had killed earlier. It bowed its head and nuzzled the carcass. It moved back a little, then tried again. A flicker of something ran across those eyes, visible even from where we were. It bowed down close and sniffed at the body, inhaling deeply, then its forked tongue flicked out and lapped at the wound where the car had mangled it. It lifted its upper body and let out a long, loud roar.

Its head snapped around and it eyed the nearest person, some poor guy in a Hazmat suit. With a striking movement like the snake we had believed it was for so long, its jaws engulfed the top of the man, then simply let him drop. There was not even an attempt at eating this victim – that was simply killing for the sake of killing. Then it once more returned its attention to the dead animal at its feet. It nudged the head with one of its talons, then uttered a lower growl and licked at the body's face.

"That's not right," Anthea murmured.

"What?" I couldn't help but ask.

"That thing is showing distress. The dead one is making it, well, upset," she explained. "We shouldn't put human emotions onto animals, but that's what it looks like.

Reptiles don't do that. Some birds, a few mammals, but not reptiles."

"What does that mean?" I asked.

"I don't know," she muttered, "but I don't like it."

The wyvern stopped what it was doing and let out another roar, this one with the distinct tone of pain about it. A car engine roared into life and reversed faster than it should have. The attention of the creature was immediately fixed on the retreating vehicle and it bounded across with one beat of its leathery wings, landing on its roof. Its weight was enough to dent the metal, and the driver lost control, the rear end ploughing through a fence and into the front of the house next door to the Robertson place. The wyvern lifted itself into the air as that section of the wall fell onto the back half of the sedan. It was close enough to us for us to see inside the car, and the driver struggling to open his door. He slid across and used his feet to force open the passenger side door and then crawl out.

The wyvern swooped down and grabbed him with those talons before it simply flew back up and let him go. He screamed as he tumbled down, landing on the edge of the tin roof of the building and then bouncing to the ground next to his car. He rolled over and continued to cry out, trying to pull himself along with his arms. The wyvern dropped down again, this time landing on his back. His squealing became louder, but one slash from a claw silenced him.

The wyvern sniffed the air, inhaling deeply.

The yellow eyes narrowed as the head now faced our direction. "Oh fuck," Anthea hissed, grabbing my arm. "Come on! Get in!" I did not need to be told twice and crawled over her as the reptile leant its head forward and breathed in once more. She slammed the door behind me and depressed the lock, which enacted automatic locking on all the doors. The animal moved forward a pace, still sensing whatever it could on the air. I sat up, panting heavily.

With one jump it cleared the gap between us and now it was smelling the front of the vehicle. The tongue lapped at the damaged front end. The head lifted slowly and the eyes narrowed. A low rumble emerged from its throat, a rumble we felt through the body of the car more than heard. It jumped onto the bonnet and fixed its gaze on the two of us through the windscreen. The side of its mouth lifted, revealing its long fang in its pocket of skin and a row of other, uneven teeth, all large and thick. It made that same noise again, and it seemed that the whole car trembled as it did so. It took a step forward, the claws pushing the metal of the bonnet down as it tried to gain purchase. It spread its wings out wide and hissed, its saliva hitting the glass like a thick paste.

"It can smell the one we hit," Anthea muttered. "It's put the two smells together – the car and the body. It knows what we did." There was no fear in her tone, just the simple statement of fact. I, on the other hand, was filled with terror, made worse with just the thought that it knew what we had done and it was less than a meter away from us, separated only by some glass and metal.

Its face moved forward slowly, the dark skin glistening, the bumps and lumps on it casting strange shadows across its surface. The end of the snout touched the glass, then backed off, its every breath creating a mist that fogged up our visibility. The forked tongue flickered out and ran over it, then the entire head recoiled a little. The steamed-up window made it difficult for us to see clearly, but it did appear that it made its way once more to the front of the vehicle. Then it jumped, rocking the whole vehicle crazily. I grabbed the dashboard; my grip grew stronger as the thud hit the roof. The tail hung down outside my door and once more we felt that deep rumble vibrating through the whole car. I looked at Anthea and she returned the gaze.

"What?" I asked.

She looked behind us, past the equipment that filled the rear and out of the back window. Creek Road ran onto the Main Road a few dozen meters that way, the deserted general store facing us with its covered windows and mostly empty interior. Her gaze returned to mine and her hand slowly drifted down towards the ignition.

A solid thump came from above us again. We looked up with a start and saw that it had collapsed downwards just a little. The next one jolted the whole car, bouncing it on its shock absorbers, and increasing the size of the indentation.

Anthea gritted her teeth and turned the key. The engine roared into life and she rammed the gear stick into reverse, then draped one arm across and looked over her shoulder. Above us came a roar that could only be described as angry, and she floored the accelerator. The car bounced a little as the thing on the roof lifted off. Anthea kept on going, though, faster and faster. I saw what she was planning and braced myself.

We slammed into the curb and were propelling upwards before, in a shower of breaking glass, we slammed through the doors of Jessop's. She continued until the back of the car hit the counter, splintering the wood and plastic and steel. She slammed on the brakes in a squeal of rubber and rammed the car into first gear and waited. "What are we doing?" I whispered.

"It worked once," she muttered and sat with the engine idling like a menacing beast, her face a mask of angry determination.

We waited there for a few moments before the animal dropped down and stood in front of the opening. It regarded us coldly, but didn't make any attempt to enter the building. Anthea waited for a few moments, as if she and the creature were having some sort of Western movie stare-down, and then she let the brake off and floored the accelerator. We rocketed forward with a jerk, and shot out of the hole we had already made, the side mirror on my side flying off as we went through. The wyvern tried to lift up into the air, but it was too slow, and I'm sure Anthea clipped one of its legs as she passed beneath it. She planted her feet on the brake and pulled the handbrake on at the same time as she swung the wheel around, swinging the car into a wild semi-circle so we were now facing the shop.

The monster landed in front of the opening and glared at us, as if daring us to do it again. It was tentative on one of its legs, but held its ground, wings outstretched. It leant forward and roared at us with that deep, throaty sound that echoed throughout the entire town. It was challenging us. I know that's anthropomorphising an animal, but that was exactly how it felt.

And Anthea was willing to take the bait. She gunned the engine and then rushed forward. This time the wyvern rose high enough to avoid a collision and the car merely increased the size of the hole in the front of the building. Anthea swung the wheel so that it was the side of the car that slammed into the shattered remains of the counter this time. She managed a three-point turn so that she was once more facing the entrance. "This is ridiculous," she growled, watching the gap, waiting for the monster to reappear.

"I agree," I returned, "but this is at least giving everyone else a chance to get to safety."

"Wonderful," she muttered, her voice dripping with sarcasm, her eyes not leaving the hole in the wall. The creature was taking its time this time, as though it knew what it was doing, heightening the fear. Then Anthea's eyes fell on the side of the front wall we hadn't demolished. I looked across as well. "Those German soldiers had a dead one that was burnt," she muttered.

"What are you saying?" I asked.

She pointed at the gas cylinders that were lined up there. "That's what I'm saying." She dropped the car into neutral, then threw open her door.

"What the hell are you doing?" I asked.

She reached across and kissed me. "You said it was up to us," she smiled.

"But this…" I started.

She covered my mouth with her hand. "Just go out and try to draw it back in here," she ordered. She reached into her pockets, and dumped a pair of drink coasters, a policeman's revolver and a few other things on the floor before she pulled out something small and colored. Then she jumped out of the car and ran across to the furthest cylinder where she crouched down. I didn't even have a chance to tell her not to, to not be crazy, but it also made sense, in a warped sort of way. So, I did as I was told – I slid across into the driver's seat, slammed the door shut and drove back out into the night.

It was waiting for the car.

It swooped down from the left and slammed into the side of the four-wheel drive with enough force to rock it off-balance. I felt the vehicle lift onto two wheels and tried to steer into it without losing what little control I had. I swung it around and saw the wyvern staring at me from the middle of the road. I knew what it wanted me to do, and so I decided to give it exactly what it wanted – I aimed for it. It waited until the last possible moment before it moved, but this time it went sideways instead of up. I ignored it and managed to get the car in through the hole we had already made in the building, slamming in the counter hard enough to break all the way through this time, only just stopping before reaching the back wall.

The wyvern was on the back of the car before I could change gear.

Its claws raked at the rear windscreen and then it was on the roof. It must have been close to the ceiling of the store at the same time, but it still managed to work its head down so that it could peer at me through the passenger side window. It growled and slammed its head against the glass. I shielded my face as it exploded inwards. The jaws slammed shut over the passenger seat, purple liquid dripping down onto the material.

I did not think. I threw open my door and hurled myself to the floor, rolling over a shoulder and making my feet as the monster tried to extricate itself from the vehicle.

The smell struck me immediately.

I spun quickly and saw that Anthea had managed to open all of the gas cylinders, her top pulled up over her nose. She indicated the front door and I nodded and ran for it. I reached it as the snake-creature finally got its head out of the window and roared, long and loud and low.

Anthea started to jump up and down. The snake's eyes fixed on her. I stopped my flight.

Anthea slowly moved backwards. I ducked around the corner of the shop, hoping it could not see me. But its attention was focused firmly on Anthea, now in the corner of the store. The creature jumped down to the ground, landing with a solid thud. It sniffed the air and a look of distaste crossed its reptilian visage; however, it seemed that it did not want to lose sight of Anthea. It moved slowly forward. I watched it go past my position, the long tail whipping from side to side, the wings folded on its back, its gait having a distinct limp, the head shaking as it went.

It slowed down. I think the odor was getting to it.

I saw the flash of light as the paper that covered the windows caught alight.

"Holy fuck," I whispered and ran. I started to move away from the building, but then changed direction and ran to the corner where I'd last seen Anthea.

The explosion showered glass over me. I covered my head and face but felt too many pieces cut into me. A ball of flame erupted inside, tongues of fire bursting out of every opening and reaching for the night sky. I sprinted for the corner. The glass inn that section had not burst outwards, but there was too much fire in there for my liking. I did not stop to think; I ran at it, arm across my face, and hit it side on. I burst inwards and landed awkwardly on the floor, but quickly made my feet.

The wyvern was wreathed in fire, moving back and forth, trying to find its way out of the building, but I dragged my eyes from it as I looked for… There! I scooped Anthea into my arms and jumped back through the hole I'd made in the window and just ran as far as I could from the fire. The disposable cigarette lighter she had pocketed at George Barker's place fell from her fingers. She was warm to the touch and there were tendrils of smoke coming from her, but I did not stop until we were far enough away for me not to feel the heat from the shop. Only then did I risk coming to a halt.

I carefully lowered her to the ground and sat beside her heavily. Her face was red but smoke still rose from her body. I carefully rolled her over and winced. The clothing on her back was burnt, her skin blistered in huge red welts, burns running along her body in dark lines that looked like cooked meat. "Shit," I muttered and placed my fingers on her neck.

I relaxed. Her pulse was steady and strong. I sat down and watched the building in front of us burn. Absently, my hand drifted to the back of her head and started to toy with that short lock of hair that covered the nape of her neck.

"Much as I appreciate the thought, not the time or place," came a soft voice.

"Thank God," I whispered and helped her turn over. She gripped me about the neck and curled up into me, careful to ensure her back did not touch anything.

"Shit, Bray, this hurts," she managed.

"You did it… uh-oh," I muttered.

The front of the store collapsed as the burning shape emerged. It opened its mouth and let out a long, pained hiss. Its body continued to burn as it stumbled forward. It stretched its wings out but they were just a mass of fire; however, it still attempted to lift itself off the ground but it could hardly move the upper limbs at all. It more fell than walked across the road, slamming into the house on the corner and falling through the front window. Flames caught hold inside immediately as the residents fled screaming out through the back door.

I noticed more and more people gathering around to watch the final death throes of this creature. No one said anything, they just became a silent crowd of onlookers, not sure what to think or do. The wyvern thrashed about in the remains of the house. The flames grew higher and wilder as the burning body made its way through the building. Then it burst through the front again. The gathered people screamed and many fled, running into the night, but Anthea and I stayed right where we were. It lifted its head, but did not even have the strength left to let out a roar.

It fell sideways, landing across the front yard of the next house in line. It rolled over as if trying to extinguish the flames that were consuming it so painfully, but it was too little too late. It fell against the building and soon that, too, was burning. The head lifted and roared at nothing; the tail gave a final spasm and fell still.

Then the whole animal collapsed and the conflagration finally took hold completely. Still Anthea and I watched and waited.

And we stayed there until the Country Fire Service vehicles arrived. They took one look at Anthea and immediately took her away to treat her.

I stayed by her side until the ambulance arrived and she was taken away to the Maitland Hospital. She smiled and held my hand as long as she could before they closed the doors and whizzed off. I just watched it disappear in the light of the burning buildings.

"Brayden?" I looked at the source of my name and groaned. I did not need this now. But Leroy came right up to me. "Where's Anthea?" he asked. I pointed at the departing ambulance. His face fell. "Is she…?" he started.

"She'll be okay," I mumbled.

He looked at me for a long time. "How are you?" he asked carefully.

"Fine," I said, but my voice was hardly my own. I continued to stare at the road.

"Brayden?" I faced him slowly. "Seriously, man, are you okay?"

I shrugged. "I have to call her mum, let Emma know," I said.

"Where's her car?"

I pointed at the shop, now a bonfire reaching high into the night sky. "Yeah, car," I repeated.

"Come with me," he said. He grabbed my arm and almost dragged me to his car. He sat me in the passenger seat and then headed off, past his sister's place and towards the

Yorke Highway. He did not say a word until we were in front of Anthea's house. Mrs Bowman's car was parked there, next to mine, and there were lights on inside. We stayed there for a few moments, just looking at the place.

"Well, thank you," I finally muttered, opening the door.

He grabbed my arm. "Brayden, look after her. Please." I could see it in his eyes. He was being serious. There was no hint of a threat about him, just his sincerity.

"I intend to," I replied.

He managed a smile, a sad one, not quite formed, but a smile nevertheless. "Thank you," he whispered.

I watched his car reverse out of the driveway and stood there until I could no longer see his car's lights on the road. Then I went to the front door of the house to deliver the news about what had gone on this night…

Chapter 34

The final day of the inquest into what had happened at Wills Creek was completed almost six weeks after the death of the creature. Anthea and I had been required to be there, but there were no real conclusions reached. While we were acknowledged as having seen the end of the beast, the dead Dr Jeremy Boyle was the one accused of withholding information while the dead Inspector Wallace was accused of running an inefficient investigation, focused more on his ego than on trying to find the truth. I felt sorry for Dr Boyle who had finally seen his life's beliefs come to fruition, but did not feel anything for the police officer.

No one found out about the animal that still lived in Anthea's snake room, nor the egg that even now sat in a refrigerator in the same place. One day, she told me, she would let some scientist with an open mind have a proper look at them, but not for a while. They also never found out about Dr Boyle's missing iPad. I relayed his death to his thousands of followers on his blog site – he had a list of passwords on the tablet, which made life easy – but made sure I commended him for following his beliefs and even strongly hinted that he had proved at least something he had told everyone was a possibility. Anthea and I shared our secrets with each other and no one else. It was as though we instinctively knew that no one was going to believe us, so we kept ourselves to ourselves. Needless to say, these things were therefore never brought up by the Queen's Counsel in charge of the inquest, was never mentioned in the media, nothing at all.

Anthea and I walked out into the late afternoon air and watched as the surprisingly small media scrum accosted the two lawyers who had been representing the people of Wills Creek and the police force, leaving us, two unknown people, alone. It had not been a public inquiry, and for that we were both grateful. We had a two hour drive back to Ardrossan, but neither of us felt like hitting the road straight away, so we went to a small pub near where we had parked my car.

"That's that," Anthea muttered. "All over."

"Yeah." I reached across and took her hand and squeezed it. She smiled at me. The only way we had coped after her two days in hospital and the constant barrage of questioning, both formal and from the people we knew in our local area, that we had been forced to suffer through had been by spending our time together. What had started as a week-long whirlwind romance had developed into something much firmer and very comfortable.

"So it really is all over?" she went on.

I lifted my hand and cupped her cheek. "Not yet," I whispered. "We're not going to forget this for a long, long time."

She laughed a little. "Yeah, when people ask about our first date, we're going to have to say we went killing snakes that couldn't exist," she grinned. "It's certainly unique."

"Oh yeah," I replied, returning her smile.

She swept her hair back out of her eyes and then gazed at the mirror on the wall beside us. "It's getting longer again," she said. "You like girls with longer hair, don't you?"

"Normally," I shrugged.

"Okay," she said, her smile fading a touch. "That's cool. I did think that shorter style suited me, though.

I looked at her for a few seconds, then stood. "Come on."

"What? Where to?"

"You'll see."

It took the hairdresser a good half an hour to get the style just like the pictures on the Internet, but when she had finished, it was almost identical to the way Lucinda Dickey looked in that film, almost picture perfect. Anthea's face beamed at the mirror, then she turned and kissed me and it was intense and filled with love. I played with the little lock that covered the nape of her neck and she groaned a touch.

We bonded properly over a haircut. It seems juvenile, not the sort of thing thirty-something-year-olds would do, but that was us. Far better that than bonding over a mythical snake burning to death in a tiny seaside town on the Yorke Peninsula in South Australia.

Acknowledgments

I would like to thank:

AM Ink Publishing for taking a risk on an unknown Australian.

Meagan for being an encouragement while writing and an extremely helpful beta reader. Her support was vital in this book being completed.

Kyle "Krimson Rogue" Martin who has no idea I exist, but whose YouTube videos taught me how not to write. I watched them many times before submitting this to make sure I did not do everything the writers he talked about did wrong.

About the Author

Steven Streeter is from rural Australia and has been writing since childhood. He is a former professional wrestler, with two children and three university degrees. An unabashed fan of pulp fiction and escapist entertainment, he has a number of books and short stories available from various publishers around the world.